Praise for *Where Sea Meets Sky*

"*Where Sea Meets Sky* combines one-night stand with coming-of-age to glorious success, one that makes this not just a read, but an experience . . . Halle's writing also stands out, poetic and vivid, then starkly honest."

—*Heroes and Heartbreakers*

Karina Halle takes us on another epic adventure . . . a journey of self-discovery and love, of taking chances and redefining futures . . . I absolutely loved Halle's ability to whisk us away and make it seem as if we were in a faraway place . . . It felt like an adventure.

—*Vilma's Book Blog*

"A luminous love story fraught with serious angst and impossible odds against the backdrop of a stunningly beautiful location . . . *Where Sea Meets Sky* is Karina Halle's most flawless writing to date."

—*Angie and Jessica's Dreamy Reads*

"Karina Halle, where have you been all my life? . . . [The] descriptive writing made the entire book so vivid! . . . If you're looking for an insanely sexy book to pick up, grab *Where Sea Meets Sky*!"

—*Once Upon a Twilight*

"Emotionally beautiful, inspiring and unforgettable, Karina Halle has yet again touched my heart with her poignant writing and her beautiful stories, and I can't wait to read Amber's story coming soon this summer!"

—*Shh Mom's Reading*

RACING
THE SUN

a novel

KARINA HALLE

ATRIA PAPERBACK

New York London Toronto Sydney New Delhi

ATRIA PAPERBACK
An Imprint of Simon & Schuster, Inc.
1230 Avenue of the Americas
New York, NY 10020

First Atria Paperback edition July 2015

ATRIA PAPERBACK and colophon are trademarks of
Simon & Schuster, Inc.

For information about special discounts for bulk purchases, please contact Simon & Schuster Special Sales at 1-866-506-1949
or business@simonandschuster.com.

The Simon & Schuster Speakers Bureau can bring authors to your live event. For more information or to book an event, contact the Simon & Schuster Speakers Bureau at 1-866-248-3049 or visit our website at www.simonspeakers.com.

Manufactured in the United States of America

10   9   8   7   6   5   4   3   2   1

Library of Congress Cataloging-in-Publication Data

Halle, Karina.
   Racing the sun : a novel / Karina Halle. — First edition.
      pages ; cm
   ISBN 978-1-4767-9644-4 (softcover)
1. Young women—Fiction. 2. Americans—Italy—Fiction. 3. Man-woman relationships—Fiction. I. Title.
   PS3608.A548286R33 2015
   813'.6—dc23
                                        2015018187

ISBN 978-1-4767-9644-4
ISBN 978-1-4767-9648-2 (ebook)

To Stephanie and her two giant suitcases.
Thank you for making Italy such a memorable
adventure. Stay away from the "brown nuts."

AUTHOR'S NOTE

This book was originally meant to be set in Brazil, a place I really wanted to visit, especially as I was set to take my assistant, Stephanie, along with me—she's Brazilian and would've been a giant help with the language. But the visa process and bureaucratic hoops to get into the country proved to be too much, so Stephanie and I went back to the drawing board for the research trip. Or, rather, I brought the drawing board to my readers. Since Brazil was out of the question, I asked readers where my next book should be set. Wherever they told us to go, we would go.

An overwhelming number voted for Italy's Amalfi Coast. Since I'd only been to Venice and Rome before, they didn't need to tell me twice; we packed up our bags and headed for the land of lemons.

Our trip took us from Naples, to Sorrento, to Positano, to Ischia, to Capri, and I fell in love with each of these places— some more than others. The Italian people of the Southern region are very charming, as you might imagine, and we made it our daily goal to find the best caprese salad we could. (Interestingly enough, the best caprese salad isn't on Capri, but at the Hotel Mare Blu Terme on the island of Ischia.)

At one point, we even saw Derio—no kidding. He was tall, dark, and handsome, with that same swoop of hair, Chucks, long shorts, and a tattoo on his leg. We were in Sorrento and I walked past him and then did a double take. We spent the rest of the night sitting curbside at a cafe, drinking wine and wondering if we'd see him again. Guess what? We did. He was walking with his mother, which made us both squee and swoon from afar. So, Derio does exist somewhere on the Amalfi Coast! If you find him, take his picture; the ones we took are too grainy. (No, we aren't stalkers . . . much.)

On the way back home from our trip, I had bad luck with the planes, as usual . . . and by bad luck, I mean there were always delays. (They didn't crash, thankfully.) I got stuck overnight in Dublin, Ireland, which was so not part of the plan (especially as I was supposed to be in New York for a signing). The airline comped us food and hotel, though (unlike some airlines, *cough*, Westjet) and at dinner I sat with a fellow traveler who had also been uprooted on her journey. While we ate and drank, she told me she had just been in Positano, too, and that she had met a girl there who had gone on a whim and fallen in love with a local Italian police officer. She had to leave Positano when her time was up but was moving back once her visa was secure. It was mad, passionate love at first sight.

Obviously, you'll recognize that I put part of that in the book—authors are the ultimate opportunists. But what really struck me, and what always strikes me about traveling, is that when you're out there on your own, in a new culture, you open yourself up to so many things—love included. People may roll their eyes at the love-at-first-sight stories, or the ones where someone takes a chance on someone they don't really know, or the ones where people move overseas for someone. And the thing is . . . it happens in real life! And that's why I love writing about love and travel, because I believe when you put yourself out there in the world and embrace it whole-heartedly—like Amber in *Racing the Sun*, Josh in *Where Sea Meets Sky*, and Vera in *Love, In English*—you open yourself up to a world of possibilities, including a love you might only have dreamed of.

So, if you're not inspired by *Love, in English*, *Where Sea Meets Sky*, or *Racing the Sun*, go out there and travel. See the world for yourself. And find love . . . not just with someone else, but within yourself and within the world.

RACING
THE SUN

CHAPTER ONE

We've all thought about how we're going to die. My friend Angela Kemp, whom I've known since we played in saggy diapers together, is convinced she's going to choke to death on something. Every time we go out to eat, she searches the restaurant for the person most likely to know the Heimlich maneuver and tries to sit by them. It doesn't seem to matter that *I* know the Heimlich maneuver; she just wants to know she'll be safe if it happens.

Personally, I've always thought I'd fall to my death. I think it all started when I was seven or eight years old and had dreams of my house turning over and me falling from the floor to the ceiling, dodging couches and tables. After that, my dreams turned to me falling off of balconies, getting trapped in collapsing elevators, and being in horrific plane crashes. Actually, it was never the crash that killed me, nor was it the scariest part of the dream; I was always sucked out of the airplane before the impact and fell to my death in a horrible rush of cold air and mortality.

It shouldn't surprise me, then, that I think I'm about to die in this moment, and by falling, no less.

In fact, I'm sure there's no way I can possibly survive this. It's not just that I'm in a taxi that seems to be coughing black fumes out of its tailpipe every two seconds, or the fact that the driver, with a mustache so big that he looks like a walrus, is looking more at me and the two other backpackers in the backseat than at the road. No, it's because, as we round the corners of the "highway" toward the postcard-worthy town of Positano, we're going full speed and there's nothing but a sheer cliff on my side of the vehicle.

"Shit," I swear, trying to hold on to something, *anything*, that would keep me in the car and prevent me from falling to my death, like my sordid dreams foretell. I look over at Ana and Hendrik, my Danish traveling companions for this leg of Southern Italy, and they don't seem all that concerned. I'm especially not going to grab on to big, blond Hendrik since Ana has a problem with random girls touching him.

Not that I'm random at this point. I met up with the couple in Rome and spent a few days with them there before we took the train down south. I know they have plans to keep going all the way to Sicily and hunker down in some beach hut with a bunch of goats (I don't know, but whenever Hendrik talks about their plans, goats are involved somehow), but I'm starting to believe that Positano is the end of the line for me.

And it's not just because I'm certain I'm going to die on the way there. It's because I am flat fucking broke. We all knew this day would come (and by *we*, I mean my parents and I). After all, I've been traveling for six months around the world and even though I've been trying to spend as little as possible, the world isn't as cheap as you'd think.

It probably doesn't help that I went a little overboard in Europe and had a mini shopping spree in every city I was in. But I like to think of my new shawls and sandals and jewelry as souvenirs, not just clothes. I mean, do you get to wear your postcards or ceramic doodads or tiny calendars with pictures of the Eiffel Tower on them? No. But you can wear a scarf you picked up from a market in Berlin.

But, of course, in hindsight, maybe I should have managed my money a bit better. I just thought that my savings were enough. And then, when my parents started bailing me out, I thought I could coast by on that. Just for a little while. Until I found out they sold my shitty 1982 Mustang convertible to help pay for this trip. After that, they just stopped putting money in my account.

I've now eaten into the money that was supposed to pay for my return ticket home, a ticket I didn't think I'd have to buy until I got down to Morocco, or even Turkey.

So, Positano, Italy, on the Amalfi Coast, might just be the end for me.

If I even make it out of this cab. As we round another bend, I can see crazy people parked on the road and selling flowers. Not the side of the road, but parked on the *actual* road. So now people are swerving around them, but when Italians swerve they don't slow down—they actually speed up.

I decide to close my eyes for the rest of the journey and hope I get there in one piece.

Even though the journey from Sorrento to Positano doesn't translate into many miles, it still feels like it takes forever for us to finally get there.

The walrus-mustached cab driver pulls to a sudden stop, abrupt enough that I fling forward, my curly blonde hair flying all over the place.

"Amber," Ana says in her deep accent. "We're here."

"I gathered that," I say, and awkwardly pretend to search through my messenger bag for euros, though I don't really have any euros to spare. Thankfully, Ana thrusts some bills into the driver's hand and we clamber out of the cab.

And so here is Positano. I'd been so busy closing my eyes and praying that I'd never really gotten a good look at the town.

It's fucking charming. I mean, it's beautiful and stunning and photogenic as all hell, but its charm is the first thing that comes to mind. The cab dropped us off at the top of a hill and you can see just how packed the town is, with building after colorful building crammed below the cliffs, staggered down the hillsides, tucked into every nook and cranny. It makes you wonder what crazy person decided to put a town here, of all places.

The one-way road leading down to the beach is narrow, with cars and pedestrians and patio seating vying for space, and lined with stores that beckon you to come inside. Actually, knowing Italy, the minute you walk past, some shopkeeper will come out and literally beckon you to come inside. Like, you can't say no (maybe that's how I've ended up with so much stuff). In the distance, the Mediterranean Sea sparkles from the sunlight—glitter on water—and hydrofoil ferries glide over it with ease.

"Wow," I say softly, trying to take it all in. "This is like the movies."

"Yes, it's very nice," Hendrik says blankly. He's never really impressed with anything. When we saw the Colosseum, he said he thought it would be bigger. Well, I thought it would be bigger, too, but that didn't stop me from being overwhelmed by the structure and history of it all. "Luckily the hostel is at the top of the hill."

That *is* lucky, considering if it were at the bottom of the hill on this one-way road, I'd have to lug my overflowing backpack and duffel bag uphill to catch a cab or bus when it's time to leave. Then again . . . I have a feeling I'm going to be here awhile. I have enough money to stay at this hostel for a week, and then I'm officially fucked.

I try not to dwell on that as I follow the Danes down the

road for a few minutes as cars and the ubiquitous motorcycle zoom past, narrowly missing me. Even being on foot and walking at your own pace, there's something so dizzying about this place. All these houses, the color of burnt orange and pastel yellow and faded rose, looking down on each other. When I turn around and look behind me, the steep, rocky hills rise up into the sky.

It feels like the entire town could topple over at any minute.

This could be a metaphor for my life at the moment.

After we've settled into a rather pleasant-looking dorm room (pleasant compared to the fleabag we stayed at in Rome), Ana and Hendrik invite me to go with them down to the beach. I really do want to go and explore, but I have a feeling they'll want to eat at some restaurant, and that would cost more euros than I can afford. As much as I hate it, I have to stick to my weird Italian granola bars and fruit for as long as I can. Besides, I'm sure the lovebirds would rather stroll on the Positano beach with each other and not have some broke, frazzle-haired American girl tagging along.

So they leave and I take my time exploring the hostel. It's small, but even though it's the only one in town, it's not as packed as I thought it would be. It's the beginning of June, too, so I thought all college kids and post-college kids (like myself) would be flocking to this area. I guess not.

That's fine with me. After living out of a backpack for months on end and never really having any time for myself, strolling around a quaint but quiet hostel would be awesome—just one of the many little pleasures of a traveler's life.

I end up back at the reception desk where a girl with shiny, poker-straight, chocolate-brown hair is sipping some lemon drink. I get major hair envy over anyone with straight strands.

"*Buongiorno*," the girl says with a smile once she notices I'm there. Then she remembers I checked in a moment ago. "I mean, hello. Amber, right? From San Francisco?"

"San Jose," I correct her, finding her easy to talk to already. I've always been a fairly quiet girl, but that changed real quick once I started traveling by myself. "Listen, I was just wondering. Well, I mean, I know you work here, right?"

She nods. "I hope so, otherwise I'll be in a lot of trouble."

"Right. I was just wondering, how did that happen?"

"Oh," she says and leans back in her stool. I notice how sun-browned her skin is and gather she must have been in Italy, or at least someplace warm, for a long time. She breaks into a wide smile. "It's kind of a long story."

I lean against the counter. "I've got time."

And so the girl—Amanda—launches into the story of her current life. She came here on a whim with a friend of hers but fell in love with Positano so badly that she didn't want to leave. Her friend ended up going back home and she asked the owners of the hostel if there were any way she could work for them. They told her she could work the front desk full-time in exchange for room, board, and little bit of extra money—all under the table, of course. She jumped at the chance.

"So how long are you staying here for?" I ask.

"My three months is up in a month."

I make a frowny face. "That sucks."

She shoots me an impish smile. "I'll be back. Luca is making sure of that."

"Who is Luca?"

"The man I'm going to marry."

And then she launches into another story, this one far more exciting than the last one. On her second week of working here, she ended up running into a local cop. He was hot, and it was love at first sight. Now that she has to leave the country (Americans can only be here for three months at a time), Luca is building a case to bring her back in seven months. If they can prove they're serious about each other and intend to marry one day, she can get a permit to work here for longer.

"Wow," I tell her when she's finished. "I was just thinking this town was like a movie set, and now this is like movie love."

She blushes. "I know it's rather fast. No one takes our relationship seriously, not even his mother. But I do love him and he loves me and I know this is the right thing to do. So why not take the chance, you know? If it doesn't work out, at least I'll have a hell of a story."

"You already do have a hell of a story." I'll admit that even though I think it's sweet and romantic, the jaded and cynical side of me thinks it is a bit ridiculous that she's doing all of this for a man, that you could even fall in love that fast. But that's probably because I've been screwed over by men a few times already on my travels.

"See," she says, pulling out her phone and showing me a picture. "This is Luca. You'd stay for him, wouldn't you?"

I let out a low whistle. Luca *is* hot. Dark-skinned with piercing, light eyes. And he's tall, too. Not that that's too out of the ordinary—it's just that everyone warned me that Italian men would be short and hairy. So far, I haven't found that to be the case at all.

"Nice," I say to her. "Well, I wish you both the best and hope it all works out."

She shrugs. "Life works out the way it wants to."

"Uh-huh." And then I remember the real reason why I

came to talk to her. "Listen, I'm having some financial diffi-
culties at the moment. You know, overdid it a bit in London
and all that. Anyway, I was wondering if you knew if there was
any work available for someone like me?"

Her eyes narrow slightly. "Well, there's no work here."

Relax, I think. *I'm not after your job.*

"Oh, I don't mean here, per se. I just meant in town. Or
in the area. Even Sorrento or Salerno."

She purses her lips and thinks. "Well, there would be jobs
in Salerno, but you don't want to work there. Have you tried
the English café down the street? Sometimes they need English speakers. There's also a work notice board for foreigners.
Usually the jobs posted are one-offs for guys, like a day spent
painting a house or something like that. But sometimes you
can get lucky."

This sounds promising. "And it's just down the street? It's
a long street . . ."

Amanda smiles, pulls out the hostel map, and begins to
mark up a path for me. "Follow the road all the way to here
and then take these stairs here. You'll come to Bar Darkhouse.
Beside it, kind of tucked in the back, is Panna Café."

"Thank you," I tell her, folding the map before shoving it
in my bag.

I walk down the streets with an extra spring in my step.
The air is fresh (when you're not inhaling diesel fumes) and
the sun is warm, baking my bare arms. I'm feeling a bit opti-
mistic about the whole money problem now. If Amanda can
find work here, I can, too.

That should also go to say that if Amanda can find love
here, I can, too. But thankfully, that is the last thing I'm looking for. I've had enough fun and heartbreak during this trip,
falling for boys who either have their hearts set on someone

else (like Josh in New Zealand) or who love you and leave you (like the Icelandic boy, Kel, who I spent a sex-filled week with in Prague). No, the next guy I was going to fall for was going to be a Nor Cal boy when I returned back home to San Jose. No drama, no heartache, no tragic goodbyes.

No fun either, I think to myself, but I quickly push that thought away.

The café is easy enough to find but it takes me a while to get there. The town is so pretty and tightly packed with storefronts, and I want to linger in every single one of them. Eventually, I get there and order an espresso at the bar. Unlike most cafés in Italy, this one actually has tables and chairs where you can sit down and sip your drink, obviously catering to tourists. But at this point I've gotten used to doing quick shots of coffee while standing up. It's at least more efficient.

After I ask the British barista if they're hiring and get a big fat no, she points me to the corner of the café where the notice board is. Though most of the postings are actual flyers for parties or advertisements for ceramic sales, there are a few work notices.

One of them looks fresh—none of the phone number and e-mail strips on the notice have been torn off.

It reads:

> Need help. Want English speaking woman. Two children. Must be good to young children and help with language. Fluency needed. Italian is helpful to have. Please e-mail Felisa. Locate to Capri.

I quickly take the notice off of the board before anyone else notices. Like hell I'm going to compete for this job. Even though I'm not really sure what it entails other than possibly teaching English to two kids, or what it pays, or if it includes room and board, I'm not going to give up the opportunity. If it doesn't work out, then I'll just put the ad back.

I immediately connect to the café's Wi-Fi on my cell phone and write an e-mail to Felisa. I make myself sound as good as possible: Graduated from San Jose State with a B.A. in English. Worked as a receptionist for a prestigious manufacturing company (before I was fired). Great with children (I think I babysat once when I was fifteen). Willing to work on Capri, provided help with housing is included. Spent a great deal of time building up life skills while traveling Southeast Asia. Know how to bake a mean tiramisu.

That last part is a lie but I thought they might find it endearing.

I press send and then wait.

And wait.

And when I realize I'm not going to get a response right away, I head to the bar next door, taking the work notice with me.

I don't get a reply until the next morning. I didn't sleep well, between obsessing over how to get home and trying to ignore the sounds of Hendrik and Ana having sex. You'd think I'd be used to public dorm room copulation by now, but I'm not. It's one of those things you don't want to get used to because then that means you should probably reexamine your life.

When I check my e-mail on my phone, all bleary-eyed, I see that Felisa wants me to meet her at the dock at four this afternoon. It doesn't say anything else. Not what she looks like or if I need to bring anything or where we're going. I mean, the dock? She's not actually thinking of doing the job interview on the island of Capri, is she?

But as many questions as I have, I'm also excited. Because this is promising. And it was so easy. One e-mail and bam! I might just be teaching English to two cute Italian children. I bet they're just darling and say *mama* and eat politely. Sure, I don't have a lot of experience with children, but I figure I might become a mother one day so this is good practice. I mean, the maternal instinct has to be in me somewhere.

I tell Ana and Henrik that I'm meeting someone down at the dock. I haven't told them about my financial problems and don't plan on it, so they're a bit suspicious about this meeting, even when I try to play it off as if I met a guy yesterday and I'm meeting up with him again.

I mean, it could be true, in a way. I assume that the children will have a father and he might want to interview me, too.

I leave at three o'clock because the hill takes its time to wind down, and Italians walk slowly (yet drive frighteningly fast). I'm at the dock with plenty of time to spare.

Positano is absolutely gorgeous from the water and the pebbled beach is packed with bronzed men in Speedos and brightly-striped umbrellas and chairs. Tiny boats and Jet Skis zip back and forth, sloshing the low dock with water. I stand there and wait, my face to the sun, still pinching myself that I'm here, in Italy, and it's a gorgeous day.

Time seems to drag on a bit. I look across the dock and slowly realize that no big ships are docking here, only small boats. I look over to my left and notice a large hydrofoil pulling out from the area around the rocks.

Oh shit. Is that the dock she meant? Have I been standing in the wrong place this whole time?

I whip out my phone and look at the time. Four ten. Just fucking great.

I'm about to start running across the beach toward the bigger ships when a woman yells out. "Hey you!"

I stop in my tracks, pebbles flying everywhere and getting in my sandals, and see a woman striding toward me. She's short and round with gray hair pulled off her face, showcasing her very sharp nose. She's still beautiful, though, in an older, classy woman way. Or she would be if she didn't look so scowl-y.

"Show me your hands," she says in a thick accent, stomping over to me, and for a moment I'm afraid that this is all a misunderstanding. Is she mistaking me for a thief or something?

But I have no time to say anything. She grabs my hands, turning them over and back again. "Okay, fine," she says and peers at my face. Her eyes are a light gray. "You will do. Come on."

And then she starts to storm away, hiking up her skirt so it doesn't brush against the pebbles.

What the fuck was that?

"Um, excuse me," I call after her, unsure whether I should follow or who she even is. "I think you have me mistaken for someone else."

She shakes her head and keeps walking. "No. You are Amber. Come or we miss the boat."

"Felisa?" I ask and then run after her, my soles slipping all over the place. "How did you know who I was?"

"Only tourists would go to wrong dock," she says. She eyes me over her shoulder. "Also, I Google you. You have many pictures."

Well, I have been updating my travel blog quite often. At least I know someone's looked at it.

I walk fast to keep up with this woman. I'm a short girl with short legs, and though Felisa seems to be the same height, she walks like a giraffe, with impossibly long strides. It's not long until I'm panting, totally out of breath, and we're standing in front of one of the hydrofoils. A few people are dragging their luggage onto metal ramps that move with the swell of each wave.

"What are we doing?" I ask.

Felisa hands two tickets over to the man collecting them.

"You come to the house, you meet the children. And Signor Larosa."

So many things happening at once.

"Wait, wait," I protest, reaching out to grab Felisa's elbow.

She shoots me daggers so I quickly let go, but at least I've stopped her.

"Sorry," I say quickly. "I didn't know I would be going to the island. How would I get back?"

"Tomorrow there is a ferry. Many ferries."

The ticket guy is eyeing us warily now.

"But where do I stay? I don't have any money. I've paid for my hostel here in full."

"You stay in the house."

"What house?"

"Signor Larosa's. Where the children are."

"Is he their father?"

She shakes her head. "Older brother. Long story."

"How much older?"

"Older!" she yells. "Now come on, we will miss it."

The ticket guy clucks his tongue in agreement.

I sigh, feeling all out of sorts, and follow Felisa onto the ramp and inside the ferry. She takes a seat on one side of the main aisle in the middle of the ship. I notice that everyone is kind of arranged the same way, with few people on the outer edges. I wonder why but there are bigger things to wonder about.

I sit down next to her. "Okay, let's start again."

"You start tomorrow, when you get your things back from Positano."

"But you haven't interviewed me yet. You don't know if I'm right for the job."

"You are on the ferry right now, aren't you?" she asks, giving me a sharp look. "Then you are right for the job. You could have said no. Also, you have nice, strong hands and you need those when handling children. Now I have to bring you to Signor Larosa and see how you are with him. And the children."

"Why is it important to see how I get along with him?"

She sighs, as if I should know all of this. "He is difficult. So are the children. But he is even more so. Hopefully he will pretend you don't exist. If you annoy him, you will know it well."

"And who are you?"

"I am the housekeeper," she says with a slight tip of her chin. "I have kept the children and the house in line since their parents died. But now is time for the children to learn proper English. Signor Larosa speaks it well, as do I, but it is not good enough for them."

"Them?"

"His parents, who made it their wish in their will. So we are looking for a teacher. The last three we had all left. Stayed one week."

Oh, Jesus. This is starting to sound like the beginning of a horror movie.

"In the ad I asked if you were good with young children. You said you were."

Actually, the ad said, good *to* young children. And of course I thought that meant if I spoiled them with candy and gave them gold stars for effort.

She waves her wrinkled hand at me. "It doesn't matter. They will be less of a problem."

"Than?"

"Their brother. Desiderio Larosa," she repeats impatiently. She turns her head and peers at me, as if searching for cracks. "If you can handle that man, then you can handle the children. Then you can handle anything."

At that she presses her lips together, closes her eyes, and appears to fall asleep right in front of me. She doesn't even wake up when the hydrofoil picks up speed and starts to rock back and forth violently, waves splashing high against the sides of the boat. I spend the whole ferry ride wondering if I can make it to the bathroom to puke in time and if we're all going to die on the high seas. That would be a change from falling to my death.

I'm also wondering who this mysterious Desiderio Larosa is, and just what the hell I've gotten myself into.

CHAPTER TWO

Amalfi Blue. It's a color that's been used to describe shades of wall paint and eye shadow and nail polish, but even then it doesn't hold a candle to the real thing. The water around the Amalfi Coast is an extremely jewel-colored, saturated blue that literally takes your breath away.

The water around the island of Capri takes it one step further. It's so clear and vibrant and changes from the richest royal blue to shimmering aquamarine; it looks like a pool of sun-splashed glass. I'm so engrossed with the color of the water as we approach the narrow marina that I barely notice the island rising up from the ocean in front of me. When I finally do look up as I'm getting off the ferry, I feel as if I'm being hit over the head with it.

"Come," Felisa barks at me as she stomps off the teetering ramp and onto the cement dock. If it wasn't for the couple behind me, bumping into me with their giant suitcases, I probably would be standing in one place, staring straight ahead forever.

I know I've been here for a second but Capri is fucking gorgeous. Brightly colored gondolas dot the turquoise water while pastel houses crowd the bustling shore, stretching up onto terraced green stone hills. The focal point is Mount Solaro, an overwhelming monolith smack in the middle, like a jagged tooth sticking out of a giant's jawbone. If I squint, I can even see cars navigating its razor-thin curves.

I shiver despite myself, remembering the road to Positano, and quickly hurry off the boat before Felisa yells at me again. Since it's the start of summer, the crowds are thick and anxious and I feel like I'm being swept down the dock, losing sight of Felisa, until I see her stern eyes peering at me from beside a taxi. Not just an ordinary taxi but a convertible.

"Are we taking this?" I ask her, super excited about riding in a topless taxi. Now, this is something to put on Instagram.

"No," she says coolly. "Come, hurry." And then she turns, crossing the street filled with a melange of awestruck tourists, fast-talking locals out to make a buck, and an array of cabs and motorcycles. Somehow they all seem to clear a path around her. This woman must be known about town, or she has some supersonic people-repelling shield around her. I wouldn't be surprised if the latter were true.

I adjust my purse on my shoulder, suddenly aware that a crowd like this could be a breeding ground for pickpockets, and race across the street after her, bumping into people and nearly colliding into the wall of a street-side café.

She walks through an arcade, and when I follow I discover we are in some half-underground tunnel, and a streetcar is slowly sliding down a track toward us.

Felisa quickly pays for our tickets—which I guess is nice of her, since I'm so discombobulated by everything—and soon we're in a packed funicular car, gliding up a hill. Within minutes we're out of the dark and into the light, the wide windows of the car displaying the island below. I can see the marina with its myriad of ferries, hydrofoils, and boats and the rustic houses that cling to the sides of the cliffs.

When we reach the top and exit the funicular, I find myself stupefied once again at the view. It's much more apparent at this height that Capri is one giant, magical place filled with villas, culture, and pretty people. Oh, and shops. All the shops. As I follow Felisa through the pedestrians-only street through the maze of what is known as Capri town, I'm floored by the shopping opportunities. Dolce & Gabbana, Fendi, Gucci, Balenciaga line the elegant paths, beckoning even the cheapest person to peruse their window displays.

I am that cheapest person, especially now, but Felisa's glare overpowers my urge to see Prada's latest offerings, so I hurry after her down the long winding lane until the shops turn to cafés and restaurants and the tourists begin to peter out.

Here I am again stunned by the views. The so-called "street," Via Tragara, takes us past house after gated house, where glimpses of the dramatic south coast of the island come into view between patches of lemon trees and climbing vines. The houses here all have names like *La Gentilina*, *Villa Celeste*, and *Villa Grotta Azzurra* and tease you through the gates. I want to stop and marvel at them and think about who lives in them and what it must be like to wake up each day with a view like that, to have breakfast and coffee on the edge of the world.

But Felisa is now making a clucking noise like an angry chicken and I keep up the pace. I've only got my handbag on me and I'm starting to wonder, if I have to spend the night here, what the hell I'm going to wear. I don't have my face wash, my toothbrush, deodorant—nothing. It's enough to send me into a bit of a tizzy but I take a deep breath and keep walking.

"Do cars ever come down here?" I ask. The lane seems barely wide enough for even one car.

She shakes her head. "No cars here, only carts."

"Like golf carts?"

"Only carts."

"How do you move, though? Like, with all your furniture?"

"Carts," she repeats, exasperated. "Hurry."

I don't know why we're hurrying. It's not like I had an appointment or anything. In fact I think it's pretty commendable on my part that one moment I was standing on the beach in Positano and the next moment I'm here on a job interview gone rogue.

As the road dips down a bit toward massive outcrops of rocks that jut out over the sea, the houses that flank the hill above and below us spread out. Soon, it's just cypress, eucalyptus, palm trees, and fragrant periwinkle bushes. The air hums with cicadas.

Finally, we stop by an impressive cast-iron gate, bookended by a massive stone wall. The number 33 is done up in fancy tile and a copper plaque reads *Villa dei Limoni Tristi*.

"The house of sad lemons?" I ask, doing a poor translation in my head, but Felisa is ignoring me, sticking a giant skeleton key into the lock. I'm about to ask why she doesn't have a modern keypad but realize she'd ignore me anyway.

The gate swings open with a dramatic creak and I step inside. While she locks the gate behind us, I take it all in. It's like we're in the middle of a garden run wild. The grass is coarse and knee-high, weaving around overgrown shrubs and pomegranate trees. There are lemon trees, too, and in keeping with the house's strange name, they do look a little sad. The lemons are huge—the size of your hand—and weigh down the trees, their boughs reaching out to us. Overripe fruit litters the ground, bees swarming happily around it. Back when I was in high school and full of hopes and dreams and shit like that, I actually fancied going into botany, or at least flower arranging, so all the beautiful flora here was doubly exciting for me.

Through the middle of it all is a crumbling cobblestone path that leads down a slight slope to the house itself. From where we are and the angle of the hill, the house doesn't look all that big. It's built of flat stones stacked on top of one another, similar to the wall running around the grounds, with vines and deep orange Campsis flowers climbing its rugged planes.

But as Felisa bustles past me and I follow down a path that turns to stairs, leading us past fragrant lavender and rosemary bushes at the side of the house, I realize there is so much more to the house than I thought. A lot more. From the front it looks like one story, but from the back it's two, with what looks to be an additional attic area above the second story. The house is enormous and the ceilings have to be well over ten feet high. And that's just one surprise. Before us is a large outdoor area made up of red brick and tile that stretches from the open back door all the way to what seems to be the edge of a cliff. There's a blue swimming pool here that appears to be only half full and a wooden bench overlooking a stunning view, hidden by chipped and cracked terracotta pots of unkempt flowers. Grapevines climb over a pergola, which shelters a massive outdoor dining area that looks like it hasn't been used in a long time.

The whole place is stunning in a shabby-chic way. It's like an old-school millionaire built the house of his dreams on the side of cliff, the blue sea at his feet, and then thought of a new dream and kind of forgot about this place. It all looks a touch neglected, which I guess would be creepy if it wasn't so charming.

And stunning. Because holy hell. No matter that the tiles need some power washing, I could totally see myself sitting on that bench in the mornings and having a cappuccino while watching the boats head to and from shore. The breeze wafts in from the sea and carries the scent of fresh herbs and bracing salt and lemons, the way I imagine sunshine should smell. I close my eyes and breathe in deep, trying to capture it somewhere in my brain.

"Sit here," Felisa says. I look over and see her gesturing to the table and chairs underneath the pergola. "I'll go get the children first."

Oh right. The reason why I'm here. She disappears into the house and suddenly I'm beyond nervous. Even though it's been a bit strange and an inconvenience, now that I'm here I'm curious about the position; even a weird job would be better than no job at all.

I sit down on the chair, the linen cushion starchy and stiff under me, and wait. After a few moments of grappling with the view—some places are just too much for a person to absorb all at once—I crane my head to look at the house. A few wide, brick-lined steps lead up to a smaller patio and to an open door, through which I can kind of see inside the house. The walls are bright white and the floors look intricately tiled. I can just glimpse the end of a gilded frame on the wall.

A movement on the second floor catches my eye. Near a set of French doors that open onto a small balcony, I see someone staring at me. He doesn't seem to care that he's been caught. I stare at him and he stares right back.

It's hard to see him properly because of the glare of the sun on the glass, but he seems to be quite tall and slim, with dark, brooding features. A little *too* brooding. It almost looks like he's giving me the stink-eye. I wonder if this is Signor Desiderio Larosa? And I wonder if I'll have to say his full name every time I address him. It's quite the mouthful.

"Amber." Felisa's harsh voice makes me tear my eyes from the window. She's standing at the back door with two children on either side of her, a hand firmly grasping an arm on each one. The children are cute—you know, for kids—but they look just as brooding as the man at the window. In fact, I know they're giving me the stink-eye.

"This is Alfonso and Annabella," Felisa says, yanking the children forward toward me. Both kids let out little grumbles and cries—not from pain, it seems, but from having to come over and meet me. Can't say I blame them.

Up close they are both cuter and angrier than I thought. They are also clearly twins who look to be about six or seven years old. Both of them are in uniform: white polo shirts with a crest, navy pants for him, pleated skirt for her. Shiny shoes. They both have the same bright brown eyes, thick dark hair, full lips, strong noses, and prominent brows. I have a feeling they'll grow up to be classic beauties when they're older, though they're already very striking right now.

They are also striking out. Alfonso smacks Felisa's arm with his hand, yelling, "*Non mi tocchi!*" Which I gather means, *Let go, mean lady.*

Felisa's grip is tight and she smiles at me grimly. "Alfonso doesn't know his manners yet. We have been trying, but he is very disruptive at school. Likes to push kids down. Always in trouble."

Oh great. I'd be taking care of a bona fide bully?

Felisa jerks her head at Annabella, who is staring bitterly at an empty spot on the ground. "Annabella doesn't talk much but is the same. You have to be more careful with her. She's very smart."

At that, Annabella lifts her eyes to look at me. It's like staring into the fiery pits of hell. Or into the face of a female Damien from *The Omen*. I half expect a Doberman to come trotting out of the house and lie down beside her.

Didn't Felisa say the children would be the easy part? Charming house, stunning view, and Capri location aside, I'm starting to rethink the whole job. There better be a hell of a benefits package. Of course, I know there won't be, and I'm one step closer to leaving.

As if sensing my hesitation, or simply reading the blatant fear in my eyes, Felisa lets go of the children. They quickly run back into the house without giving me a second glance. For the first time today, Felisa looks worn down and I notice the exhaustion pulling at her crepey eyes.

She sighs and sits down across from me, folding her hands on the table. "You seem like a strong girl, and only a strong girl will be able to handle those two. They aren't normal children, not like the ones you might know."

Oh my God, they're vampires, I think. Funny where the mind goes.

"When their parents died, everything changed," she continues. "They were five when it happened, two years ago. They were very different. Always very bright, but that is because their mama and papa were bright, especially mama. But they were kind, too. Considerate. Very well behaved. People would walk past this house and talk about the mama and how successful she was, how papa was such a strong figure in town. They would talk of the house and how beautiful and well kept it was, and of course about the Larosa children. 'What darling children,' they would say. 'What a brave, handsome older son.' Now they hurry past this place, either in disgust or in pity. 'It is such a shame,' they say now. And they shake their heads and carry on their way."

There's real pain in Felisa's voice and I have so many questions to ask that I don't even know where to begin.

"How long have you been working for the Larosas?"

"Since Desiderio—Signor Larosa—was born. Twenty-nine years ago."

So the brother is twenty-nine. Interesting. "And you've been here ever since?"

She nods. "And I am getting tired. The kids are getting to be too much."

"But my job is just to teach English, right?"

She nods again, sharper this time, not looking at me. "Yes. They need better English than they get at school."

"And how long should these English lessons go on for? How often? And if you don't mind, I'd like to talk about getting paid and my living situation."

Her eyes briefly flit to the window and back. "I'm afraid that is for Signor Larosa to decide. I can assure you he will be fair, though he has, how you say, pinched a lot of pennies lately." She gestures to the backyard. "The gardener was let go six months ago. The cook and housecleaner went before that. Signor Larosa is in charge of the estate but he is needing to be careful with the money that was left. The Larosas were wealthy but things cost money here. Capri is very expensive."

"Why doesn't he sell the house and move somewhere cheaper with the children?"

She tilts her head to the side and gives me a look that says I have no idea what I'm in for. "Because Signor Larosa has not left the island since the accident."

He hasn't left the island? Is this turning into an episode of *Lost*?

"The accident? You mean, when the parents . . ."

She shakes her head. "No, not that accident."

Not *that* accident? What the fuck is going on in this crazy house?

She looks over my shoulder and straightens her spine. I

turn my head to look and see the tall brooding man standing by the back door. He doesn't look too happy. I wonder if he overheard what we've been talking about. I try not to look sheepish.

He raises a finger at Felisa, and without saying a word, walks back into the house.

I look at her for an explanation.

She gets out of her chair. "Come, come, he wants to meet with you now."

I swallow hard. At my last job the interview process had been conducted by my supervisor—Larry Groberman—who wore a too-tight tie, never smiled once, and made me feel ashamed for even being alive. I survived that one and got the job after all, but I don't think I'm going to survive this one. As I follow Felisa up the brick steps to the back door, I feel like my legs are going to give out. Holy hell, I'm nervous.

Being inside the house doesn't help either. I'm over-whelmed as we step into a hallway that opens onto several different rooms, including a giant chef's kitchen, living area, dining room, and eating nook—plus I can see other doors lingering in the background leading to who knows where. The bedrooms are upstairs, accessible by a giant staircase. The walls are white; the chandeliers are brass and crystal; and the floors are shiny ivory tile, sometimes with splashes of yellow and blue, sometimes with black. The sun streams in through large radius windows, with thick gold curtains drawn back with velvet rope, but even though it's all very bright, it's also a bit sterile. The decor should be warm but it comes off as cold, for some reason. This definitely doesn't seem like a house for two small children. I can't detect any signs that children even live here.

"This way," Felisa says, taking me to the left and past the

dining room to a brown wood door that looks weathered and worn. She knocks then clasps her hands at her waist. Considering Signor Larosa had walked into the house moments before, you'd think he would have left the door open or something, expecting us.

"*Entri*," a commanding voice says from the other side. I take in a deep breath as Felisa opens the door. I remind myself it's just a job, and a crazy-sounding one at that. If it doesn't work out it's probably for the best. And then some.

I step into a room that takes my breath away. If the rest of the house doesn't have a soul, surely one resides in here. We're in a library of sorts, a room of light and dark, a delicate balance between glass and wood. There are dark mahogany bookcases upon bookcases, all packed with books, broken up by floor-to-ceiling windows through which the light streams in, as well as a set of French doors that lead to the patio overlooking the pool and the sea. Another wall contains French doors that look out over a dry fountain in the middle of a small, overgrown courtyard, complete with iron chairs and table. In the middle of the room is a giant teak desk, stacked with papers, file folders, and overflowing trays. A laptop rests among the chaos. This is where Signor Larosa is sitting, ramrod straight in a leather chair.

I'm so taken with the room—it must stretch the length of a whole side of the house—that I almost dismiss Signor Larosa. I say *almost* because once my eyes do settle on him, they bulge right out of my head.

Signor Desiderio Larosa looks like he just rolled off the model runway in Milan and then hitchhiked his way here. I don't even know where to begin, how to take him in. He's handsome as hell, for one thing. He's a got a face that makes you stare, maybe do a few double takes. His eyes are a golden brown, really clear, framed by perfectly arched black eyebrows and long eyelashes. His nose is very Italian and strong, but it suits his features. His cheekbones are high and razor sharp, his lips full and smooth, and his chin has a slight dimple in it. He's got a ten-o'clock shadow running along his jaw, which just adds to his aura of masculinity.

Then there's his hair. I've seen this cut on so many men since I've set foot in Italy, but so far he wears it best. Short sideburns, close-cut on the sides, and then a swoop of long hair on top. It's thick and dark and almost rockabilly. I kind of want to run my hands through it and give his strands a tug.

But of course that would be entirely inappropriate since he's staring at me like he wants to toss me off the side of a cliff. Man, can this guy glower. I'm not sure whether to be scared or turned on. Or both.

"Signor Larosa," Felisa says, her hands still clasped in front of her. She treats him so demurely and respectfully for someone who has probably been working at this house since he was in diapers. "This is Amber MacLean. She is one of the first applicants for the tutor position."

I try not to look at her in surprise. There were more applicants? How stupid of me to think there was no competition for this job, that I was the only one who applied.

Signor Larosa is studying me. Nothing moves except for his eyes, which are roving all over my face and body like he's trying to figure me out. If he likes what he sees, he doesn't show it. He's still got the brooding-meter turned up to the max.

"I would like to speak to Miss MacLean alone," he says to Felisa in perfect, albeit accented, English. He doesn't look at her.

Felisa isn't all that surprised but when she nods at him and turns to leave, she gives me a look that says *good luck*. She actually looks anxious for me. I remember all the things she had said about him before we boarded the ferry.

The door closes behind her and it feels like I've been sealed inside a vault. Suddenly the library seems darker than before and my whole body is aware that I'm alone in this place with this smoldering, stupidly hot man.

"Please, take a seat," he says, nodding slightly. I look behind me to see another desk against the wall, an even bigger stack of papers on top of it, as well as an Underwood typewriter. Thick dust has settled everywhere, and the desk looks like it hasn't been touched in years. I walk over and pull a leather chair from it, and as I do my eyes briefly rest on a stack of paperbacks. They're all the same book, *Villa dei Limoni Tristi*. I try to make out the author but the spines are hidden by the typewriter.

"If you please," Signor Larosa says harshly, and I nearly jump where I'm standing. I shoot him an apologetic smile and immediately feel my face go red as I pull the chair to rest across the desk from him. I make a point of not sitting too close. I want to be able to run if I need to.

I sit down quickly, folding my hands in my lap and crossing my feet at the ankles. I can see now why Felisa's brash demeanor changed when she knocked on the door. Suddenly, she seems like a ray of sunshine.

"I must tell you," Signor Larosa says, pulling out a piece of paper from the desk. It's a printed copy of my résumé and he already has a red pen in hand, as if he's going to cross the whole thing out and tell me everything about my life is wrong. "I don't think you are right for this job."

Well, that's encouraging.

I raise my brow. "And why is that?"

He gives me a sharper look. That is to say, he gives me an *even sharper* look. His eyes slice into mine like razor blades, but I refuse to look away. Telling me that I'm not right for the job is a surefire way to bring out all of my Taurus tendencies.

"I had asked Felisa to make sure the applicants were older and more mature. You seem very young." His eyes trail down my body again and back up to my face. I try not to show the fact that my hairs are standing on end.

"I'm twenty-four," I tell him.

"But you have no experience with children or teaching English," he countered smoothly, his face a mask.

"I have a degree in English," I say, raising my chin a little, "so I know more than most people do. I've been told I'm a natural teacher. And I have experience with children. There are many in my neighborhood." Sometimes I yell at them to get off my lawn.

He glances at the résumé. "In San Jose, California?"

"That's right. Have you ever been there?" I ask, hoping to enliven the conversation.

"No," he says simply, looking over my résumé again. "I don't want to have to trust Felisa on this one, though she hasn't let me down before."

I chip away at my neon yellow nail polish, not really sure what to say to that. I have a million questions and this man is going to be even more difficult to get answers from than Felisa was. Still, I have a feeling I should wait for him to say something.

Silence cloaks the room; you can really feel its presence in here. Meanwhile, the sun has started to descend to the horizon, the light through the radius windows becoming a pale gold. It's beautiful. I wish I could open the French doors and let the breeze in. I wish I could just snatch the résumé out of his hand, leave the room, leave the house, and go back on the ferry to Positano. I wish I had the money to walk away.

"So you met the twins, did you?" he asks, finally putting my résumé away and folding his hands in front of him.

I nod. "Yes, outside."

"And how did you find them?"

"They are very cute."

"There must be a better English word than that. Try me. I know English very well."

"Then why aren't you teaching them?" I blurt out. I didn't mean to say it but it has been on my mind ever since he opened his mouth.

He tilts his head, considering me. "I have a difficult relationship with them. You see, they are my brother and sister and they are in my care. I am all the family they have left. You have parents, am I assuming correct?" I nod. He goes on. "Do you think you would learn anything if your parents tried to teach you another language?"

I shake my head and make a face. I was traveling to escape my parents. "No way."

"Well, then that is the same case here. Alfonso and Annabella . . . already our roles are too twisted. Besides, it is easier to learn from a native English speaker. There is less chance to cheat. With you, they will have to learn English or not talk at all. I assume you are not a great speaker of Italian?"

"I know some," I tell him. And that's true. It's just hard to define what *some* is.

"Yes, some, of course," he says in his jackass condescending way. It rankles me and helps me ignore how pretty his eyes are. "So, Miss MacLean—"

"You can call me Amber," I interject.

"Perhaps," he says. Still no trace of a smile. "So, Miss

MacLean, give me the right word to describe the twins. In English."

I sigh inwardly. "Do you want the truth, a lie, or a white lie?"

For a moment he almost looks impressed. "Give me all three."

Here goes nothing.

"From what I observed of them, Alfonso and Annabella seem very precocious."

"That is the white lie. Though also truth."

"They are bold and confident."

"Bold, yes, confident, no. What is the truth?"

"They seem excitable."

"Still, this is not what your first thought was."

I'm not sure if he's trying to get me to call them spoiled brats. That was one of my thoughts, but actually not the main one.

"They seem to be troubled and are lashing out in anger," I tell him sincerely.

He nods. "Yes. That is the truth. You can see how your first choice, the word *cute*, wasn't very honest."

"They *are* cute, though," I say, picturing their features and then studying their brother's in front of me. There are some key differences—the twins have lighter hair—that make me wonder if perhaps they are step or half siblings. But that's just another question to add to the pile.

"I suppose they are cute," he says, as if the subject is weighing him down. For a moment he looks extremely tired but then it lifts away. "Now tell me, how do you think you would be able to teach English—something you have never done before—to these two troubled, angry children?"

I swallow. I actually don't have a good answer to that. I

feel like I've been totally caught unaware and I'm not sure if I can bullshit my way out of this one like I have on other job interviews.

I clear my throat and sit up straighter in my chair. "I don't know, to be perfectly honest with you. I don't really know the first thing about children. I know English but I've never taught it. The last thing I taught was how to use Excel and PowerPoint to the person who had taken over my job. Which I was fired from, by the way. I'm not even sure if I want to move to Capri to take this position, should it be offered to me, and I'm really not sure if this is the job for me, considering the children have issues, your housekeeper has issues, and I can guarantee that you have issues. No one has discussed money, or where I'm supposed to live, or even where the hell I'm supposed to sleep tonight. This house is borderline creepy and I won't be surprised if you tell me it's haunted. And I can't make tiramisu worth shit."

His eyes brighten at that. It's almost as if he wants to smile but can't.

"Then why are you here?" he asks slowly.

"Because I don't have any money. And I don't want to go home." I can't even afford to go home, but I don't tell him that part. "And even though this job sounds a lot like trial by fire, I really like a challenge. I think it would be good for me." I raise my chin even higher. "We both don't think I'm right for the job. I'd like to prove the both of us wrong."

He stares at me for a beat but his handsome face gives me nothing. I can't tell if I've impressed him or bombed the hell out of this interview. Oh well, if anything, at least I got to see some charming, creepy villa on the cliffs of Capri up close and ogle a really hot Italian Stallion. That's something to cross off my bucket list.

He presses his lips together and nods at the door. "Miss MacLean, thank you. Would you mind telling Felisa to come in? I would like to speak to her now. Alone."

"Where should I go?" I ask.

"You can wait in the kitchen. Feel free to help yourself to water."

Water. How generous.

I give him a stiff smile and then quickly get out of my chair, glad for an easy exit. I open the door, just as heavy as it looks, and see Felisa standing across the hall, practically motionless.

"He wants to speak with you alone," I tell her.

She's trying to read my face but I'm not sure what it's giving her. She walks into the library and shuts the door behind her.

I collapse against the white wall and let my body sink to the cold tiles. I breathe out a sigh of relief that it's over, though my nerves are still hissing with adrenaline.

Now, I wait.

CHAPTER THREE

Felisa and Signor Larosa are taking a long time in the library. I don't know why. Either you hire someone or you don't. Then again, I guess teaching two troubled children requires more thought than the average job, and I certainly didn't sell myself. I basically told him I needed the job because I needed money. Oh, and that I wanted to prove us both wrong, which was true, but mainly that I wanted to prove *him* wrong since he seemed to have made up his mind about me. Not exactly the most compelling reasons to hire someone.

Tired of sitting on the tiles like some reject, I get up and wander into the kitchen. It's twice the size of my parents' kitchen. (My mother was so proud when we got the house all those years ago because she could finally bake her heart out.) This kitchen is part modern with gleaming chrome, and part rustic—thick marble countertops and vibrant pottery. I think about having a glass of water after all when I hear feet on the staircase. I turn to see Alfonso standing at the entryway of the kitchen, staring at me with his hands on his hips.

Ah shit.

The little boy rattles something off in Italian and it strikes me that he still has his uniform on. Hasn't he ever head of playtime? And just what the hell is he saying?

"Hi," I say to him, trying to smile as big as I can. "I'm Amber." I point to myself. I point to him. "You're Alfonso."

He frowns, and he's the spitting image of his brother. He's going to grow up to be one brooding, glowering model dude himself.

"I know," he says in the cutest, angriest, most heavily accented English ever. "You are to teach us English."

I cock my head at him and keep smiling. "Well, I hope so."

"Where you from? America?"

"Yes, I am. From California. Do you know where that is?"

"You are a movie star?"

Now my smile is genuine. I shake my head. "No, I'm not."

"Is it because your face is too small?"

I can't help putting my hand on my cheek. I *do* have a small face.

The little jerk has a smug smile on his face. I'm trying to think of an appropriate insult to hurl back at a seven-year-old when I hear the door to Signor Larosa's office open. A second later, Felisa is looking at us with a wry expression on her face. She says something in a warning tone to Alfonso that makes him run away and then beckons me with her finger to follow her. I feel like I'm going to the principal's office.

Back in the library, Signor Larosa stands at the French doors at the front of the room, staring at the sea. Felisa and I stand by his desk but don't say anything. I wonder if maybe I should clear my throat or something when he speaks.

"Do you really think you can handle this job, Miss MacLean?" he asks without turning around, his voice low and foreboding. I can tell he wants me to say no, but as difficult as it sounds, it's also not rocket science.

"Yes, I do," I tell him.

He sighs and then turns around. Now that he's standing up I have a much clearer view of him. I know why my first thought was that he was a model: He's dressed impeccably.

Fashion in men isn't something I really notice, unless it's a hipster who's trying too hard, but Signor Larosa's style looks elegant and effortless and just plain cool. He's wearing a blue blazer with the sleeves pushed up to the elbows and a white dress shirt. A thin orange-and-blue-printed silk scarf is knotted around his neck, just visible beneath his collar. I'd been focusing too much on his face before to even notice. His long legs are clad in stone-colored, slim-cut denim and his shoes are blue Converse to match his jacket. Like most men here, he seems to eschew socks.

He's also taller than I thought, maybe six feet, with a slim but athletic build. His pants hug his hips just enough to outline a bit of a visible bulge. Or maybe it's just the lighting in here. Or maybe I'm just a pervert.

And again, I'm aware that I'm gawking at him. Was I supposed to say something else? How much time has just passed? Am I being really obvious? I jerk my eyes upward.

He purses his lips, his brows drawn together. I stare at him dead-on, keeping my face as attentive as possible. I can feel Felisa's eyes looking between the two of us.

Signor Larosa walks toward us, surprisingly light on his feet for such a moody man, hands behind his back. He stops behind his desk and gives me an exaggerated nod.

Please don't look at his junk, please don't look at his junk, I beg myself. My eyes have been known to have a mind of their own around the male species, especially when tight-ish pants and/or big appendages are involved.

"Congratulations, Miss MacLean," he says. "You have the position if you so wish to receive it."

His statement begs for innuendo but I'm too much in shock to really notice.

So I say, "Seriously?" Because he does seem like the type

of man to mess with you for his own enjoyment. Not that I could imagine him enjoying anything.

"I am very serious," he says, unnecessarily. His long fingers wrap around the back of his chair and he leans against it slightly, still watching me. "I would like you to start tomorrow. You are more than welcome to stay the night. Felisa will make up your room."

"Wait, wait, wait," I say, and he raises his brows at me. I blunder on. "I'm happy that I have the job but I'm not accepting it until I know a few more things. For one, what are the hours? Are room and board part of the deal, and if not, will I make enough money to rent a place here on Capri? Is there even a hostel or a cheap backpackers in the area?"

Felisa snorts beside me. Signor Larosa looks at me like I'm the child who needs lessons of some sort.

"There are no such places on Capri, not for the prices I am sure you're looking for," he says. "If you have the option of another place, you are free to take it, however it would be best if you stayed here. We have the extra room. That way you would be a part of the children's lives outside of their lessons."

"Like a nanny?" I ask, and I know I sound horrified. I'm already wrapping the ends of my curls around my fingers in anxiety.

"Felisa is the nanny," he says. "Your job is to teach the children English for two hours every evening. On occasional Saturday afternoons, Felisa may ask you to watch them while she does errands. That will be worked out ahead of time. Your room and your meals will be included, if you so wish. Though perhaps with Felisa's cooking, you may want to make your own."

Oh my God. Did he just crack a *joke*? I look at Felisa, who doesn't look impressed. Not that that's anything new.

He goes on. "There will be an extra allowance of one hundred dollars per week for you to use for whatever you wish."

I do quick calculations in my head. Legally, I have to be out of the country in two months. I spent two weeks in the UK, which doesn't count toward the European Union's tourist visa, but I'd already spent one month in Holland, Germany, and France, plus other parts of Italy. Which means I can only save up eight hundred dollars for a plane ticket at this rate, and that is not going to be enough to get me home.

Still, my instincts tell me to take what I can get. With free room and board, there's still a chance I might find a part-time gig when the kids are at school. This is as good of an opportunity as I'm going to get.

"What about beyond the two months?" I ask him.

He looks at me curiously. "Two months?"

"Well, the whole Shenanigan Visa thingy."

"You mean the Schengen Visa?"

I nod. "Yes, that's what I said. I've been in Europe for a month already, which leaves me two months to stay here legally. Is there any way I can stay beyond that? I mean, unless you only wanted me to stay here for a short while."

He frowns. He clearly hadn't thought of this little predicament. "We'll take it as it comes. That is the saying in your country, is it not?"

I nod. All righty. Well, as long as he's okay with it then I'm okay with it. "Sounds good," I say as I feel all the pieces fall into place. I can do this. I can live here and tutor a pair of brats under the watchful eye of a deliciously grumpy Italian dude and an old spinster housekeeper. I can save up money. Then I can go home. I don't like the idea of returning to reality and responsibilities and my parents, but I'm sure in two months I will be dying to get out of this place.

I smile brightly at Signor Larosa and Felisa. "So, who is going to give me the grand tour?"

They exchange a look.

"I will," Felisa says, unable to hide her sigh.

I keep my eyes on Signor Larosa and offer my hand. "This will make it official."

He eyes my hand, then eyes me. I swear he squints a little. Then he shakes my hand. His grip is strong, hot, and I swear to God I feel a tiny zing of electricity from his palm to mine. I know it's dry and staticky in here, but still. His handshake is as impressive as he is.

He lets go of my hand first and I quickly withdraw mine. His face gives me nothing but handsome lines.

"Come," Felisa says, grabbing my elbow. "I will show you."

I'm escorted out of his office and back into the hall. She shuts the heavy door behind us and then gives me a stern look. "Now that you are hired, you will learn the rules."

"Rules?"

"There are many rules of the house," she says and jerks her pointy chin at the door. "You are never to disturb Signor Larosa when he is in his office."

"What if I need him for something? Like, important?"

"Then you find me."

"What if I can't find you?"

She eyes me with impatience. "You will find me. But if you don't, knock once. If he doesn't answer, don't knock again."

"What does he do in there?"

"That is his business," she says and motions for me to come along. But now I'm staring at the wooden door to his office with even more curiosity. "And," she adds, "the room is off-limits if Signor Larosa is not home. You are never to go in there."

My eyes widen. This is starting to sound like *Beauty and the Beast*. Oh my God, am I Belle? Is he an Italian Beast? Did I just stumble into the best scenario ever? My inner nerd is having heart palpitations.

"Never," she repeats, probably recognizing the dreamy look in my eyes. "He is a very private man. And in that way, don't be hurt if he doesn't want to talk with you. He keeps to himself. He's good and just but he . . . It is best if you concentrate on the children and stay out of his way."

"You must know him very well," I say. I want more info on my new boss and I want it bad.

She looks me square in the eye. "I was practically his second mother. But even mothers don't know their boys all that well. Now, come on. There are more rules."

More rules?

While she shows me the downstairs guest bathroom (complete with Jacuzzi tub, because you know, your guest may want to take a dip after dinner), her room and en suite, the laundry room, the breakfast nook, the living and dining rooms, the exercise room, family room, and kitchen—the tile and gold practically give me a headache—she rattles off more rules.

She is not to be disturbed between the hours of eleven p.m. and six a.m.

I am not to disturb Signor Larosa when he is in his bedroom, at any time.

I am not to disturb the children between nine p.m. and seven a.m.

If the phone rings and someone asks for Signor Larosa, the call is to be passed to her. If she is not home, I am to take a message. I don't bother pointing out that it would be impossible for me to write in Italian but I think that's the point.

If someone comes to the door, they are not allowed in the house unless she is there to authorize it. So really, don't answer the door, ever.

I am not to have guests over without asking permission first. The way she says that one makes me think she wants to add, *No boys in your room either*.

The children are not allowed to leave the property unsupervised.

I have a curfew of one a.m.

And if I hear funny noises or screaming in the house, I am to ignore it.

"Wait, what?" I ask as we climb up the stairs to the second floor. "Screaming?"

She swallows hard, looking uneasy. "It is nothing to worry about. Sometimes . . . sometimes Signor Larosa has nightmares."

My hand flies to my chest. "About what? Has he seen a doctor about them?" Because, uh, that's not normal.

She nods but doesn't say anything until she takes me down the upper hallway and gestures toward the door in front of us. It's situated right above Signor Larosa's office and I'm guessing it's just as big. "This is the master suite. It was his parents' room, before they passed. It is his now. You will have his old room. It's at the other end, so it shouldn't be a problem for you. Here."

She grabs my elbow again and leads me to a room next to Signor Larosa's. The door is partly open so she pushes it the rest of the way. It's a large room, with blue-edged tile and a big indigo rug in the middle. There's a desk in the corner, a few bookcases, and a small bed with a cartoon shark-print bedspread. That's the only sign that this is a child's room.

"Alfonso sleeps here," she says and points at a door inside. "That leads to a bathroom that he and Annabella share." We walk down the hall and look into Annabella's room. It's pretty much the same as Alfonso's but she has more books and there are a few dolls sticking out of a box. Her bedspread is leopard print. Sassy.

"Where are the kids?" I ask, since they aren't in their rooms.

She leads me to the end of the hall to two doors. She opens one of them and pokes her head in. It's carpeted—gasp—and the kids are sitting on the floor, flipping through coloring books. They have a TV playing in the background with what seems like Italian-dubbed *Dora the Explorer*, and the room is full of organized chaos. Suddenly they seem like little kids, and they aren't in their uniforms anymore either. Annabella is wearing shorts and a zebra-print top. Guess she likes the prints. Alfonso looks like a mini version of his older brother in a dark polo shirt and knee-length khaki shorts.

"Alfonso, Annabella," Felisa addresses them. "Signorina Amber MacLean will now be your tutor. She will be living in the room next door and will help you to better your English. You must behave for her, listen to her, and do as you're told."

Alfonso looks upset, says something in Italian, then gestures to the room that's to become mine. Annabella's lip quivers and she promptly sheds big, sad tears.

Holy cheesus, what is going on?

Felisa says something sharply to them—no sympathy from this lady—and then shuts the door to their muffled cries. I'm staring at her with big eyes, my maternal instincts that I didn't even know I had all tied up in knots.

She avoids my stare for a moment then gives me a look that says she's more affected than she lets on. Her eyes are watering and she takes in a deep, steadying breath.

"They are still upset over their parents' death," she explains in a low voice.

"Well, of course they are," I tell her. "I can't imagine what that would be like."

She nods, considering that. "You are to sleep in Signor Larosa's old room. The one he was in before he married."

Married? *Married?!*

"Married?"

She grimaces as if she's said too much. She probably has since she barely divulges anything. "Was married. They are divorced now. Not long after the accident. But that is his story to tell, not mine."

One story he'll never tell since you told me to basically never talk to him, I think.

Sighing, she continues, "The children still hope that Signor Larosa will go back to his room. But now that you will stay there, it means that . . ."

"Their parents aren't coming back," I fill in sadly.

She shakes her head. "Alfonso seems to be the one who knows this but sometimes Annabella has a hard time. It's been two years but she remembers them as if they were here yesterday. She knows the truth but she prefers to live in a dream world. When that dream is no more, she has problems. You will see. The doctors say she needs time."

"It sounds like she needs therapy," I say, crossing my arms and feeling a bit cold.

"She has someone at school she talks to," she says. "Signor Larosa thinks that is enough."

I frown. To be fair, Signor Larosa has only been taking care of them for two years. He's only twenty-nine. I'm not sure how much he can know about any of this. But then again, I am not one to talk. This is a house where I should definitely keep my opinions to myself.

She opens the door to my room and we step inside. It's

bigger than I expected. The tiles are terracotta, giving it some warmth, and there's a large, fluffy, white throw rug in the middle. The queen-size bed fits into a bit of an arched alcove in the wall, framed by fancy moldings. There's also a love seat and coffee table right in front of a window that overlooks the front yard, with its bower of lemon trees, and the towering hill on the other side of Via Tragara. It's almost completely dark now and the lemons glow yellow in the fading light.

I look to Felisa for permission before I open the door to my right. It leads to a nice en suite bathroom, complete with a shower and tub, marble counters, and gilded faucets.

Yup. I could live here. Oh wait. I will be living here.

"This is very nice," I tell her. "Are you sure you don't want this room?"

She dismisses me with a wave. "This is too much for me. My room is just fine." She looks around and points to an ancient-looking armoire. "There should be some spare clothes in there. This is usually an additional guest room, though we don't have them anymore. I'll let you settle in. I have a meal to prepare."

"Do you need any help?"

"No, thank you," she says and then closes the door, leaving me alone in the room.

I stand in the middle of the room for a moment, trying to take it all in, but it's too much. I throw my purse on the love-seat and then collapse, starfish style, onto the bed, facedown. It's comfortable. Signor Larosa must have had good sleeps in here.

At that I start thinking about him and everything I've learned. He has night terrors that might wake me in the night. His parents are dead. He's been left in charge of his much-younger brother and sister. He was married, now divorced. There has been more than one accident. He seems to not like me very much but obviously likes me enough to hire me. I'm not allowed to really talk to him, let alone look at him.

But I do want to look at him. A lot. And I want to talk to him, too. I want to know more about him, what happened, why he got divorced. I want to know what his dreams are about. I want to know what he does in that beautiful library-turned-office all day long. I want to know about the *Villa dei Limoni Tristi*. I want to know everything.

My brain is working on overdrive. In the room there is silence except for a warm breeze that comes in through the window, rustling the gauzy curtains, and the hum of crickets and cicadas.

I shut my eyes for a second.

....

There is a knocking sound. It's in the darkness but I can't tell if I'm asleep and dreaming or awake. I can't see anything.

"Amber," I hear Felisa say, her voice sounding disembodied. "Signorina MacLean."

"Yes?" I croak, my throat feeling like it's been stuffed with cotton. I suddenly remember where I am. Sad lemon house. Capri. New job. Traumatized twins. Hot, mysterious Italian boss.

What a crazy fucking day.

I pry myself off the bed and stumble over to the door, nearly sliding on the rug. I feel for the handle and then open it.

It's completely dark out in the hall except for Felisa, who is holding a lantern in front of her face, her wrinkled features black in the shadows. She looks straight from a Gothic thriller and I have to blink a few times to remember what century I live in. But then I notice the lantern is battery-operated and the flame is phony, like one of those fake candles.

"The children have gone to bed and like to sleep in complete darkness but must have their doors open," she explains. "They complain if the hall light is on. I am off to bed soon. I wanted to let you know that I saved you some dinner. I tried to wake you up earlier but couldn't. I didn't want to disturb you if you needed your rest."

I don't want to be a bother to her but since she saved me some dinner and I'm absolutely starving, I nod my head. "Thank you, I would love some food."

I follow her out into the hall quietly as we pass by the twins' rooms and head down the stairs. I notice that there's a light visible under the door to Signor Larosa's room. I wonder if he's gone to sleep already as well.

Once in the kitchen, Felisa pulls out a bowl from the fridge and puts it in the microwave. I sit on the barstool at the giant island, waiting for her to tell me not to sit there but she doesn't seem to care. She's tired and seems a bit defeated, which is a change from earlier.

I feel the urge to say something, to fill up the silence as the microwave clock counts down. But surprisingly, she beats me to it.

"Signor Larosa is a very nice man," she says softly, resting her hand on the counter and staring blankly at the dish in the microwave as it goes around and around. "And the children are lovely. Please don't hold who they are now against them. They were not always angry. Once, everything was different. This was a beautiful house. The children were happy, always smiling. Signor Larosa had his own career. He was a motorcycle racer, you see. Their mother was a famous novelist, and their father owned the newspaper in Sorrento. This family was very successful, very happy. Then, one horrible night, it was all gone. Taken by God. Things have never been the same.

Sometimes I am afraid they never will be. And that is a difficult thing for me to watch. I have been here for twenty-nine years, but now I am losing my courage."

There are so many things I want to say, want to ask, but Felisa seems to be having a moment. I feel like she's talking more to herself than she is to me.

The microwave finally beeps and she takes the dish out, placing it in front of me. It's full of large ravioli in a creamy red sauce. It looks amazing and smells even better. She grabs a fork from a drawer, and as she hands it to me I catch her eyes.

"How did they die?" I whisper.

"They drowned," she says. "One night, the elder Signor Larosa and the Signora took their private boat to Sorrento for a benefit dinner. Signor Derio, who lived in Positano with his wife at the time, was to meet them there. The sea was rough, as it usually is in November, but they made it. After the benefit, Signor Derio decided to come home with them to visit the children. His wife remained in Positano. They were halfway across when the waves got too bad. They radioed for help but the boat was overtaken and capsized. Signore and Signora drowned, yet somehow, Signor Derio did not. They found him hours later hanging on to a seat cushion that he must have ripped off."

I almost drop my fork. This is far, far more horrible than I imagined.

"Didn't they have life jackets?"

She shook her head. "I assume there was not enough time to get them. Signor Larosa doesn't talk about it," she goes on, her voice softer now. "He refuses to talk about it, to anyone. But the nightmares, the screaming. I know he suffers in his dreams. He might be reliving it over and over." She pauses, clearly moved. "He is a good man. I've said that before. His parents were the world to him. He would have fought to keep them alive. It must be horrible to try and save the people you love and to fail in the end."

A tear runs down my cheek, and I'm suddenly overcome with emotion. My parents drive me absolutely nuts. My dad's harshness, my mother's inability to cope with her emotions without food. But I still love them to bits. I don't know what I would do if I were in Mr. Larosa's shoes, if I saw my parents drown before my eyes.

"Don't cry," Felisa chastises me, her features growing hard again. "To be in this house, you must become tough. You cannot let your emotions for the children and what happened get in the way. They deserve your sympathy but they, too, must move on. They are stronger than they think they are."

"And what about Mr.—Signor—Larosa," I say. "Am I not to have compassion for him?"

Her mouth quirks up into a dry smile. "Many women have compassion for him. They try to get him out of his shell, to make him feel. But they do not succeed."

"That's not really what I was talking about," I quickly say. "I mean in a . . . friendly way."

"He is your boss now, the master of the house. He is not your friend. The sooner you realize this, the better. Amber, he has not left this island in a year. He refuses to cross the sea. He has a lot of damage deep inside. Your job is to help the children learn English. It is not to solve all the problems of this house. If I can't solve them, neither can you."

Well, that sounded like a challenge, if I ever heard one.

"But . . ." I say feebly.

"No more," she says with a shake of her head. "I have told you more than you should know. Eat your dinner."

"But if they died at sea two years ago, why is it only in the last year that he hasn't left the island? What is this other accident you spoke of? Is that when his wife left him?"

"Eat your food," she repeats. "You have to go back tomorrow to Positano for your things. The first lesson will begin tomorrow night. You have a long day ahead of you."

"I don't know if I feel comfortable leaving the island now either."

She gives me a look. "I will see you in the morning. We eat at eight thirty a.m. if you wish to join us." And at that she turns and walks out of the kitchen. I'm grateful she left her little lantern behind so I can find my way back to the room without falling down the stairs.

I take in a deep breath, trying to wrestle with all this new information. My heart feels heavy, sinking at the thought of what they've all been through. I know Felisa's advice was to toughen up, but I don't want to if I don't have to.

I slowly finish my food—delicious, though I don't take any pleasure from it—and look around. Suddenly, I'm aware of how big and dark the house is. I put the dish and fork in the large sink and decide to leave the light above the stove on. I pick up the lantern and am about to head up the stairs when something just outside of the back doors catches my eye.

I carefully walk across to the breakfast nook that opens onto the back patio and look through the glass and into the darkness. The sky is clear and the crescent moon shines just enough to bathe the sea in stripes of silver light.

There's a tall silhouette at the edge of the patio leaning against the railing and staring out into nothing. I can tell it's Mr. Larosa. A small light burns, flickering in and out, and a puff of smoke follows. So he smokes. That doesn't surprise me. Everyone in Italy smokes. They know the warnings and they don't care. It's part of their lust for life.

I watch for a few moments, wishing I could turn off the lantern so I can observe him unseen. But I don't want to risk not being able to turn it on again, and when I look back out the window, I can see his position has changed. He's watching *me* now.

I raise my hand, just enough to qualify as a wave. He doesn't move. The cigarette burns orange red in the darkness.

I quickly lower my hand, feeling stupid, and scurry away through the house and up the stairs. I close the door to my room and breathe in deeply, actually feeling kind of angry. It was just a wave. I shouldn't feel so rankled by it but I do. Damaged or not, it's just plain rude not to return such a gesture.

There's not much else for me to do, so I take off my pants and climb into the soft covers of the bed. I leave the lantern on, even though it creates creepy shadows on my wall. If I'm this annoyed by him already, there's no telling how I'm going to survive the next two months.

This is your ticket home, I tell myself.

I repeat it again and again.

CHAPTER FOUR

I wake up slowly, blinking my eyes at the sun streaming through the windows. I already know where I am, even half asleep. When you travel all the time, spending nearly every night in a different bed, you adjust quickly.

I'm in my new room at the *Villa dei Limoni Tristi*. For the first time in a very, very long time, I realize what this means: my own room. I have privacy. It was just me, alone in the room. No snoring Canadians or smelly Swiss boys. I smile to myself and settle into the bed even further. Normally, when I wake up I get up and get ready. Sleeping in doesn't really exist in a hostel. But it can exist here.

Then I hear the muffled yells of the children from downstairs and I realize that I probably can't sleep in here either. I have to get back to Positano and then I'm on the job.

I slip on my wrinkled clothes from yesterday, even though they smell kind of rank, then head into the bathroom to try and make myself look presentable. It's not easy to do with a small cosmetics case and no toothbrush, but I manage to find a spare toothbrush and toothpaste still in the wrapper in one of the many drawers and douse myself in a lemon-smelling perfume that livens me right up.

My hair is a disaster and only Carrie Bradshaw can get away with the crazy curly bedhead I have going on right now, so I pull it back into a low braid and slick on some anti-frizz serum that I carry in my purse at all times. My face is looking a bit puffy—I'm probably not drinking enough water—but there's not much I can do about that. I know I can look quite pretty when I put some effort into it, but today I don't have any ammo. Plus there's no one to impress.

Who am I kidding. There *is* someone to impress. It's just that I doubt Mr. Larosa would notice even if, I don't know, Beyoncé was standing in his house, naked in front of him.

Once I am somewhat satisfied I head out the room and walk down the hall, peeking over the railing at the open living area below. The voices are much louder now, drifting up from the kitchen. Alfonso is protesting something or other and Annabella is making whining noises. Felisa is chastising both of them. I can see how I will need to walk a fine line with those two. On the one hand I feel so terribly sorry for them because of all they've been through. On the other, they can't go through life acting like delinquents.

When I round the staircase I glance out the windows and doors to the patio and backyard. The day is bright and sparkling, so beautifully alive. It's amazing how sunshine can clear away the doubts that night bring.

I try to keep that thought in mind as I approach the kitchen. Alfonso and Annabella are at the round table in the breakfast nook, picking at their food. On the kitchen island is a lavish spread of cold cuts, cheese, and bread—a typical Italian breakfast.

"Espresso?" Felisa asks me, already reaching for the tiny cup. Coffee—dark and so strong it's nearly painful—is a way of life here, so I don't dare refuse. Plus, I need it. My head is still a bit in a fog.

She starts making the espresso from a fancy, gold-toned machine and eyes me over her shoulder. "Do you know how to use this?"

I nod. Luckily I do since I worked at Starbucks part-time during my first two years of college.

"Good," she says. "Help yourself to the breakfast."

I grab a plate and pile meat and cheeses on it and pour myself a cup of orange juice, sneaking a glance over at the table. Do I sit here at the kitchen island or do I go and sit with the children? Part of me wants to just drink my coffee and try to wake up, but the other part realizes that if I am to teach these kids I should start making an effort to befriend them right now.

I wait until Felisa hands me my espresso cup. I shoot it back in the customary fashion, wincing as it burns down my throat. This stuff isn't to be sipped; it's something to get over with, like hard liquor. Then I take the juice and the plate to the table. I draw a deep breath, smiling at the children, who aren't looking at me, and sit down. Annabella shoots me a furtive glance and concentrates on spreading honey on her bread. Alfonso takes a messy sip of his juice and then spits it right back into the glass. He looks at me defiantly, waiting for me to get angry with him.

Instead, I smile even wider, gulp back most of my juice, then spit a little back into the glass. Yeah, it's gross, but at least it makes him giggle. Felisa turns around at that, staring at us with hostile curiosity. I look down and busy myself with my prosciutto.

After that, Alfonso goes back to being grumpy and it's not long before Felisa is gathering the twins together to take them to school. She tells me it won't take her long, but if I wish I can leave as soon as Signor Larosa gets back from his ride.

"Motorcycle ride?" I ask as she ushers the children out the front door.

"Yes, he goes every morning."

I wonder where he rides since the island isn't very big, but she's already closing the heavy front door on me, the kids halfway up the lemon-strewn path to the road.

I sigh and grab my purse from the bedroom before heading back downstairs. I try out the espresso machine, finding it just as simple, albeit more compact than the ones at Starbucks. Then I briefly eye the door to his office and pause. If he were to come home from his ride, I would definitely hear a motorcycle. I reach for the door but stop myself. It's probably locked, and if it's not there're probably cameras or some shit set up. He may even be inside the office right now and the whole motorbike story was a ruse to see how curious and disobedient I am.

Well, I won't give him that satisfaction. I swiftly head out the back doors by the breakfast nook and into the backyard.

It really is a shame that the area is in a bit of disarray. Unless the pool is half full for safety reasons, it really should have more water in it. The outdoor furniture needs some sprucing up and the flowers and plants need a lot of attention and care. Now that I'll be living here, I know what I'll be doing in my spare time: bringing the villa back to its former beauty. If the plants are pruned and thriving, then maybe everything in the house will fall in line.

I walk to the edge of the patio and carefully peek over the railing, ever conscious of my fear of heights. The slope beneath isn't too steep and I marvel at the cacti and bright purple bougainvillea clinging to the earth among fragrant sage shrubs and wiry grass. Beyond that, the sea beckons—deep, beautiful, blue. Small boats weave between the sharp spires of the Faraglioni Rocks, possibly carrying tourists up the coast to the famous Blue Grotto, a sea cave I read about in my Italian guidebook and am dying to see for myself.

Time slips past me. With the dry air, the salty breezes, and the hot sun bursting through a few low-lying clouds, I feel as if I could stay here forever. Here, in this moment, it's just me and this earth and this sea and this sky. There is no uncertain future to head home to, no fear—fear that I won't be able to find a good job, that if I do find a good job I'll be stuck in it forever, that I'll never be able to move out of my parents' house and live on my own, that I'll turn into my parents. Fear that I'll never lose those last ten pounds, that I'll never find someone to love who will love me in return, that I'll never really grow up.

Fear that I'll never truly be happy.

Because what this trip has taught me so far is that the happiness I'm seeking can't be found at home. And while it's been hit or miss on my travels, I'm at least one step closer to it on the road. When I'm traveling, I feel like the secret to my life, to myself, to really becoming, is one step ahead. It's in the next destination, the next town I get lost in, the next stranger I talk to. It's always next but never here. But when I go home, back to the way things used to be, there is no *next*. It's all over. The wonder and the hope are gone.

I like having hope. And I hope I find what I'm looking for before I have to leave.

"*Salve.*" I hear a deep voice from behind me. Somehow I resist the urge to jump out of my skin.

I whirl around to see Mr. Larosa approaching me. He's wearing aviator shades, big black moto boots, dark jeans, and a dark gray T-shirt, with a leather jacket slung over his shoulder. A cigarette hangs out of his mouth. He looks like an Italian James Dean.

I really want to stop referring to him as Mr. Larosa.

"Hi," I say to him. "Nice morning."

He nods. "Do you know what *salve* means?"

Time to quiz me on my Italian? "It's the formal way of saying hello. I mean, *ciao*."

He takes a drag from his cigarette and I can feel him watching me, even though I can't see his eyes. "I'm surprised to see you here."

"Good surprise or bad surprise?" I find myself asking. I don't know why my mouth has a mind of its own whenever he's around.

His own mouth twitches as if supressing a smile. "It's just a surprise. It doesn't have to be either, does it?"

"Just like luck," I say.

He nods and blows smoke away from me. I watch the muscles in his neck strain as he does so. He has one lovely neck, the kind you want to suck on for a moment or two. I bet he tastes like spices.

"Yes," he says slowly. "Just like luck."

"Felisa said you were out on your motorbike."

He nods again, coming to stand beside me. One of his hands wraps along the railing as he stares out at the view, his back ramrod straight.

"I didn't hear it come in," I note, trying to keep the conversation going.

"I park it on the street. There is a gate for it." He turns his head in my direction. "You were in your own little world here."

I sure was. "I was lost in the view," I say.

He takes a slow drag, not saying anything. I can see my reflection in his glasses and wish that I could have put maybe a bit more effort into my appearance. Also my purse is pulling on my shirt and making my cleavage pop out more than what's considered classy. I think about adjusting it but don't want to call attention to myself.

"It is beautiful," he says, and at first I think he's talking about my cleavage. Then his head swivels back to the sea. "Angry sometimes, but still beautiful."

"Just like a woman," I remark.

He actually breaks into a full grin. It's so gorgeous—his teeth, my God, his perfect white teeth—that I actually suck in my breath. "Yes, I suppose you are right," he says, his voice sounding the most lighthearted it has been since I've known him. Then the smile vanishes and the clouds settle again. "Tell me, Amber, do you really think you have what it takes to do this job?"

I swallow hard, wishing I had more confidence. "I'm going to find out."

"Have you ever really been tested before?" He flicks ash to the ground and the breeze blows it away. "Not by children. I mean by life."

I frown at him, feeling a bit pissed off at the question. "Of course I have. Who hasn't?"

He shrugs. "Some people go through life without a single true trial."

"Not me."

He runs his hand under his jaw, his stubble making a scratchy sound, and then says, "Good. Trials make you stronger."

Yet as he says that I wonder why he doesn't take that to heart. His own trials, his brother and sister's trials, it all seems to have made them weaker. But here I go again, making assumptions about things I know nothing about. I've had my tribulations in life but they don't compare to what he's been through.

"You called me Amber earlier," I point out. "Not Signorina MacLean. I know you're my boss and everything, but I'd really rather not call you Signor Larosa. And I really hope you'll address me with *ciao* instead of *salve*."

He cocks his head at me. "You are a very bold woman." Then he nods, as if affirming something to himself.

I try not to beam at that. "But what should I call you? Desiderio? What do Alfonso and Annabella call you? Desi?"

"Actually, they call me Derio. And you can, too, if you wish."

"All right, Derio," I say to him and hold out my hand. "My name is Amber, pleased to meet you."

He arches a brow but shakes my hand again. There is no electric shock this time but the feel of his warm palm against mine is doing something funny to my insides. My nerves feel carbonated. "*Incantato*," he says in a low, charming voice, and the feeling intensifies.

He finally lets go of my hand and I try to compose myself. Damn it, when did I turn into such a girl? Swooning over a handshake?

He clears his throat. "You better hurry if you want to catch the next ferry back to Positano," he says. "That is, if you wish to be back here tonight for the first lessons."

I nod, feeling that moody distance creep back into his tone. He's right, though. Not only do I have to get back to the mainland and hike all the way up that damn hill to get my stuff, I have to find a bookstore somewhere that has something that might tell me the first thing about teaching English to Italian children. I have a feeling that won't be so easy, though. Thank God for my Kindle and the ability to buy just about any book at any time. I've always been a lover of paperbacks and hardcovers, but eReaders really save your ass while traveling.

"I will see you later," I tell him, then add, "Derio." I love the way it rolls off my tongue.

Despite what we just shook on, he doesn't seem all that pleased to hear me calling him that. His mouth draws together into a thin line and he nods curtly. I trot off, ignoring his personality change. I hope he's not Moody McMooderson when I get back.

Going back to Positano seems a lot more dramatic than the trip coming over to Capri. Maybe it's because there's a slight swell to the seas and I'm extra conscious now of the way that Derio's parents died. Maybe it's because once I step foot on the mainland, I know I never have to go back to Capri if I don't want to. I can stay in Positano and avoid responsibility and spend my days lounging on the beach with a few good books.

But the fact is, that scenario would only last a week. And then I would really be shit out of luck. I'm cut off from my parents, and I have no friends to loan me money (they're all as broke as I am). I can either find another job or I'm really fucking screwed. And the chances of me finding another job that supplies me with a hundred euros a week, plus room and board, is next to impossible.

So while I slog up the hill in Positano, past all the little boutiques overflowing with ceramics and limoncello, past vine-covered restaurants and lumbering tourists, I make up my mind.

Once I arrive at the hostel, I manage to get my money refunded for the rest of the week. Amanda, the front desk girl who fell in love with the hot Italian cop, gives me her phone number and tells me to call her if I ever want to meet up or if I have any problems. Then I say goodbye to Ana and Hendrik, who happen to be cooking lunch in the communal kitchen.

They were kind of worried when I didn't show up last night but figured I'd met someone. Funny how they keep on figuring this about me, even though I've never hooked up with a boy since they've been around. Maybe they figure it's long overdue. I can't argue with that. I tell them to e-mail if they happen to go to Capri and I wish them luck on their journeys.

Ana seems sad but I know the minute I'm gone they'll continue on like nothing has happened. That's the thing about traveling couples. They never really integrate into the backpackers' way of life the same way the solo traveler does. No matter where they go or who they see or what they do, they will always have each other. Me, I sometimes feel like I lose a bit of myself every time I have to say goodbye to a person or a place.

But this time I don't feel any loss or sadness. I feel excitement. As I watch them make cheap packaged meals in the kitchen, I'm reminded that all of my meals are taken care of now. I don't have to eat like a pauper off of borrowed plates. I don't have to share my room with seven other people or wait in line for the toilet or—as has happened a few times— shower with other women. I don't have to watch my stuff all the time or feel like it's seconds from being stolen.

At that thought I go and get my backpack out of the lockers, pull the straps over my shoulders, and get out of the hostel. It may be the last time I see one for quite a long time.

....

I get back to Capri a bit earlier than I expected, benefitting from good timing with the hydrofoils. There's a bit of a pinch in my throat when I see the mainland disappear in a haze. I wonder if I, too, will be like Derio now, trapped on this rock in the middle of the Tyrrhenian Sea.

Maybe because of this isolated feeling, I drag my feet a bit as I head back to the house. When I take the funicular to the crowded streets of Capri town, I decide to explore a bit. Everything is so expensive and posh and geared toward locals and well-off tourists that it's hard to find some place to go. It's the afternoon now and I'm dying for a pint of beer or a glass of rosé to take the edge off but I don't want to spend five euros on a small glass, even though I got about a hundred euros back just by canceling my stay at the hostel. I need every penny for the plane ticket back home.

I go down one path, which leads up some stairs past a church and out of the busy town center and find my holy grail, finally: an Irish pub. In all the countries and cities I've been to, no matter how lonely I've felt or isolated because of language barriers, I have always found my English-speaking brethren either drinking in or working at an Irish pub.

Here seems to be no exception. I walk into the small joint, all dark wood walls, brass accents and green leather seats, and see two white boys who look at me and smile. One with a shaved head seems half drunk and gives me the overly appreciative up and down. Well, at least I've impressed someone today, though once again I'm conscious that I didn't even change clothes at the hostel. After this drink, the next thing I'm doing is taking a two-hour shower.

"Hello, Blondie," the drunk guy says with a thick English accent. "Can I buy you a drink?"

Wow. That was fast. I eye him and then his friend. His friend is quiet, smiling shyly at me, and kind of cute with thick brown hair and small blue eyes.

"Sure," I say to him, satisfied that they're just a couple of drunk and soon-to-be drunk backpackers. "I'd like that." I sit down across from them and am promptly introduced to Cole from Birmingham, England, and Charles from Louisville, Kentucky. They met in Amsterdam, bonded over weed, and decided to see the Mediterranean together.

"So cute," I comment.

"Hey, I'm buying you a beer, not *him*," Cole says, slurring enough to make me think he doesn't need another beer. But according to him, he does. He stands up and walks over to the empty bar. So far we're the only people I've seen in the place.

Cole hollers, "Yo, pretty bird!"

Pretty bird?

At that the bartender pokes her head around the corner, her eyes trained on him in a decidedly evil manner. "What did I tell you about calling me that?" she says in a slight New York accent. "My name is Shay and if you can't call me that then I can't serve you."

Shay crosses her arms and throws a rag down on the counter in a huff. She seems like a tough little cookie. She's also absolutely gorgeous, and I can see why Cole has stooped to calling her nicknames. She's tall, curvy in all the right places, with long, thick, golden-brown hair and Brigitte Bardot bangs. She's even got the Bardot pout going on, with full lips and pale lipstick, though her skin is dark bronze and her eyes are strikingly hazel. She's definitely got a Middle Eastern bombshell thing about her.

"Sorry, sorry," Cole says. "I was just buying a beer for my new friend here, Andrea from San Francisco, California."

I give him a stiff smile. "Actually, it's Amber from San Jose, California." I look at Shay. "I promise I won't call you any nicknames."

She laughs at that and I'm glad. When I first started traveling I felt too shy and unsure of myself to let loose with people I didn't really know. That's one of the main things that has changed about me. I'm more eager to make friends, more confident talking to strangers, and I can eat at a restaurant or go to a movie alone without feeling like a loser or caring what people think.

"Go sit down," she tells Cole. "And I'll be buying Amber her drink, not you." She smiles at me. "First drink here is on the house, so what will it be?"

I give Cole an apathetic shrug and then go over to the bar, where I can see the selection. I usually accept drinks from guys because it saves me money but only after I'm sure the guy knows that nothing is going to come out of it. With Cole drunk, I can't be sure if he does or doesn't expect anything, even if it's only two in the afternoon.

"Whatever is on tap is fine," I say, quickly adding, "but something light. No Guinness."

"I like easy customers," she says and pours me a pint of Peroni. She passes it to me and wipes her hand on her apron. "So, Amber from San Jose, I'm Shay from Brooklyn."

I raise the beer at her. "Nice to meet you. So how did you get this gig?" I ask, nodding at the bar.

She shrugs. "My boyfriend and I came here three months ago. We drank at this bar every night for a week, not wanting to leave. The previous bartender was going back to Ireland so we just kind of swapped."

"But what about the whole Schengen Visa thing?"

She shrugs again. "Italy is really relaxed about people over-staying their welcome, or so we were told. When we flew into Europe, we made sure to fly into Rome. They never stamped our passports for entry there so there's no real proof of how long we've been here."

"Lucky," I say. "I have to leave in two months."

She makes a face. "Well, you can probably stay a bit longer. A lot of the people I meet, the customs officials don't even look at their passports when they leave."

"*Ciao, bella!*" A singsongy voice comes from the door. I turn to see two Italian girls enter, all long limbs and even longer hair. They wave at Shay and sit down at a table by a window. I spy a Fendi purse being placed on an empty chair. So chic.

"*Ciao! Un momento*," Shay says and then starts pouring two Guinnesses. She nods at the girls and eyes me. "Those're Utavia and Lenora. They come here every Friday for their cheat day. They love Guinness but I guess it doesn't mesh very well with their diets."

I look back at the girls. So much for Italians being able to eat everything and anything. These girls obviously have to work to stay slim.

Shay runs the beers over to them and comes back to me. With only a few people in the bar we get to talking, and soon I'm two beers in and feeling a bit buzzy. She tells me all about her boyfriend, Danny, and how they were a lot like me—couldn't find a job after college so they decided to work boring jobs and save money and just travel instead. As I talk to her, I get to thinking that maybe I'll just do that again when I go home. Forget about using my English degree, I'll just work at Starbucks and travel all over again. Or maybe I can even use the experience I get at the Larosas' and teach English somewhere else in Europe.

I'm daydreaming about this when Shay asks me, "So how long are you planning to stay in Capri for?"

"Well, unless I can get a work visa or something like that, two months."

"Oh, I thought you were traveling in Italy for two months. You're going to be on Capri for that long?"

I nod. "I got a job as of yesterday. Teaching English to children. Of course, I don't know the first thing about teaching or teaching English to Italian kids, but they seem to know enough already, so I'm hoping it won't be too hard."

"Where will you be living?"

I gesture in the direction of the Faraglioni Rocks. "Down the Via Tragara. *Villa dei Limoni Tristi*. House of sad lemons?"

She frowns and looks over at the Italian girls who are still nursing their beers and chatting away.

"*Scusi*," Shay says in broken Italian. "*Dove si trova Villa dei Limoni Tristi?*"

The girls exchange a look and leave their chairs, coming over to us.

"Why do you ask?" The taller one says in English, eyeing me suspiciously.

"I'm staying there," I tell her. I tilt my head at Shay. "I was telling her I have a job teaching English to the two children who live there."

"Larosa?" the other girl asks. "Annabella and . . . and . . . Alfonso, yes?"

"Yes," I say, somewhat excitedly. "You know them?"

Another brief exchange and then the taller one says, "Yes. I know their brother, Derio."

Is that bitterness I detect in her voice?

"Oh," Shay suddenly says. "That's where the motorcycle guy lives! Yes, okay, I got it now." Then she looks to me. "Oh my God, you're living there? That house has so many rumors around it." She catches the look on my face. "Sorry, don't mean to put a damper on your new job."

My eyes go wide. "What kind of rumors?"

"First of all," the tall one says, "Derio has to be gay."

"Gay?" I repeat. "But he was married."

The woman raises her hand. "Gay. Not interested in women."

Her friend elbows her and laughs. "Not interested in Lenora."

Lenora rolls her eyes. "Anyway, he has mental problems."

"So handsome, though," Shay says somewhat dreamily. She grins at me. "Sometimes I see him riding his bike in the mornings. Danny hates it when I'm trying to sneak a glance."

"The house is so ugly now that Sophie and Adamo are dead. They were their parents. Very nice people, very classy. Derio isn't. He shouldn't have been left in charge. The poor housekeeper, she'll die next if she continues to work so hard."

"Felisa?" I ask, not really appreciating Lenora's callous tone. "She's tough as nails."

Lenora purses her bright pink lips and shrugs. "It's all a shame. The children are orphans, all of them. Even Derio. They should be in the care of people who know what they are doing, not some divorced motorcyclist."

"Ex-motorcyclist," Utavia adds.

"That's right. He doesn't even make money anymore. You know, he was very good at what he did, very famous here in Italy. Had a beautiful wife. But she left him when he quit racing. Went for another racer. That must have hurt, but what did he expect? The money was gone except for what was left in inheritance. But what sort of man lives off of that?"

"And he's gay. She probably left him for that, too," Utavia says jokingly.

"Why, what happened?" I ask. "Why did he quit?"

Lenora sighs as if she's suddenly tired of talking to me.

"There was an accident. About a year after they died. He was racing and his bike spun out. He was favored to win the race but then it happened. He broke his arm and ribs. He wasn't that badly injured but it was enough for him to decide to never race again. He wouldn't really say why, but he quit. Lost the sponsorships, everything. And for nothing."

"But he still rides on the island."

"It's a small island. He doesn't race here. One of the rumors is that he hasn't left Capri since then. Who knows why? That's why we think he is not all right in his head. What kind of man gives up everything to take care of his brother and sister?"

Um, a really good man? I want to spit at her.

"Tell her about your date with him," Utavia says.

Lenora rolls her eyes again. "I would rather not. We went out for dinner to a very nice place in Anacapri. He got too drunk and then ignored me. That's another thing, he drinks too much." She pauses and looks me up and down. "I don't think you're going to last long."

I paste on a smile. "As long as I last two months, then I'll be golden."

She gives me a derisive snort. "You'll see. They've never had a nanny before other than the old woman. What a horrible person she is."

"I'm not the nanny," I point out. "I am teaching the children English."

"Why?" Lenora asks. "They learn that in school."

"Apparently it was the wish of their parents," I say.

"So they were a bit crazy, too. She was an author, you know, Sophie Larosa. Very famous, though she kept to herself. Who knows, maybe she thinks learning more English will make them little writers in all languages." She looks at Shay, who has been listening intently this whole time. "What do we owe you?"

"Ten euro," Shay says and Lenora fishes out a twenty from her Gucci wallet.

Lenora wiggles her manicured nails at me. "The extra ten euro is for you, for the next boat out of here. You'll thank me later when you have no choice but to leave that crazy family."

She turns around and leaves the bar with Utavia.

"I forgot to mention," Shay says carefully and with a smile, "that aside from ordering a Guinness, they also like to indulge in their bitchy tendencies. Don't worry, though, most people on the island are really nice."

I nod, feeling out of sorts and strangely defensive about the Larosas, especially Derio. I don't doubt what she said is true. He could be gay, I guess. His wife probably did leave him over money. He might drink too much. He might have mental problems. But none of that makes me like him any less. Maybe it should, but it doesn't.

"Have another pint?" she asks, just as a few more people enter the bar and sit down next to Cole and Charles.

I glance at the clock on my phone. "I wish I could but I guess I should get going."

"Hey, don't let those girls scare you. You've already been hired right? That means you're right for the job. And anyway, it's just for a couple of months, not a lifetime commitment. You can do anything for a couple of months, I believe that. Besides," she says, and pulls out a paper coaster. She takes her pen out of her apron and writes down her phone and e-mail address. "You have any problems, or just want to talk or have a beer, just call me, okay? You're one of the few Americans I know staying on this island. It would be nice to have a friend."

I take the coaster, tell her I'll be in touch, and attempt to pay for the second beer I had.

She shakes her head. "Just come in next time and maybe I'll let you pay."

I gratefully agree and take off, heading toward my new job and the scary unknown.

CHAPTER FIVE

It's been one week since I was hired to work at the Larosas', one week since I've called the *Villa dei Limoni Tristi* home, and one week since I've seen Shay or really anyone else outside of the household.

During that week I've managed to make Alfonso and Annabella cry. They've made me cry. Felisa has yelled at me. Felisa has yelled at them. I've thought about quitting, especially when notebooks and pencils were hurled at my head by angry Italian children. I've had too much espresso at breakfast and too much wine at dinner. I've spent all my spare time reading up on how to teach these damn kids better, how to be better, and I've spent a lot of time trying to bring the grounds around the house back to life. I've also become convinced there's a ghost in the small attic upstairs.

And yet, during all the trials and tribulations of the first week, I've barely seen Derio at all. Sometimes in the mornings I'll see him walk up the path to the road and bring his motorcycle out of a gated shed to the left of the property and then zoom off. Sometimes I catch him on his bedroom balcony smoking. Sometimes I just see the door to his office closing, as if the ghost I think lives in the house is passing through. But I have not conversed with him, nor exchanged any sort of smile or acknowledgment.

In some ways it's good. It keeps me focused on Alfonso and Annabella. In some ways it's bad, for those same reasons. After one week, the two don't seem to be warming up to me at all. The good news is that their English is at least improving a little bit. So far I've let them choose the topics. For Alfonso, it's sharks; for Annabella, it's everything involving Africa. Turns out her obsession with animal print is because she loves the idea of safaris, not because she's making a fashion statement.

It's Friday afternoon and I'm sitting on the floor in the kids' playroom, going through my day planner and trying to think of what to teach them. I've turned the place into a partial classroom, complete with a whiteboard on an easel, plastic chairs, and a box of "mystery" (aka, weird things of mine or things I find around the house that might make for good show and tell). It's the end of a long, difficult week and I want to make things interesting and fun—then I want to hightail it to the Irish pub and have a few pints with Shay and get hit on by drunk British boys. Anything to take my mind away from here.

There's a knock at the door, and as I say "Come in," I expect to see Felisa telling me she's about to pick up the kids from school. Instead, the door opens and I see Derio poke his head in.

I immediately get to my feet, feeling like the president has just walked into the room.

"Am I disturbing you?" he asks. He still hasn't come in.

I shake my head, smoothing down the front of my yellow maxi dress. "No. Not at all. I was just planning the lesson."

He nods and then comes in. He walks right over to me, hands behind his back, mouthing whatever I have written on the board. I get a whiff of his scent, musk and sage and lemons. I try not to inhale too deeply.

"So this is where you teach them?" he asks, eyeing his surroundings.

"Uh, so far," I say, quickly tucking my hair behind my ears, but being the unruly beast it is, my hair springs forward. "I'm working it out as I go."

"How about teaching them outside, in the sunshine?"

I bite my lip. I considered that. "Perhaps. I just wanted to establish a routine first."

"Very good," he says, his eyes sliding to mine. They're so dark and intense that I feel very small and exposed next to him. I've gone from never seeing him to having him extremely close. It's jarring. I'm not sure I like being jarred.

"And how has your first week been to you?" he asks, his voice lower now.

I'm a horrible liar. "It was okay."

"Just okay?" he asks, sounding a bit amused.

I shrug. "Alfonso is better at throwing pencils than he is at using them. I'm afraid of what will happen if I let him use his iPad."

"But you believe writing by hand is important?"

"It's easier for me," I tell him, honestly. "I guess I'm kind of going by how I've been taught."

A rare smile glimmers across his lips. "But you are barely more than a child yourself."

I want to laugh. I throw my hands out to the sides. "I told you, I'm twenty-four. Just turned it last month." I pause. "And you're only twenty-nine. You're not even thirty yet. We're practically the same age."

"But you look very young," he says.

"It's the hair," I explain.

It looks like he wants to reach out and touch it—his hand moves slightly—but he doesn't. "Yes. And your face. It's a very innocent face for someone with such wild hair."

I'm not sure what to say to that at first. I feel like he's

paying me a compliment, which is a rare thing. I want to clutch his words to my chest and hug them and never let go. But then my mouth opens and I say, "I only look innocent, believe me."

He takes that ballsy comment in stride and moves away from me toward the door. "I've been quite busy this week. I wanted to apologize for that," he says. He pauses and looks at me over his shoulder. "I thought perhaps it might be nice to do something different for the last day of the week."

"Like what?"

"Can you swim?" he asks. "Do you like to?"

I would have thought that would be an extremely loaded question coming from him but he says it casually. "Uh, yes I can swim. And I love to. I haven't since I've been in Italy, though."

"No?" he asks, brows raised. "We will have to change that, then. Sometimes I take the twins to the beach. I haven't done that for a while now. I was thinking we could go now and pick them up from school. Give Felisa a night off. Does that interest you?"

I nod. Hell yes it interests me. No teaching and an evening at the beach? Count me in.

"There aren't many beaches on Capri, and they are not like the ones you have in America. I have an aunt who lives in Florida and it is not the same at all. Very rough stones here. But the water is warm and so clear you can see the bottom without goggles. The beach I take them to is by the light-house, Punta Carena. It is the only beach that has sun all day, until it sets."

"How do we get there?" I briefly imagine riding on the back of his motorcycle, my hands wrapped around his chest. Maybe we can stick the kids in a sidecar.

"I'll call a taxi to meet us by the Piazzetta and I'll call the beach as well. You must reserve a spot ahead of time."

What kind of a crazy-ass beach is this? I nod anyway. "Okay, let me just throw together a little bag." I follow him out into the hall and while he goes to make his call I pop in to my room next door and start packing a tote with a towel, bathing suit, sunblock, hat, and my Kindle.

Ten minutes later we're saying goodbye to Felisa, who looks tired but relieved, and I follow Derio up the path through the lemon trees and through the gate to the road.

We walk along the Via Tragara at my pace, though his long legs could carry him much faster. He's got his shades on and another fashionable outfit—blue untucked dress shirt, knee-length tan cargo shorts, tan Converse shoes. He slips a cigarette in his mouth and lights it.

"Does no one tell the Italians that smoking is bad for you?" I ask.

He smirks at me. "They do. We just don't care. We like all of the bad things." He inhales, his nostrils flaring, then breathes it out. "Smoking, racing, drinking, sex. All bad. All very good."

And is that sex-with-a-woman sex? I want to ask but as I'm staring at him, despite his loner tendencies and his fashionable ways, I'm just not getting that vibe. Sometimes his eyes seem to smolder with something, though it's probably wishful thinking on my behalf.

"Tell me, Amber," he says, playfully pronouncing my name. "What are your bad habits?"

"Bad habits?" I repeat.

"You must have some," he says.

I ponder that and pull my shades out of my bag. The sun is hot and glaring off the sea in the distance. "I guess I eat too much," I tell him honestly. "I try not to, and I'm always worried about it. So I guess that's a bad habit, too. Worry. I worry about a lot of things. I'm really bad with money. I spend recklessly. I'm impulsive with things and don't really think them through. I also make snap judgments with people and I know I shouldn't. I guess I used to think I was entitled but I got over that one pretty fast. I'm stubborn. I think I know more than I do. I tend to look for split ends in my hair and pull them apart. I pick at my nail polish. I don't exercise as much as I should, mainly because I hate exercise. When I have wine, sometimes I have too much. I forget to put on sunscreen. I kiss all the wrong boys." I pause. "I'm pretty sure I'm just a person composed of nothing more than good intentions and bad habits."

"Wow," he says quietly. "That is a lot. I didn't really expect you to be so honest. Most women—most people—are never honest about their faults. But really, it sounds more like you are more human than made of bad habits. Though I don't really understand the last one. You kiss all the wrong boys. How do you know who the right boy is?"

I raise my shoulder. "I don't know. I haven't met him yet."

"Like the story with the princess and the frog."

"Maybe," I say, and suddenly I feel vulnerable for sharing all my worst qualities with him. Vulnerable, but free.

We walk along the road, passing the other fancy houses and tourists. I nod at them and smile but notice that Derio keeps his head down, his focus in front of him, as he puffs away on his cigarette. I wonder if he knows what the people in town say about him. From his cagey demeanor as he passes people by, I gather he does.

Once we head into the clean, impossibly narrow streets

of Capri town, Derio sets off down a small street to the left, grumbling to himself in Italian as he goes.

"Not a fan of the crowds?" I ask him.

He makes a *tsking* sound. "No," he says gruffly. "I hate living here this time of year. You should see Capri in the winter; it is heaven. All the Prada and Louis Vuitton stores and overpriced tourist joints are closed and only a few bars, restaurants, and grocery stores are open. Even hotels are closed. That is the real Capri, not this."

I try to imagine Capri with dark gray clouds instead of stunning sunshine, with just a few locals milling around instead of the throngs of sunburned visitors. "It must be very lonely," I say, picturing the isolation. This is just a rock in the middle of the sea.

"Yes, but it is good to be lonely sometimes," he says. "There is one bar in the Piazzetta, the square here, that remains open. Everyone goes there. If you are lonely, you can go there and be with people."

But something tells me he doesn't do that.

We come to a stop outside of a large stone building. Through the windows I can see a chalkboard, like schools used to have before iPads and computers replaced everything.

"Is this their school?" I ask.

"Yes," he says. "There are two small schools on the island. One here, one in Anacapri. Have you been there yet?"

I shake my head. "To be honest, I haven't really left the house until now."

He tilts his head at me. "Oh? Then I am especially glad we are going to the beach. We will take the cab through Anacapri. Perhaps on the way back we can stop somewhere for dinner. I prefer it to here, less crowded and more charming."

The sound of a bell ringing, almost like a church bell, comes out of the building, and suddenly the air is filled with children yelling and laughing. But I'm thinking about what he just said and the way it made me feel. Going out for dinner with Derio? Granted, the kids will be there, but somehow that almost makes it more intimate. My stomach does a little flip at the thought.

"Derio!" Alfonso says as he comes out of the building. Annabella trails behind him, her thumbs hooked around the straps of her backpack, her head down. Another child races past us, yelling something at Alfonso that makes him smile but Annabella seems to be totally shut off from the world around her.

I think Alfonso asks what we are doing picking them up instead of Felisa, but when Derio tells them they are going to the beach instead, even Annabella's face lights up a little.

Soon we're hailing a cab just outside of the funicular, and I can't stop an internal *squee* as one of the convertibles pulls up to us. Alfonso wants to sit up front with the driver so Annabella goes in the backseat, followed by Derio in the middle. I'm glad for that because my fat ass would be a hindrance to both of them if I had to ride in the bitch seat.

I squish myself in, trying to buckle the seat belt and leaning against Derio to do so. I hear him inhale and for a second I think maybe he's trying to smell my hair. I freeze. *Don't look up, don't look up,* I think, while also thinking, *What shampoo did I use? What does my hair smell like?*

The seat belt goes in with a click and when I do raise my head, Derio is facing the other way. Hmmm. Maybe my imagination is running away from me. He doesn't seem like the type of guy who would smell my hair.

The taxi starts and we jet off down the hill. I casually take a strand of my hair and run it under my nose. The faint note of coconut lingers on it. At least I smell good.

Driving in Capri, like the rest of Italy, is nearly a full-contact sport. I close my eyes as the car winds down the hill and overtakes pedestrians in the narrow lanes, orange buses squeezing past us with a hair-width to spare while people on scooters tailgate us. Once we're out of the congested city streets, the road begins to climb, up and up, and curve some more. Soon the houses drop away and it's just lush foliage, rock face, and a serious cliff edge on my side. We must be hundreds of feet up, and I know I saw this very road from the marina when I first arrived. If I were brave enough to look, I would've seen nothing but space.

I close my eyes again, feeling my body freeze up on the verge of a panic attack. I get pins and needles all over my limbs as I experience vertigo, that falling sensation, again and again.

"You're not looking at the view," Derio says, his voice so close to my ear, but even that doesn't help. Instead, I turn into him, burying my face into his shoulder, my weight against his side. "Are you okay?" he asks.

I nod against him but I still don't move. It's crazy what the fear can sometimes do to me, especially if the drop is sudden and I'm up really high. It's almost like if I don't hold on to him or if the seat belt isn't tight enough, there's a chance I'll be sucked away, pulled over the edge. Sometimes I even fear that I'll jump on purpose. It's fucked up, but it happens occasionally. (The fear, not throwing myself out of cars or off of balconies.)

Derio doesn't say anything. Instead he puts his arm around

me. His grip is firm and strong and somehow that centers me, knowing that he has me and is holding on. I know it's not a romantic gesture and that's okay. I just want to feel anchored.

And I do feel anchored. I feel protected and warm. And though I know he wasn't smelling my hair earlier, I'm inhaling the fuck out of him because honestly I can't get enough.

CHAPTER SIX

After about five minutes of closing my eyes and burrowing myself into Derio's arms, I can feel the air around us change. It becomes more dense, less open, and street sounds become louder. I carefully raise my head and look around, the wind whipping about my hair. We're driving past large resort-like buildings and white-washed residences. We seem to be inland enough that there's no chance of us falling to our doom. It pains me to think we have to take that road back home. Maybe I can hitch a ride on a boat.

I swallow thickly and straighten up, afraid to meet Derio's eyes. I know they're studying me underneath those sunglasses. With deliberation, he slips his arm away. The breeze feels cold for a moment before the sun goes back to searing my skin.

The cab takes us through Anacapri, which does look like a cuter, less touristy version of Capri town, past olive groves and tiny vineyards in the looming shadow of Mount Solaro. Finally, the island flattens out, opens up, and we're parking at the base of a pink lighthouse.

"This is the *Faro di Punta Carena*," Derio explains as we pile out of the cab. "We are at the most southwestern part of the island."

It's absolutely beautiful. The startlingly clear water, with its millions of shades of vivid blue, laps against the dramatic rocks and craggy coves. After Derio pays the driver, we walk down toward a restaurant perched on the edge of the cliff. He motions for me to stay put with the kids while he goes in to talk to someone.

Alfonso tries to follow him but I reach out and grab his arm.

He glares at my hand and says something along the lines of "You are not my mother!" in Italian.

My head jerks back at the ferocity in his voice but I don't let go. I can't let them do whatever they want, especially when their brother is around, and especially in public.

Thankfully, Derio returns and when he sees me holding on to angry little Alfonso, he stoops down to his brother's level. He talks to him in a low voice, gentle but firm. Then he eyes me and takes my hand off of him. He holds it for a moment, squeezes it so that Alfonso sees this, and then lets go of me. He finishes by asking Alfonso, "*Capisci?*"

Alfonso looks at me. I give him a small smile, not wanting him to think of me as the enemy. Eventually he nods.

Derio sighs and straightens up. "I am sorry," he says.

"It's not a problem, really," I tell him. "They're just kids. They do this kind of stuff."

He shakes his head slightly, seeming lost in his own mind. "Yes, but they are raised to be better than most kids. They need to show you respect."

I have to admit, I'm a bit touched by all of this. Derio grabs on to Alfonso and Annabella's hands and takes them around the side of the restaurant. I watch their silhouettes, black against the sun, for a beat before I follow.

Though the area below and around the restaurant's patio is made up of different platforms, all with well-oiled people relaxing on loungers, Derio takes me to a private deck with its own umbrella, lounge chairs, and even a brightly colored bathhouse for changing. He hands the kids their swimsuits and they disappear inside, hooting and hollering and making noises in the echo-y space.

I take a seat next to him, pondering if I should use the bathhouse after them or put my bikini on underneath my maxi dress. I can do it fast and without anyone seeing parts of me they shouldn't, but doing it next to Derio doesn't seem right either. Somehow it's more intimate to undress next to him that way than to just strip naked.

"Heights," he says to me as he opens the bright blue umbrella between us.

"What?"

"You have a fear of heights," he says. "That is why you were hiding on the ride over."

I nod, looking away. A seagull wheels down toward the loungers beneath, trying to steal bruschetta off of someone's plate. "Yeah. It's not that bad, but sometimes it just hits me, you know?"

"I know," he says gravely, his focus now on the sea.

"You're not afraid of swimming?" I ask him carefully, unsure of how much to let him know that I know. It's definitely not a secret and I don't think Felisa was sworn to silence, but it's the first time I've talked about it with him. Hell, it's the first time I've really talked to him since I got here.

He stiffens and I know I've probably done the wrong thing by asking him. I wait, holding my breath. Finally he shakes his head, ever so slightly. "No, I am not afraid of swimming, provided I am not too far from shore."

But I guess boats are a different story. I don't say anything more, of course.

Alfonso and Annabella come spilling out of the bathhouse, dressed in their swimwear, and gather around the rails of the deck, pointing at things below. I gather up my suit and a blousy caftan that I use as a cover-up for all my jiggly bits and disappear into the dark bathhouse.

It smells like heat and wood and sea inside and I take a moment to just compose myself. Some days I'm ashamed of my body, others days I'm loud and proud and couldn't care less what people think. But today is one of those days that I feel my pale skin will be on display in that bright sunshine and I'll be exposed more than ever before. My bikini is black-and-white striped and very flattering, but having Derio there makes me wish I had the lean, tanned, tall body of someone like Lenora instead of the pale, dimpled, curvy, short body that I seem to be stuck with. My mother always harps on me that I need to change my diet and exercise more, and while I think she's right, she's also one hundred pounds overweight and hard to take seriously. If anything, *her* nitpicking over *my* body aggravates me more than anything else.

I ignore her comments in my head and step out into the sun. Even though I put the caftan on I still feel exposed. It isn't until I put my dress down on the lounger that I realize I'm not the one exposed here. Derio is standing beside Alfonso and Annabella, leaning against the railing and pointing at a passing yacht.

He's in a goddamn Speedo.

I kind of freeze. And then I ogle. Because his back is to me and I have a mighty fine view of his body, I feel the need to soak it up while I can. Derio Larosa, without his clothes on, in practically nothing.

As I suspected, his body is pretty much perfect, at least from the rear view. His skin is this uniform reddish brown shade from his feet to the nape of his neck. His legs are firm, muscular and lean, and his ass is jaw-dropping. Like, he definitely has some well-sculpted, high and tight junk in his trunk. It makes me want to bite one of his cheeks.

Then there's his back, long and rippled with lean muscles, leading up to broad swimmer's shoulders.

Thankfully my eyes are at his upper portion when he turns around, about to say something. For a moment I forget I'm in a bikini and then I notice he's kind of staring at me. God, I wish he wasn't wearing those glasses because I would die to see his eyes. I have no idea if he likes what he sees or not but I bet he can tell that I do.

He smiles, just briefly. "Are you ready to go for a swim? I'm afraid if I don't take them now they will plot my murder in my sleep."

"Sure."

He takes off his sunglasses and turns around, walking toward me to put them on the chair. And now I have a full view of his front. I try not to stare but it's hard when it's even more gorgeous than the back. His chest and abs, of course, are trim and well muscled in the way that an athlete's are, complete with a dusting of trimmed chest hair and treasure trail, but it's his damn Speedo that has all my attention. The stereotype of the Italian Stallion is not lost on this man. He's packing heat, and a lot of it, in those tight red bottoms.

Somehow, and I don't know how, because that banana hammock is just begging for people to stare, I manage to tear my eyes away from him just as he looks up. I can only pray that my face only feels hot and isn't turning a beet shade of red. *Blame it on the sun, blame it on the sun*, I chant to myself.

I decide to lead the way, even though I don't really know where I'm going. I head down a ramp that ends at a platform. A few people are sitting on the edge, their legs dangling off the side, while others jump in. There's a set of stairs that leads from the platform down to the water. It's only then that I realize he's not the only person in this little swimming area who's in a Speedo. He just happens to be the only man in the history of the bathing suit to make it look oh so fucking good.

I pause at the edge of the steps and then move out of the way as a heavyset woman in a swim cap comes past. She gets halfway in and then launches into a rather elegant crawl. The water does look inviting, and though it's late afternoon, the sun is bearing down on me.

I turn around, about to ask Derio and his penis whether this is the place to go in the water, but he strides to the edge of the water and does a perfect swan dive off. With a gasp I glance over the edge and see him perfectly enter the water with nary a splash, just where the blue deepens between the rocky crags.

When he surfaces, he's smiling, white teeth against bronzed skin against azure water. He looks like he's straight from a damn Dolce & Gabbana ad. Behind me, the twins let out a squeal and then run down the stairs toward the water's edge.

"Be careful!" I yell after them, wishing I knew it in Italian. Of course they don't listen but they're sure-footed and brave as anything and go down the stairs and into the water as fast as they can. I sigh and make my way down the steps, careful not to slip.

The twins swim over to Derio and try to climb on his shoulders, although they're a bit too big for that. He treads water, trying to keep them above the surface before he shucks them off with a laugh. They splash and kick for the shore, climbing up on the rocks. I watch them carefully, wondering if we have a first aid kit and chastising myself for not bringing one, just in case. I might just be their teacher but I can't not look out for them.

"Are you coming in?" Derio asks, swimming closer to the edge. He wraps his long fingers along the edge of the stairs and looks up at me. I hate the view of myself that he must have at the moment but he doesn't seem to mind. "*Leoni possono nuotare.*"

"*Scusi?*" I ask.

"Lions can swim," he translates, though it still doesn't make much sense. He gestures to my head. "Your hair is like a lion's mane. You are a lion. *La Leonessa.* Lions can swim, can they not?"

Lion, huh? I can live with that.

"They sure can," I tell him proudly. I am a California baby, after all. With a deep breath, I take off the caftan and wedge it between rocks for safekeeping then head down into the water. It's surprisingly warm, at least compared to the Nor Cal ocean, and soon I'm weightless and immersed in the clearest water I've ever swum in.

"Beautiful," he says to me, swimming closer.

I can't help smiling. "What is?"

"Everything," he says, looking around him. Then his eyes lock on mine. "All of this."

"It's stunning," I say briefly, tilting my head back to take in the sun. "It's like living inside a painting."

"Yes, that is what everyone says about Capri," he comments. He swims over to the side to keep an eye on the twins, who are splashing near the steps now, and I can't help watching the water glide over his dark skin, the look of his well-honed muscles. He moves so fluidly, gracefully, and it strikes me that he moves somewhat the same on land. I wonder what he's like on the back of bike, racing at full speed. I bet it's almost supernatural.

He glances at me, treading water in place for a few moments. A wet piece of hair flops onto his forehead, making him look boyish. "What do you think about Capri?"

"I love it," I say, but it's an automatic response. I'm not sure if I love it, per se, but I am loving parts of it. I don't love my job—yet—but this is the setting we're talking about. And how can I not love it after what he's shown me today? I feel like I'm swimming in God's pool. "It's almost mythical."

He nods and spits out some water. "Yes, there are many myths about Capri. You have heard of the Grotta Azzurra? Blue Grotto? That is here. You will have to go some time."

I'm about to say something cheeky like, "Will you be the one to take me?" but then I remember that the Blue Grotto is only accessible by tiny boats, like gondolas, and that probably wouldn't go down so well with him.

"Where else should I go?" I ask instead.

He points up at Mount Solaro. "Up there. Picnic among the flowers. Great views."

I give him a look. "Don't you have to take a chairlift up there? Fear of heights, remember?"

He nods. "I remember. Perhaps you will face your fears."

"Are you going to be there holding my hand?" I say, half jokingly.

He smiles softly. "The chairlifts only fit one person. So, no. My arms don't reach that long."

"Then no fucking thank you," I say. Then I immediately clamp my hand over my mouth, realizing I swore in front of the children. Somehow this is the first time it's happened.

Alfonso bursts out laughing at my profanity and then

launches himself off the step and into the water, splashing us. He's yelling, "*Merda!*" which I'm pretty sure is Italian for *shit*.

"*Eh, smettila,*" Derio admonishes Alfonso. Alfonso just giggles and swims back to Annabella, who is poking her fingers into the rocks near my caftan.

"Sorry," I apologize to Derio. "I forget I say bad words sometimes."

"Just another bad habit," he says. "Apparently I have the same one. Maybe we are more alike than I thought. Of course, you don't smoke."

"No."

"But alcohol and sex, that's okay with you?"

I nearly sputter in the water. My mind reels, trying to think of something clever and witty to say to that. "I like both those things," I say, like a total noob.

He gives me a grin and then swims away, doing a fast front crawl through the water, slicing through the shades of blue and around the corner of the rocks.

"Where are you going?" I call after him but he can't hear me.

"He comes back," Alfonso says from the steps. I eye him in surprise, not only because of his English but for being so forthcoming.

I swim over to him, finding a non-jagged part of the rocks to hold on to. I'm amazed that these kids aren't bleeding all over the place from cuts and scrapes.

"Where does he go?" I ask slowly, in my teacher voice.

He gestures. "Around the . . . the . . ." He points at the lighthouse.

"Lighthouse," I tell him. "In English we call that a lighthouse."

"*Si*, lighthouse," he repeats. "Then he comes back."

"And he leaves you alone like this?"

He shakes his head. "Oh no, Felisa, she is here. He never leaves me, Annabella, alone."

"Good," I say. "He takes good care of you, you know."

Alfonso shrugs and kicks at the water. "*Certo*," he says noncommittally. I think it means *sure*.

Suddenly, Annabella bursts into a fit of laughter and I look to see her waving my caftan in the air before she lets go. The breeze hooks it and carries it away, floating down to the rocks on the other side of the narrow cove.

"Annabella!" I yell at her. "That isn't very nice!"

She only smirks at me and makes the motion of a bird flying away.

I sigh and say, "Stay here," to the twins, repeating, "*Non si muovono.*"

I swim across the cove and reach the rocks. I look over my shoulder at them before I start climbing. They're sitting side by side on the steps and watching me in anticipation.

I'm not so bad climbing up things as I am climbing down things, and the lump of rock isn't high enough to give me vertigo or anything like that, but I don't really like how my ass is probably hanging out of my bikini while I try to lift myself up. I'm glad that Derio has decided to go for his lighthouse swim so he doesn't have to see this.

Once I'm close to the caftan, which is snagged on a sharp rock, I steady myself, my toes hooked into one small ledge. I grab on to a solid rock with one hand to balance and stretch across to my caftan, my breasts smushed painfully against the rock, my arm reaching as far as I can. The caftan suddenly lifts, about to be blown away, and I make a grab for it.

At the same time, my whole body tips to the left, completely off balance, and as my fingers wrap around the edge of the cloth, I know the victory will be short-lived. I let out a cry as my body dips toward the sea and I try hard to twist away from the rock.

Despite my efforts, my left shoulder and the corner of my head still hit the rock, and I feel a sharp stab of pain at my temple and scraped skin at my shoulder bone before I plunge into the sea.

I'm not knocked out but I'm in deep water and disoriented. I let go of the caftan, which has wrapped itself around my head underwater, obscuring my sight. I don't know which way is up or down, and in a moment of panic I open my mouth to breathe. Water seeps into my lungs and I try to cough but I can't, and my arms and legs don't seem to be working. I don't know where the surface is. I want to scream but I'm drowning and I can't breathe.

I can't breathe.

I can't breathe.

Suddenly, arms hook underneath me, pulling me up to the surface, and I'm gasping for air, still choking on water. I try to get it out, violently puking the water back into the sea, my lungs feeling as if they have been scraped with pumice stones. I cough and cough and cough, but still so thankful that I can, that there is air and my head is above water.

I am dragged to the steps and only then do I realize that Derio has rescued me. His face is absolutely pale, his eyes frozen in fear as he keeps repeating my name.

I can only nod at him to tell him I'm okay. I hear Annabella and Alfonso crying and the murmurs and gasps of the bystanders watching it all unfold.

A man comes down the steps and aids Derio in helping me up to the platform. I stand there, shivering for some reason, while a woman wraps a big towel around me. I look down and see my shoulder is scraped open, a gaping pink wound, and blood is leaking from my head. I can't help feeling a bit woozy at the sight but Derio's arm is right there again, holding me up.

Soon, I am led away from the sunbathers and past the restaurant full of gawking onlookers. A tiny ambulance speeds into the parking lot and I am quickly ushered into the back by a lot of fast-talking Italians. I want to tell them that I feel fine, that I will be fine, but I honestly don't know if that's true. I'm just glad to be alive.

The hospital is located outside of Capri town but this time the ride doesn't bother me—I just keep my eyes closed anyway and figure, *What are the chances of an ambulance careening off the cliffs?* When we get there I'm amazed to see how small it is, a somewhat modern but nondescript building we could have passed by earlier, unnoticed.

The size works in my favor, though. I'm escorted into the emergency room by the attendants but there's no one there so I'm immediately put into a room. Derio and the kids aren't there either; I guess they had to catch a cab and follow since there was no room in the tiny ambulance.

There's a friendly doctor, Doctor Romano, with tiny, kind eyes who speaks perfect English and dotes on me with lots of stinging solutions and Band-Aids. He asks me lots of questions about my head, how I'm feeling, if I'm dizzy. I tell him I'm tired and in shock but my head feels fine otherwise, just hurts a bit where the wound is. Luckily he says that the head bleeds easily and it's not a deep injury at all. He also adds that I'm very lucky that someone was there to save me.

I feel horrible about that. I would have rather some random person pull me out from the sea than Derio. I saw the fear in his eyes. I almost drowned in front of him. I know I don't mean much to him, but that couldn't have been easy for him to see.

Eventually, Doctor Romano tells me I am free to go, I just need to treat the wounds like I would any cut and if I feel the slightest bit dizzy or sick, I have to come back here immediately. He also tells me I have a load of paperwork to fill out. I give a silent prayer of thanks for the travel medical insurance I purchased.

I step out into the waiting room, dressed in the blue hospital gown since I didn't think to bring my dress, and see Derio sitting there. He's in his shorts and shirt, his hair still wet. His hands are clenching and unclenching by his sides. When he sees me, he immediately gets to his feet and comes over to me, his brow knitted together.

He says something to Doctor Romano, who smiles and says something reassuring. It doesn't seem to soothe Derio, who looks to me with an even more worried expression.

"I'm okay," I tell him. "I'm fine. Really. Just a scratch." I lift up the side of my hair and show him the bandage on my widow's peak. "I'm a lioness, remember?"

He doesn't smile. His dark eyes are almost smoldering in their intensity. "I heard screams as I was swimming back and came around the corner just as you hit the water. I thought I wouldn't reach you in time."

I give him a small smile, not wanting to make a big deal about this at all. "But you did. Thank you." I reach out and touch the side of his arm. He doesn't move. "Where are the kids?" I ask.

"Felisa came and got them," he says, "while you were in there. Alfonso told me what happened, what Annabella did."

I shrug but the skin on my shoulder stings. "It's fine. She was just being funny."

He shakes his head. "It wasn't funny at all. I'm sorry she's like that with you. I'm sorry they both are."

I meet his eyes. "They have reasons to be," I say sincerely. "I don't blame them." *And I don't blame you*, I think. "So I guess we aren't going out for dinner now, are we?" I ask, attempting to change the subject.

"No," he says in a low voice. He clears his throat. "Maybe we can take what you call a rain check?"

"Of course," I say. "Does it ever rain in Capri?"

"Sometimes. And it's beautiful when it does. It's like the island has been holding on to it for too long and she finally lets it all go. Usually in the fall, after the summer season, we get the heaviest rains."

I breathe out in relief, happy that he seems to be relaxing. "You, uh, wouldn't happen to have my dress, would you?" I ask him.

He raises a brow. "You mean you don't find this to be the height of fashion?" He tugs at the sleeve of the gown. "It shows off your legs."

Before I can say anything to that, he goes back to the chair and gathers our beach totes. He hands me mine and our fingers brush against each other as I take it from him. I really need to pretend it's nothing, that there isn't this potency between us every time we touch. It's all in my head. My crazy, knocked-around head.

I head into the bathroom, laugh at my reflection—wild eyes, wet hair, bandaged head—and get dressed. It seems both Derio and I faced a bit of our fears today. I just don't know if either of us came out any stronger.

CHAPTER SEVEN

The next morning I wake up feeling groggy, my head and shoulder burning like they're on fire. But I don't feel nauseous or dizzy so it's safe to say I escaped the event without a concussion. I also see that it's eleven a.m. when I finally pull myself out of bed, and I've missed breakfast. I know I should take the fact that I'm injured and use it to my advantage to get some much-needed rest, but I'm curious about Derio, as well as Alfonso and Annabella. I don't want any of them to worry about me.

When I get dressed and go downstairs, I find the house to be completely empty. At least it seems that way.

"Hello?" I call out as I walk into the kitchen, which is usually the hub of activity in this house. Everything is put away neatly, spic-and-span.

I decide to make myself an espresso and after I wrestle with the noisy machine, I pull up a stool to the island and sip it. In a week, my body has gone from barely tolerating the stuff to finding it delightful and kind of addictive.

Though I can hear the usual birds chirping merrily outside, the house hums with silence. I've actually never been completely alone in the house before. It's kind of nice, albeit spooky in a way. Despite the sunshine that pours in through all the windows, I guess the dramatics of yesterday are casting a bit of a shadow on my subconscious, and when I think I hear something thump from upstairs, it scares the bejesus out of me.

I finish the last bit of dark espresso and slowly put the cup down, listening hard now.

Another *thump*. Coming from the attic.

Well, actually, it's a storage space, accessible from a narrow hall between Alfonso's and Derio's rooms. I've obviously never been up there but this isn't the first time I thought I heard something funny coming from there. There was a reason why I ended the first week somewhat convinced that there might be a ghost in the house.

I've never actually seen a ghost in my life, and even though I believe in them I've always been a bit skeptical. But old villas on Italian hillsides kind of get your imagination running. I listen again and hear the same *thump*. It sounds like something being dropped or knocked over. The other night it was more like a scratching sound as I passed by it in the hall. It was probably a rat, if anything, but in my imagination in the dark, it was the sound of someone trying to claw their way out.

I had a brief notion of Derio keeping his ex-wife locked up in the attic, but then decided that sort of thing only happens in books.

I get off my stool and look out the windows again to the patio. It's sunny, bright, and the sea gleams blue. There is absolutely nothing scary going on. I take in a deep breath and head to the stairs.

Once I get to the second floor I pause, holding my breath and listening.

Thump.

There. Above me and down the short hall, almost where the ladder pulls down from the ceiling.

I wish I had something to defend myself with, like a candlestick or something, but I'm not really sure what the protocol is. My knowledge stretches as far as those ghost hunters on YouTube, like that crazy guy with the mustache and the girl who screams a lot, who never really seem to solve anything.

I creep down the hall, my bare feet sticking to the tiles, and then I wait below the attic door, the pulley hanging above me. I inhale, reach up, and with one go jerk it down.

There's a cry and then the door opens, the steps slamming down onto the tiles. Suddenly, it's raining books as paperbacks hit the tiles and echo loudly—*bang, bang, bang*.

When it finally stops and I'm able to swallow my heart back down my throat, I poke my head around the stairs, looking up.

Derio is in the attic, staring down at me with the most exasperated expression on his face.

"Oh, hi," I say, feeling foolish all of a sudden. "I didn't know you were up there."

He swears in Italian then says, "Well, who did you think was up here?"

He's pissed off. This isn't good.

"A ghost?" I say, helplessly.

He makes a disgusted face. "A ghost?"

"Yeah," I say. "I didn't know anyone was home."

"You think I would leave you alone in the house after what happened?"

I shrug. Not when he put it that way. "I thought you were all out."

"Felisa took the twins to the gardens," he says, his voice hard. "I was up here attending to some matters."

I look at the books at my feet. They are by his mother, Sophie Larosa, but I don't recognize the titles. Almost all of them are different, too, in the small mass-market format you might find at a grocery store. "Your mother was a writer," I say, stating the very obvious, though I know he knows he's never told me that himself.

He makes a disgruntled sound and comes down the stairs in a huff. "I was organizing these," he says, gathering all the books into his arms. I try not to look at his muscles or his angry, handsome face.

"What for?" I ask. "How many books has she written?"

He shoots me a look that says it's none of my business. But I have the power of Google and I can make it my business if I want to. "She wrote a lot," he concedes.

"What kind of books?"

"Does it matter?" he asks.

"I love books, I read all the time," I tell him. Of course it matters. "Have any been translated into English?"

"No," he says, somewhat bitterly. "Not yet."

I reach for one of the books on the pile. "Can I have one? Maybe it will help me learn Italian."

He holds the books away from me. "These are not for sale."

"I'm not going to buy one, I'm going to borrow one."

He narrows his eyes into mahogany slits. "You're not going to borrow anything."

I take my hand back and put it on my hip. "Why do you hate me so much?"

He jerks his head back. "I don't hate you."

"Then why are you acting like an ass?"

"Because you act like a little girl," he says without hesitation.

My eyes widen. "You're the one playing keep-away with books."

"I do not know what keep-away is," he says. "Now, please go make yourself breakfast or something." He takes the books and goes back up the stairs into the attic.

"Little girls don't know how to make breakfast!" I yell after him. Not my best comeback.

Still, I sigh heavily and head down the stairs and wrangle up some toast and olive oil to get me through the day.

....

Because Derio was in such a rotten mood, I was happy when the kids and Felisa got back from the gardens. That was until Felisa started acting harsher than usual, which was saying a lot. Thankfully, Alfonso and Annabella were on their best behavior around me. I could tell that the near-drowning really scared the crap out of them and made them be a little more considerate, even nice. We spent the rest of the day in the garden, and I managed to teach them a little bit about the plants and how to keep them healthy. I decided that in the future I would get them their own pots where they could grow easy herbs. That kind of stuff always kept me occupied and hopeful as a kid.

Sunday morning was a little bit better. I was allowed to sleep in again, even though last week Felisa had insisted I accompany them to church. When I woke up they were all just coming back, and though Alfonso and Annabella were relieved to be free from church in that overly dramatic way that involved flinging themselves over couches and moaning from the residual boredom, the tension was high between Felisa and Derio.

They were both snapping at each other in Italian, and at some point I had to say, "Hey, let's all remember what we learned in church today," which I assumed was something nice, of course. But the two of them just glared at me and went back to their bickering.

After another espresso, which had Felisa shaking her head

at the noise (let's be honest, I was trying to drown them out with the machine), the two of them disappeared into his office. I had my drink and sat down on the couch with the kids as they babbled to me in Italian about something or other while I sat there saying, "*Non capisco*" over and over again, trying to get them to speak in English.

Then someone from the office yelled, a door slammed, and Derio walked hurriedly out to the living room, paused before the three of us, and then asked how I was feeling.

"I'm fine," I tell him, rather suspicious, considering all the mayhem and bad vibes.

"No concussion?"

"No," I say slowly. "The cuts are healing up, and although it was nice to sleep in this morning, I feel pretty good."

"Good," he says and gives me a smile. It's the first smile I've seen of his in over twenty-four hours, so it startles me a bit. Sometimes I remember how damn handsome he is, and it almost makes up for the fact that he's been a dick lately. *Almost.*

I squint at him. "What do you want?"

He looks at Alfonso and Annabella. "Would you like to go to Ischia today with Amber?" he asks slowly in English.

Iss-sky-*what*?

The twins' faces break out into wide, shit-eating grins. "*Si*! Yes!" they cry out and start jumping up and down on the couch.

"What's Ischia?" I ask, worried.

"It's another island, just north of here," he explains. I can hear the impatience in his voice. "Felisa has taken them once before and they loved it. There's an old castle up on a fortified hill, like an island attached to the island by a long road."

I don't know how I feel about this. "How far is it?"

"Ferries leave all the time," he says. "If you go now, you can be there for a few hours and come back on the last boat."

"But what do I do with them there?"

"I just said. There is the castle—Castello Aragonese, that is. It is just a short taxi ride from the ferry. It should occupy you all day."

I frown at him. I know he's trying to get me out of the house with the kids but the idea of going so far away with just me and them is a little nerve-racking. Hell, taking them into Capri town is nerve-racking.

"You'll be fine," he says. Then he adds, "The children will love you for it."

I eye the twins. They are both staring at me with big, eager eyes. I sigh inwardly. I can't really say no to those faces. And I can't really say no to Derio since he's my boss.

I raise my chin and nod at him. "Fine. Not a problem."

He grins, though there is something uneasy about it. "Great, good. The next ferry leaves in an hour. Pack a bag and get down to the funicular. You can buy tickets at the marina."

An hour doesn't really leave us much time. I pack my tote bag in a hurry full of things we might need for the day and the kids put on more sturdy shoes and comfortable clothes at the speed of light. We leave the villa behind us, Alfonso and Annabella tugging on my hands as we jog up Via Tragara toward the square and funicular.

Because of the accident and because they're just so damn excited, they're actually easy to take care of. They're loud—especially Alfonso—and they have a bad habit of kicking ferry seats and I have to keep telling them to keep their voices down. But they listen to what I say for the most part, and there's zero animosity on their end, unlike usual.

Surprisingly, the children don't seem at all affected by the ferry crossing. There are some waves, particularly as we hit the open stretch between the islands, that bounce the hydrofoil back and forth, but they only cry out with glee as it happens. Even though I know the twins have their own demons, it's good that they aren't as crippled in some ways as Derio is.

Derio. When I'm not thinking about the twins, I'm thinking about him. I want to know what he's doing in his office. Why the secrecy? What was he doing with all of his mother's books in the attic and why was he so angry about them? I want to know if he's ever going to trust me completely because I feel that he doesn't. Not that he should—he doesn't really know me—but I am tutoring his siblings. He's so hot and cold that it drives me nuts.

And of course this whole moody, reclusive, damaged side to him is putting my feminine instincts into overdrive. I want him to overcome his issues, his dark demons, and of course I would foolishly hope that I could help him do that. Isn't that what every woman wants? To heal the bad boy?

But thinking like that doesn't get me anywhere. It's bad enough that I find him sexy as hell, I should stop hoping that he might feel the same way about me. Besides, he's my boss, the one paying my salary, and I'm living under his roof with his rules. That has all the makings of something not only rightfully forbidden but also terribly messy.

It's too bad I have an affinity for getting messy.

When the boat docks at the tiny Ischia terminal, we push our way through the crowds with a lot of "*Permesso, permesso*," making sure we can get a taxi. There's a bit of a line but eventually we get one with a friendly driver.

Ischia is beautiful, maybe more mountainous than Capri but with a lot more greenery and on a bigger scale. There's traffic and lush gardens and rustic houses and quaint hotels and cute restaurants, yet at the same time it seems less crowded than Capri. I find myself wondering if Derio would ever settle here if he could get over his fear, or where he and the twins would one day end up. Meanwhile, the cab driver tells me something about all the spas and the volcanic mud here. He seems convinced that I am German. Must be the hair.

We're eventually dropped off near the end of a long pedestrian cobblestone road flanked by colorful stucco buildings. I thank the man and pay him with the money for the trip that Derio gave me, grab the twins, and head down it. It's about noon but the restaurants are still shuttered; they're on a weird Italian schedule that ensures you never get food when you want it.

The Castello Aragonese appears at the end of a long, stone-bordered walkway, like something out of a fairy tale. I actually have to stop where I am and take it all in. This is one of those moments when it's all too much and your senses can't really keep up.

"Come, come," Alfonso says, tugging on my arm, but I don't move. I barely hear him.

The castle rises out of the sea like some giant placed it there on purpose, like he was decorating the island and this was his crowning touch, an added gem. Buildings, gardens, walls, and fortresses are carved into the sides of the rock; a mythic, impenetrable kingdom. Gulls wheel in the air as tourists and locals alike walk to and from the castle, pausing to look at the achingly beautiful turquoise and ink-blue water and bright yellow fishing boats that surround the island on all sides.

I blink and stare and breathe, trying to be in the moment. It's nearly impossible. I know it will take time for me to feel it. Oftentimes when I'm traveling, I don't even feel like I've seen the things I have until days later when it suddenly hits me. Unfortunately by then, all I have are memories and photographs, which just aren't the same as the real thing, even if the real thing didn't feel very real to begin with.

"Amber," Annabella says politely. "May we please go see the *castello*?"

That finally snaps me out of it. "Very good," I tell her, giving her a big smile. "And yes, of course."

As we walk toward it, Annabella shoots me a shy glance. "Were you writing?"

I raise my brows, thinking she has her English mixed up. "Writing?"

"You were looking at the *castello*. My mama, she wrote a story about a *castello*."

Oh. *Oh*.

"She would write in her head? Dreaming in the day?" I ask her.

She nods. "Yes. Dreaming when awake. Making stories." She taps at her head. "Up here."

This is the first time I've heard either of the twins mention either of their parents without crying. I don't want to push too much but I want Annabella to know it's okay to talk about them. Maybe this is what they've been missing all along. Certainly Derio wouldn't indulge her since he doesn't talk about them himself.

"What kind of story is it?"

She shrugs. "She only read me . . . a little bit. There was a prince and a princess. In love. She did many . . . a lot of . . . writing."

"Are you in love with Derio?" Alfonso suddenly asks me.

I glance at him in surprise, my jaw unhinged. "What?"

"You and Derio," he says, scrunching up his nose a little. "Are you going to get married?"

"What?" I say, even louder this time. "No. No, Alfonso, we aren't like that. Your brother and I . . . I work for him. I am your teacher. I am not his . . . his . . ."

"Girlfriend," Annabella supplies.

"Yes," I tell her. Then shake my head. "But no. I am not his girlfriend. I am just a friend."

Alfonso pouts a little at that. "Oh. Okay."

What, he's disappointed?

Time for me to take this opportunity and be extra nosy. "Did you know his wife?"

Alfonso nods. "Yes. Daniella."

So she has a name. "Did you like her? Was she nice?"

He shrugs. "She was nice. She would give us candy."

Ah, candy. Always the way to a child's heart. I make a note that I should start carrying some at all times.

"She yelled," Annabella says. "At Derio, many times."

"But not at you?"

She shakes her head. "No, she didn't say much to us."

"But she gave us candy," Alfonso puts in.

"Yes," Annabella agrees, looking very serious. "The candy was good."

And I can't help smiling because even though we're talking about Derio's ex-wife, who apparently yelled at him a lot, the twins just conversed with each other in English naturally, without any prompting from me. Score one for progress. Maybe I can do this teacher thing after all.

As we enter the castle grounds and take a very tiny lift (Europe, I think, was founded on tiny little elevators) up to the top, the twins become more and more talkative. A few times I have to remind them to speak in English but they power through. Unfortunately, they ask me question after question about the castle and grounds, things I don't know the answers to, so I start making stuff up. I tell them the monastery was run by tiny elves who were exiled from the North Pole, and that a man called Winston Churchill, who could fly on golden wings, first built the castle.

"Who lived in this building?" Alfonso asks as we walk along a tiled patio past a tiny wooden door. The view of Ischia, all green hills and pastel buildings, looms in front of us, begging for Instagram photo after Instagram photo.

"Dracula," I tell him.

"Really?" he asks, all wide-eyed and staring at the small door with trepidation.

"Yes, Italian Dracula."

"That's not true," Annabella says, skipping over to the edge of the wall to stare at the view. "You lie. All the time."

"I'm writing in my head," I tell her, and she smiles at that.

We spend three hours roaming all over the castle grounds, hiding out in old prison cells, a weird creepy room full of toilet-type things where nuns used to let dead bodies rot, down pebbled roads that skirt the exterior of the island, past churches and vineyards and olive groves. I'm absolutely exhausted and my sandals have rubbed blisters onto my feet but I'm grateful to Derio in the end for suggesting it. I don't think his motive was for me and the children to bond, but regardless that's exactly what happened.

As the sun dips low on the horizon, heading for the golden sea, we race it on the hydrofoil home. Annabella rests her head on one of my shoulders and Alfonso does the same on my other. Soon they are fast asleep, and I'm feeling a bit like the Grinch did when his heart grew by three sizes.

CHAPTER EIGHT

It's just after nine o'clock when we get back to the villa. I practically had to drag the twins for the last bit down the Via Tragara, cursing the Larosa family for living so far away from Capri town. Did they really have to be so far removed from everyone else?

The path from the road to the front of the house isn't lit like it usually is, and I nearly walk into a lemon tree. The house itself is darker than usual and the lights aren't on at the front door.

Annabella says, "*Sinistra*," as I lead them to the door. It's also locked.

I fish around for the key inside my purse and eventually find it. I'm guessing that there's no one home, or Derio went to bed really early. That said, Felisa should be out and about.

A weird, tingly feeling crawls down the back of my neck. I take in a deep breath, unlock the door, and step into the house.

I flick on the hall light. "Hello?" I call out, my voice sounding small. "We're back, alive and well."

I look down at the kids as I shut the door behind us. They're staring at me, also feeling like something is off.

"No one is here," says Alfonso.

I swallow. "Well, if that's true, that's okay. I am here and you are here and Annabella is here and that's all we need." I smile at them so they don't worry. There's nothing to worry about, it's just dark and not the welcome we thought we'd get.

"Why don't you guys get into your pajamas and maybe Felisa will let you play your iPad games for a bit."

"Felisa is not here," Annabella says. She's standing down the hall and staring at the maid's quarters, where Felisa sleeps. I walk to stand beside her and look.

The door is open and Felisa's room is completely empty. The bed is made, tight enough to bounce quarters off the sheets, but the desk, the shelves—it's all completely bare. It's like she was never here.

"What the . . . ?" I step into the room. I open the closets. All her clothes are gone.

I turn around and eye the children. "Please tell me that Felisa existed and was a real person."

They frown in unison.

I step away from the closets and open drawers, all empty. "Felisa was real, right?" I repeat, feeling like I'm going crazy.

"Yes, yes," Alfonso says. "But she's not here. Where did she go?"

"Is she coming back?" Annabella asks.

I shake my head. "I don't know." She could have gone away for the night, but it doesn't explain why every single thing is gone, even her little Catholic crosses and funny porcelain doodads that she collected. A rosary and a framed picture of Alfonso and Annabella that were on the wall are also gone.

"I need to speak to your brother," I tell them, grabbing their hands and leading them out into the hall. I close the door and we go into the kitchen. "Derio?" I call out. There is no answer. I look at the kids. "Why don't you do what I said. Go get changed and then play on your iPads for a bit."

They stare at me, not moving, wanting to be part of uncovering the mystery of the missing nanny.

"Go," I say, pointing at the stairs. "I will figure this out and talk to your brother. Everything will be fine. I'm sure she's coming back."

Annabella shakes her head, looking down at the floor. "No. She won't. She once said one day she will have to leave for good. Just like mama and papa did."

Oh Jesus.

"I'll bring you candy if you go to your rooms," I tell them as a last resort.

Finally, they run off. I stand below and watch them climb the stairs and disappear into their rooms. I don't really have any candy but I know there's a tub of sorbet in the freezer that will have to do.

I inhale deeply, trying not to panic. Just because Felisa is gone doesn't mean something horrible has happened. Derio has to be here, he wouldn't just leave me alone in the house with the kids, would he? I mean, I'm not their nanny. Today was just a fun outing, not the start of something permanent.

Before I can freak myself out any more, I go to his office and knock on the door. "Derio?" I ask. I listen but don't hear anything. "Hello, Derio? Where is Felisa?"

I wait. I know that Felisa had warned me to never knock twice, but fuck that noise. She's not here right now anyway.

I knock again, louder this time. "Derio!"

I put my head against the door and listen. I think I can hear the tinkle of glass inside. Someone is definitely in there.

Against all orders, I put my hand on the knob and try to turn the door. It's locked.

I bang on the door, trying to not alarm the kids. "Derio!" I jiggle the knob. Nothing.

This isn't about to deter me. I head out to the back patio and peer inside the office. It's dark except for the green glass lamp on his desk, the kind you see in old lawyers' offices.

Derio is at the desk, slumped over.

I gasp and quickly knock on the glass to try to get his attention but he isn't moving. I try to open the French doors but they're also locked from the inside.

"Shit!" I swear and run off the patio and around the corner. I push my way through the brush, small palms whipping my face and stinging my sore shoulder as I burst through them. I end up by the dried-up fountain and the small courtyard at the other side of the office.

I try the doors there and they open so quickly I almost spill into the room.

"Derio!" I cry out, running over to him.

His head is buried in his arms and I can see the bottle of gin on the floor beside him. I push at his arms, and though it's like pushing stone, I'm relieved when I see him move a little. He lets out a groan.

Now what?

I shake him. "Derio, it's Amber. Where is Felisa?"

"*Mi lasci in pace,*" he mumbles into the desk.

"Derio," I say again. "Please." I crouch down so I'm at his level. I run my hand through his hair. I don't know why. To comfort him or comfort me. His hair is so thick and unimaginably soft and it's entirely inappropriate that I'm doing this.

"*Se ne vada!*" he yells, flinching away from my touch. He seems to agree with the inappropriateness and glares up at me with angry red eyes until I yank my hand away. "Go away!"

Fuck that. "I'm not going away," I tell him, any sympathy I had for him immediately gone. "You're drunk and I'm all alone with the kids. Where is Felisa?"

He shakes his head and closes his eyes. He starts laughing to himself.

I smack his shoulder hard. The laughing stops, and if looks

could kill, I would already be buried at sea by now. "Don't touch me," he says.

I swallow uneasily. I don't know what kind of a man he is when drunk, but I think he's an absolute douchebag. "I won't touch you," I try to say through an unsteady breath, "if you just tell me what the hell is going on. Where is Felisa? Did she leave? Everything in her room is gone and she isn't here."

He leans toward me, trying to reach for his bottle. I kick it out of the way and then take a careful step backward. He glares at me. "You shouldn't be here."

"Well, I am here," I tell him, folding my arms. "Trying to prevent my boss from dying of alcohol poisoning."

"You know nothing about me," he sneers.

"And that's your fault, not mine. I've been trying. You're a closed-off asshole half the time."

His head jerks back at that. Perhaps it was a little harsh and uncalled for, but still.

"*La leonessa esce a caccia*," he says with deliberation. "So, the lion comes out to prey."

"I'm sorry," I say quickly. "I just don't know what to do. Where is Felisa?"

He turns away from me, his chin dipping toward his chest, his eyes staring blankly at the space in front of him. "She left. She quit."

"She quit?!" I can't help roaring.

"Yes," he says, softer now. "She is gone."

"Why? What happened?"

"It was, how you say, a long time coming."

"You knew," I say, pointing my finger at him. "You knew this was happening, that's why we were sent away today."

"Yes," he says thickly. "I knew something was wrong. She

was trying to fight with me. I didn't want to fight with you all here. So I sent you away. Then we fought and she quit."

"But why?"

He eyes me and gives me a sour smile. "Because I am no longer the son that she raised. And she is no longer welcome here. I don't need anyone to compare me to the man I once was. That man is gone. I hope you understand that. *Capisci*?"

"*Non capisco*," I tell him. "And I never knew the man you were before. I barely know you now."

"Then let's keep it that way." He attempts to get up but lists to the side. I go to him, trying to help him out of his chair.

"Get away from me," he yells, violently shrugging out of my grasp. "You can't help anyone. You're useless."

I immediately let go and step back. "I am not useless," I tell him, my mouth gaping a little at the pain in my heart. I know they're just drunk words but they hit home and hit deep. My father, when angry, would call me useless all the time. Stupid and helpless. Always telling me I had to grow up. He was right about it, too—all of it—but I was trying now. I was really trying now.

"I can manage on my own," he adds, trying to get up again. "I have so far."

I take in a deep breath and try to ignore the sting of his words, which still flare inside me. "Managing is not the same as living," I tell him.

"Oh, just go to bed," he tells me, leaning with both arms on the desk, head hanging forward then rising up and down. As angry as I am, I can't leave him here in the study. I don't really trust what he's going to do; he seems too volatile, and I don't trust the alcohol in his system. If something were to happen to him, then Alfonso and Annabella really would have no one left.

I take in a deep breath and come back over to him. "I will

go to bed once I put you in yours. *Capisci?*" I wrap my hand over his arm and try to pull him up and toward me. It's like trying to move a pile of bricks. Eventually, though, he stops muttering Italian protestations and gets up. He smells like gin and cigarettes and lemons, yet somehow it's almost the best smell in the world.

Together we stumble out of the office and into the hall, nearly colliding with the opposite wall. I'm steady on my feet but he's so much larger and taller that when he goes in one direction it's nearly impossible not to go with him.

When we round the corner to the stairs, I look up and my heart grows heavy. Alfonso and Annabella are standing together in their pajamas, watching us. They don't look scared but they don't look happy either.

"Try to walk straight," I whisper harshly into Derio's ear as I adjust his arm around my shoulder. "We have company."

Derio looks up to see his brother and sister and his lips press together tightly. He swallows, his Adam's apple bobbing. He's going to hate himself for this in the morning, I can already tell.

"*Andate a letto,*" he says to them and I wince when he slurs. "*Rapidi.*"

The twins continue to stare so I repeat what he said. "Go to bed, please." I pause. "I will come see you in a minute. Your brother is fine, he just isn't feeling well. I'll bring sorbet."

Like before, the treat gets them moving. They slowly go back to their rooms just as we reach the second floor, throwing little glances at us over their shoulders. They didn't seem that upset or shocked, just worried. I wonder how many times something like this has happened. If someone like Lenora said he had a reputation in town for drinking, my guess is this isn't the first time.

I open the door to his room and manage to flick on the lights. His room is gorgeous and huge, with an enormous king-size bed, a bathroom fit for a Roman emperor, a sitting area, and a spacious balcony. I have no time to soak it in, though. I quickly move Derio over to the bed and help him onto it. He collapses in a heap.

"I'll be back," I tell him, moving him so he's on his side before I close the door and leave the room.

The children are back in their rooms like I asked so I quickly run downstairs and fill two small bowls with blood orange sorbet. Before I head up, I take a moment to breathe. My heart is racing a mile a minute, threatening to burst out of my chest. Felisa has quit, which means for the time being I'm in charge of the twins. There's no way around it. Even when Derio wakes up tomorrow hungover but sober, I'm going to be the one who has to step up. At least until they find a new nanny, because they all know that's not my job. That's not even close to my job.

But for tonight, I don't have a choice. And I really don't want the children to suffer anymore. As I run the bowls of sorbet up the stairs, I can't believe I've suddenly become one of those bleeding-heart *won't-somebody-think-of-the-children* types, but it's happened.

I go into Alfonso's room first. He's sitting up in bed and waiting. I stand by the door and hold out the bowl. "Do you want to eat this in your sister's room? I can explain to you both what's going on."

He nods and takes the bowl from me. We go into Annabella's room and he sits on the corner of her bed while I pull over the desk chair.

"Derio is not sick," Annabella says first. "He's . . . *ubriaco.*"

"Too much *vino,*" Alfonso fills in, shoving a spoonful of

sorbet in his mouth. At least they seem to be taking this in stride.

"And you've seen him like this before?" I ask.

They nod. "Yes, sometimes," Annabella says.

"Where is Felisa?" Alfonso asks.

"Yes, did she leave?" asks Annabella.

I nod slowly, not sure what to tell them, but they'd figure out the truth sooner or later.

"I am sure she will be back later," I say, adding a white lie. "But for now, she is gone."

Annabella's lower lip trembles and she stares sadly down at her bowl. "Who will love us now?"

Oh, my poor fucking heart.

"Your brother loves you very much," I tell her adamantly. "So much that sometimes it is hard for him. And Felisa loves you, too. She took your picture with her so she could look at it while she is gone."

"But he can't take care of us," Alfonso says. "He needs someone to take care of him."

Now, this is a pair of extremely astute children. "He might be stronger than he looks," I tell them. "Besides, he is trying his best. And I will try my best, too. I will look after you until we find someone else."

Annabella gives me a shy look. "We like you. We are sorry we have been so bad."

"Yes, we are sorry," Alfonso chimes in. "Please, we do like you. We want you to stay. We don't want you to leave, too."

I'm melting into a puddle, along with their sorbet. I look them both in the eyes and say, "I'm not going anywhere. Now finish up your sorbet and get to bed."

They slurp down the rest of it and I take the bowls from them. I say goodnight to Annabella, take Alfonso to his room, and say goodnight to him. I go down to the kitchen, put the bowls in the sink, and turn on one of the lanterns before I turn off all the lights in the house.

Once back upstairs, I go into Derio's room. He seems to be sleeping now so I turn on the light beside his bed, a really ornate, fancy thing of marble and gold, and then go to the washroom to fill up a cup of water for him. An Italian version of Advil would be good for pain in the morning, so even though I know it's kind of intrusive, I open the drawers on the beautiful vanity and do a quick search. I find some kind of painkillers, as well as prescription meds.

Don't be nosy, I tell myself. But I am nosy. Might as well embrace it.

I lift up the bottle and peer at it. It's a nearly full bottle of blue pills—Zoloft prescribed to Desiderio Larosa. The date it was issued was eighteen months ago. He hasn't been taking them at all.

I sigh and put it back, feeling all sorts of frustrated. I bring out the water and the painkillers and put it on his bedside table.

"Derio," I say softly. He is breathing deeply and doesn't stir. He looks so beautiful and vulnerable when he's sleeping, I can see why people creep on people at night. His lips are pressed together into a near pout, his forehead smooth of the usual lines and furrows. A strand of hair falls across his temple and I resist the urge to brush it out of the way. Knowing my luck he'd spring to life screaming, "*Non mi tocchi!*"

But still, I stand there, studying him, taking him all in without fear of being caught. I wonder what it would be like to kiss him. If he would care, if he would react. I wonder if he would ever let himself go or if he's shut down forever. I told the kids that he was stronger than they thought. I don't want to be wrong about that.

Eventually I leave his side, only to return later with a blanket and pillow and wearing the T-shirt and shorts that I sleep in. I move over to the couch in the sitting area of his bedroom and settle down for the night. I don't think he's going to die in his sleep but something is compelling me to stay by his side.

CHAPTER NINE

"Amber, where is Derio?" Annabella asks me as I give her and Alfonso their juice. They're sitting around the breakfast nook table and I'm trying to figure out what to give them to eat. They have to be off for school in ten minutes and they're half dressed and hungry.

"He's sleeping," I tell her, trying to slice a loaf of hard bread without cutting off my fingers.

"It's late," she notes in a discerning tone.

"Yes, it is. He'll be up when you get back from school."

"Are you going to take us?" Alfonso asks.

"Yes, I will, if you hurry up and eat and get ready," I say as I throw down two slices of jaggedly cut bread in front of them. They stare down at the bread and then back up at me with confused faces.

"Eat it," I tell them. Then I roll my eyes and quickly grab a jar of Nutella from the cupboard and put it beside them. "There."

The twins exchange a look. Alfonso mutters under his breath, "*Mi manca Felisa.*"

"Yeah, well, I miss her, too," I say.

Soon I'm hustling the twins out the door and taking them to their school. It's only when they disappear into the building that I nearly collapse. I lean back against the stone wall and decide to grab a coffee at one of the outdoor tables that line the Piazzetta.

It's quiet this early in the morning and the sun is casting long shadows across the square. A few other people, mainly older local men with slicked-back gray hair reading the newspaper, are scattered about, and a few pigeons dart underneath the tables looking for pastry crumbs. I pick a small table near the church tower and the charming waiter brings me a cappuccino, which I drink so fast I have to order another. And then another. I'm more exhausted than I thought.

I barely slept at all last night. The couch was pretty comfortable but I was forever conscious that I was sleeping in the same room as Derio. Then he started having his night terrors. Holy bejesus, did that scare the shit out of me. He wasn't as loud as he has been before, but his cries of anguish were so painful to hear. I don't know how he makes it through each night, let alone the twins.

I even got up and went to his side, just in case. I don't know what I expected to happen but I wanted nothing more than to wake him up and comfort him.

When he started calling out softly for his mother, I could hear the heartbreak in his voice. It undid me, cutting me to the marrow, and I couldn't go back to bed after that. There was just too much sorrow in this house.

"Amber?"

I look around me, startled that someone could know my name, and see Shay and some dude walking across the square toward me.

"Oh hey," I say, gesturing to the seats at my table. "Sit down. How are you?"

"Good," Shay says. She looks stunning, even in the morning, and I kind of hate her. My hair is pulled back into a frizzy bun and I don't have any makeup on at all. Thank God for sunglasses. "What happened to your head?" She leans forward, peering at my temple.

I forgot I had the bandage there. "Oh, nothing. Don't worry about it."

She frowns at me for a moment and then waves her hand at the boy beside her. "This is Danny, by the way."

Danny nods at me politely. He's not exactly the guy I expected Shay to be with it. He's kind of goofy-looking and meek but I'm just making assumptions again. One of my bad habits.

"Nice to meet you," I tell him and I hold my hand out for him to shake. He does so and it's like shaking hands with a jellyfish.

"So where the hell you been?" she asks me while she signals for the waiter. "You were supposed to come back to the bar." She talks to me like we've known each other for years and I'm totally okay with that. It reminds me of my friend Angela back in Cali, which then reminds me that I owe her a really long e-mail and not just the occasional comment on her Facebook and Instagram photos.

"Busy," I tell her. "Really busy."

She orders her coffee from the waiter like a pro. "Is that so? Busy with the children or with the mystery man?"

I manage a smile. "Both. And their full-time nanny, who they've had for like a million years, quit. Just yesterday. You don't want to be a nanny, do you?"

She wrinkles up her nose. "Oh, hell no. I'm not a fan of kids."

I watch a bunch of pigeons in the square take flight, their wings flapping noisily. "Yeah, well I thought I wasn't a fan of them either but these kids . . . well, they aren't as bad as I thought. Not anymore, anyway. I feel sorry for them. They've been through so much and I just don't see how it's going to get any better. I mean, how do you just get over losing your parents? I don't even like my parents and I couldn't imagine it. There's just so much pain and suffering in that house but it's all hush-hush and no one talks about it, especially not Derio, who's becoming more of an enigma the more I get to know him. Now, with Felisa gone, I know I'm going to have to step up and become the nanny until they find someone. I had to take the kids to school this morning, which is why I'm up here at this hour. Lord knows what I'm going to have to do when I get back to the house. Cook? Clean? I don't do that shit and I have no idea how I'm going to get through to Derio, especially when I need him the most." I pause, taking in a deep breath. "Fuuuuck."

Shay and Danny both stare at me for a moment before Shay puts her hand over mine. "Hun, how many cups of coffee have you had this morning?"

"Not enough," I tell her as I ask the now-overworked waiter for another.

I stay with Shay and Danny for an hour, talking about Capri and traveling and this and that before I realize I should probably head back to the sad lemon house to check on Derio. I make a promise to come to the bar sooner rather than later, and Shay says she'll put her feelers out for anyone who might make a good nanny for the children.

When I get back to the house there's this strange feeling of quiet. And calm. I like it. I walk down the hall and see Derio sitting outside underneath the pergola, drinking from a bottle of water. For once he isn't dressed immaculately—just black pajama pants and a plain white shirt. I like that look on him, too. I know I'm probably the last person he wants to see right now but I want to make sure he's okay. Besides, I still need to give him a piece of my mind. He said some pretty uncalled-for things last night, whether he remembers them or not.

I head outside and when he sees me he raises his hand in a small wave. I could be an asshole and not return the gesture, kind of like he did when I first came here for the job interview, but I decide to suck it up. Someone has to be the bigger person and it might as well be the person without the hangover.

I wave then walk over to the pergola and stop at the front of the table, underneath the bright blooms. A few bees buzz about. It's going to be a hot day.

"*Buongiorno,*" I tell him.

He's wearing sunglasses so I can't see his eyes but I know they must be red as hell.

"Good morning," he says, his voice low and ragged, like his throat has been scraped raw. "Did you take the twins to school?"

I nod. "Someone had to. You know, since you were sleeping and Felisa is gone."

He looks away and breathes out deeply. "Yes. I checked my e-mails this morning. She is gone."

I cross my arms. "You didn't do a very good job of explaining last night what had happened."

"I know," he says quietly, looking down. "I'm sorry."

"Are you?" I ask. "Because you were being a tyrant. A stupid, drunken tyrant."

He jerks his head up to look at me. "What did I say?"

"You said mean stuff."

"None of it was true."

"How do you know if you don't even know what you said?"

He swallows and licks his lips. "Because I don't think a mean thing about you. I only think good things about you. Very good things."

I'm not sure if I believe that but I sigh and sit down across from him. "Well, things were said and they were the complete opposite of very good."

"Amber," he says and places his hand over my wrist. I nearly jump at the contact. As usual, his skin is warm and the pressure of his hand is soothing. "I am very, very sorry if I said mean things. Sometimes this terrible thing comes out of me. I didn't want you to be exposed to it but you were. And I know you took care of me when you shouldn't have. You shouldn't have to take care of me or the twins, but you do."

I like his hand there. I want to grab it, lace my fingers through his, and feel that strength that I know he has inside. But I resist. "You *are* going to get a new nanny, right?"

"Of course," he says, pulling his hand away. "This has just caught me by surprise. I knew Felisa was unhappy but I didn't expect her to leave me."

I look at him. Leave *him*?

He seems to notice my expression. He pauses, chewing on his lip for a moment, before he snaps a cigarette out of his pack on the table. "This is very difficult for me," he admits. "Felisa . . . She was like a mother to me, to all of us. To lose them both . . . it's very hard. It's just as hard for the twins. Maybe more so." He pushes his sunglasses to the top of his head and looks right at me. He's a broken man.

"I understand," I tell him, not sure of what else to say.

"I don't expect you to," he goes on and sticks the cigarette in his mouth, lighting it. "I just need a few moments to get over it. And I will. Then I will start looking for a new nanny.

Don't worry, you won't have to help for long. But if you could, just until then, I would be eternally grateful to you."

My heart softens a bit. "Well, of course I'm going to help. I don't want the kids to suffer. And I don't want you to suffer either."

He snorts caustically at that. "I am sure that is true."

"I'm serious," I tell him. "More than anything I want to help you, and I will."

"Even though I am a total ass?"

I nod. "Yes. But in the future, could you try not to be? You know, if I'm going to help out I will because I care about all of you, but I won't do it if you treat me like garbage. I'm not saying that you normally do, but last night . . . Well, I don't appreciate being yelled at and I especially don't like being called helpless or useless."

Derio coughs loudly and looks at me with pained eyes. "I said that?"

"Yes." And it still kind of hurts.

He shakes his head to himself. "They are not true words, Amber. Please believe me. You are not useless or helpless. I honestly do not know what I would do without you. I need you, deeply. Madly, even."

He seems so heartfelt that it stuns me a little. He needs me, madly? Even if it's just for my services as a babysitter, I've never been needed before. My chest feels effervescent, like bubbles have been set free. He looks up at me and his features soften, from the fullness of his lips to the hardness of his eyes. "I'm extremely fond of you."

More bubbles, butterflies, everything is letting loose inside me. I'm warm, I'm golden from his words. And absolutely surprised.

Because he's staring at me in such a way that makes me feel

like he's really seeing me for the first time, I feel the need to play it all off. "Well, I'm fond of you, too," I tell him, trying to sound playful. "When you're not being an ass."

"So you forgive?" he asks in such a voice that I would be a cold, hard woman if I didn't.

"Yes, of course I do," I tell him. "Will you forgive me in advance for the absolute chaos that will come with me being a substitute nanny?"

"You will do fine," he says. "You have done beautifully so far. Their English is so much better now and they seem happier. I can see the changes in them. You're like a tonic for them."

I take that in, relieved to know that he's noticing the same changes that I am. I just hope I can keep it up and not have them revert to their old ways now that Felisa is gone. "So what exactly happened with Felisa? Last night you made it sound like she wanted to leave and you didn't want her here anyway."

He leans back in his chair and taps the cigarette. Ashes blow away in the light sea breeze. "I may have said that but only because she hurt me first. But I know she left because it was just too hard for her. I am difficult. The twins are. We are slow to change and heal, to be what she wanted us to be, to be what we used to be. Plus, she met a man, years ago, who lives in Salerno. I didn't think it was possible but I think she found an opportunity to be with him and she took it. I think she chose her own happiness over us."

"Oh."

"And I don't blame her," he adds quickly. "She has been with us for so much of her life. Always alone. Always taking care of us. First me, then the twins, then I guess all of us. You see, my parents had me when they were very young so they needed the extra help. Felisa then stuck around and became part of the family. Much later on, many many years later, my parents wanted to have more children. My mother became obsessed with it, you could say. She was older then, of course, and she had to go through many expensive treatments to become pregnant. Then finally she did. And then Felisa, who had already moved on after I turned fifteen, came back. We don't know what she gave up when she came back to us. She never talked about the life she had while she was away. But she came back to look after the twins. When my parents died, it made it impossible for her to leave. She was very loyal to my parents, you see. They would have wanted her here for as long as possible. I am sure Felisa saw herself trapped for the rest of her life."

"So do you think because I'm here now, she thought she could pass it down to me?" I ask.

He puffs on his cigarette and blows a cloud of smoke into the air. "Yes, could be. It seems that way. But I do know she would never have left the twins to someone she didn't trust, who she didn't think was capable. She could be very harsh and sometimes cold, but she thought highly of you. Just as I do."

I'm not used to him complimenting me even though I know he's laying it on thick because he feels so bad about what happened last night. "So now what do we do?" I ask.

He stubs out the cigarette on the table. "Now we try and get by until everything finds its place."

"Meaning you will hire another nanny."

"Yes," he says. "And I will do my best not to be an ass. You deserve better than that."

"Well, thank you in advance for that," I tell him, getting to my feet. "I better go inside and start making a master list or something of all the shit that needs to be done around the house."

"Do you need any help?"

I shake my head and eye his rumpled appearance with a smile. "I don't think you'll be much help in your state."

He looks down, sheepish and impossibly vulnerable. "Thank you," he says. "For staying with me last night. I woke up in the middle of the night and saw you sleeping on the couch. You . . . that . . ." He trails off, pausing. He takes in a deep breath. "It was a nice thing to see."

I give him a quick smile and then hurry back into the house. I can feel his gaze on my back and unspoken thoughts hanging in the air, like so much cigarette smoke.

CHAPTER TEN

Despite the odds, two weeks pass in the blink of an eye. Though it's insanely difficult—and difficult still—to assume the role of nanny, especially in the footsteps of someone like Felisa, who knew the family inside and out and ran a very tight ship, somehow I manage to push my way through it. It helps that the children are being somewhat understanding, although they're still prone to their extreme moments of brattiness. More than a few times I've been told my meals suck and have had doors slammed in my face when I tried to act like the voice of authority. It's hard not to take it personally, but I'm working on it, one incident at a time.

Derio hasn't been that helpful, at least not in a physical sense, and often keeps to himself. He smokes on the balcony and on the patio; he goes for his motorcycle rides. And then he locks himself in his library for hours on end. When he finally emerges, he smells like cigars and scotch and goes straight to bed. The night terrors still occur a few nights a week but I'm finally learning to sleep through them, even though his cries sometimes hurt my heart.

Except for tonight. It's a Thursday and past midnight. I can't sleep but it's not because of Derio's night terrors. My brain is turning over and over on itself, trying to think of what to cook tomorrow and what to organize. Is this what mom brain is like? It seems all I do is plan and worry and it's sucking the life out of me. I'm constantly misplacing things, like my styling products in the fridge; I've got dark circles around my eyes; and I'm always a few steps away from hysteria.

I'm about to switch on the light and maybe pull out a book since sleep seems so elusive when I hear a *thump*. I pause and then listen again.

A few beats pass. Another *thump*.

Then a scratching sound. I hold my breath and sink back into my bed. The moon shoots pale beams through the window, illuminating my bedroom in spooky shadows.

There it is again! Another *thump*, followed by smaller ones. They sound like footsteps, right above my damn bed. My eyes trail upward to the high stucco ceiling.

I have trouble swallowing and my chest feels hollow. I exhale as quietly as possible and then get out of bed. I grab the lantern and switch it on and quietly step out into the hall. It's dark, save for the slices of moonlight that cut in through the twins' open doors.

I pause halfway down the hall, listening. I can hear Alfonso breathing softly and the tick of the grandfather clock downstairs. The fridge hums. My heart pounds.

I round the corner, about to head to the stairs that lead to the attic when I run smack into Derio.

I gasp, my scream strangled in my throat as his hand goes for my biceps, holding me firmly.

"Amber," Derio whispers. "It's me."

I lean back, away from his body. He's wearing his underwear. Black. Tight. That's it. Nothing else. The ridges of his muscles stand out in the shadows of the lantern light and I hope I can pass off my gawking as fright because, let's face it, I'm a bit scared, too.

"You hear it?" he asks, not seeming to care that he's practically naked in front of me. I guess it's really no different from when he was wearing his Speedo at the beach, but this feels far, far more intimate and I'm so close to him; I'm practically at licking distance. I'd always wondered if he was a boxers, briefs, or boxer briefs guy, and I should have figured it would be something on par with that Speedo of his.

"Yes," I whisper, tearing my eyes away from his firm abs and the hard lines of his hips before my gaze goes any lower. "I thought it was you up there."

He shakes his head. "No. I was sleeping and it woke me up."

"So," I say, glancing up at the ceiling. "Are you going to go up there?"

He gives me a wry smile. "To be honest, I would rather not."

"Are you scared?" I tease softly. Then there is another *thump* and both of us stop smiling.

He gives me a determined look and holds his hand out for the lantern. "May I?"

I give it to him, though I don't want to be left in the dark either. I know I could turn on the hall lights but the children have been extra tired lately with all the stress of Felisa leaving and I don't want to risk disturbing them, even though I have no idea how they can sleep through all this commotion anyway. There's never anything louder than a bunch of people in the middle of the night trying to be quiet.

Derio reaches up and pulls down the trapdoor and the stairs as quietly as he can. Which is to say, not quietly at all.

"Shhh," I tell him even though it's pointless. We both pause, listening to see if the twins are up or if whatever is in the attic is making noise again.

Silence.

He gives me a nod and then heads up the stairs. I'm sad

that he's taking the light because it's completely preventing me from checking out his round ass as he climbs upward.

That's it, Amber, I tell myself, *focus on his bouncy ass, not on the fact that he might be murdered by the ghost in the attic.*

"What do you see?" I whisper, leaning forward on the stairs and trying to peer up. I can see his body glowing in the light and the shadows on the attic walls behind him.

"I don't know," he says uncertainly. He slowly walks forward and out of my view, like he sees something and is approaching it with caution.

I gulp and start climbing the stairs after him. I'm just poking my head above the floor and thinking of every single *Paranormal Activity* movie I've seen when Derio cries out, "*Merda!*"

It's followed by a god-awful, inhuman scream that I don't think comes from Derio. Suddenly, the lantern drops and he's running toward me and something black and angry is flinging itself at him in a whirl of fur and teeth and claws.

"Go!" Derio yells at me and I practically fall down the stairs just as I hear a loud hiss as something leaps past me. I stop, holding on to the railing, and watch a black cat barrel down the stairs to the first floor.

"Oh my God!" I exclaim. "What the hell was that?"

"What is it?" Alfonso asks sleepily, rubbing his eyes and coming out of his room. He flicks on the hall light, illuminating us.

With my hand to my chest I look at Derio, who looks both hot and ridiculous as he comes down the stairs in his underwear, with his messed-up hair and bewildered expression on his face.

"A cat was living in our attic," he says, trying to catch his breath, the whites of his eyes shining. "I have no idea how he got in." He smiles at us. "I guess we have to try and get him to leave."

"Oh boy," Alfonso says excitedly. "I'll get my gun."

Before I have a chance to ask, he returns with a squirt gun in hand. Annabella is at our side, too, now. I look at Derio and shrug.

And so the four of us spend a good thirty minutes running around the house trying to catch this cat. Alfonso has his squirt gun, Annabella has a hairbrush, and I wave spatulas around like some crazy cook who wants to make cat for dinner. Eventually we're able to drive the finicky feline out the open doors. It's only as the cat runs off into the gardens that Annabella says, "Oh, that is Nero."

"Nero?" Derio repeats.

"Yes, Felisa would give him milk sometimes."

Derio and I exchange a look. These kids were a few saucers away from having a pet cat?

After all the excitement dies down it takes a while to get the kids back into bed and asleep. I can't blame them. Even though I have to be up early to make breakfast and take them to school, it's two a.m. and I'm not tired at all.

"Would you like a, how do you say, nightcap?" Derio asks me as I'm about to walk up the stairs and back to my room after putting a few glasses away in the dishwasher; taking a cue from the cat, I gave warm milk to the twins in hopes it would make them sleepy. It worked.

I raise my brow. "You're still in your underwear."

"Does that bother you?"

I try not to smile. "Not at all." Nope, definitely not at all.

"*Buono*," he says and he gestures for me to follow him. He goes into his office and I feel a little bit of a thrill. For once I'm actually being invited in here.

He tugs on the pull-chain of the green lamp on his desk and then pulls a chair toward the desk. "Sit, please," he says, as if this is some formal business meeting in our sleeping attire.

I do so and then look around the room while he takes a bottle of scotch out from underneath his desk and pours some into two glasses. He hands me one with a wink and then sits down in his chair.

"You like this room," he notes.

I nod, taking it all in now that I can. It's so dark but even then it's not spooky. It's just perfect, all the dark wood and the books and the possibilities. "I've always loved libraries," I admit. I take a sip of my drink. "This one kind of reminds me of *Beauty and the Beast*. Especially because you have that ladder over there. I've always wanted to swing on one like Belle did."

"You are definitely the beauty," he says. I can feel his eyes burning on my skin and I feel too shy to meet them. "And I am definitely the beast."

His voice sounds so despondent over the last word that I can't help looking at him. He's staring at me but remorsefully now.

"You aren't a beast," I reassure him. "Now, the cat that attacked you, he was a beast."

He gives me a quick, small smile. "Yes, he certainly was." He licks his lips and leans in against the desk, his gaze more intense. "How are you, Amber?"

"Right now?"

He nods.

"I'm okay. Worried that I won't get enough sleep but I'll manage."

"And how have you been these past two weeks? As nanny."

I lean back in the chair and swirl the golden liquid around

my glass, watching it as it goes. "It's not been easy but I think I'm doing okay. I feel bad for the kids for having to put up with me."

"I think you're doing wonderful," he says, voice soft.

I give him a half smile. "That's because you're never around, which means you're never around to see me screw up."

"I'm around," he says. "More than you think."

I exhale and adjust myself in the chair. "Yes, well it will be a lot better once we get the new nanny." I pause. "You are still looking, right?"

He nods. "Of course. There just haven't been any applications."

"Really?"

He takes a long gulp of his drink and I'm amazed he doesn't choke on it. He seems to absorb the burn. "Yes. No one has applied. I will keep my hopes up."

I stew on that for moment and make a note to stop by the bar tomorrow and check in with Shay to see if she's found anyone. We posted an advertisement there similar to the one I had found at the café in Positano.

"Can I ask you a question?" I ask after I finish my drink and am feeling more confident.

"Yes," he says somewhat warily.

"What do you do in here all day long?"

He looks stunned that I asked that point-blank. But since we're in the office in question and he's in his underwear and we're drinking scotch, I figure why not.

"I'd rather not say," he says.

"Why not?"

His brows furrow in annoyance. "It is personal."

Damn. It's really hard to make something your business when someone tells you it's "personal."

"I won't judge you," I say, trying anyway.

He swallows and looks away. "There is nothing to judge." A moment passes where I'm sure he's about to go on, then his eyes slide to me. "You know, you don't speak very much of your home."

Now it's my turn to be stunned. "Oh. Well, I don't really get a chance to speak to you often. You know. 'Cause you're in here all the time."

"We are speaking now," he says. "Tell me about Amber MacLean's life in San Jose, California."

"Oh God," I say, my eyes widening. "What's there to even say? It's like that whole world, that whole life I had, doesn't exist anymore."

"Because you were traveling?"

"Yeah. And to be honest, there really isn't much to remember."

"You had a job," he says. "I saw it on your résumé."

Right. Résumé. He's my boss.

"I worked as a receptionist for a company that made cases for electronics, like iPads and smartphones and all that."

He raises his brow. "That doesn't seem like the place for you."

"Thank you," I say, taking that as a compliment. "And it wasn't. But I was desperate. I was one of those idiots who majored in English. I thought maybe I could get a job in marketing or communications or something and when I finally got this job they told me I would start off as receptionist and then move on up to something that used my skills. But that never happened. I worked my ass off, was paid like crap, treated like shit, and then they let me go, saying they didn't have the budget." I push my glass toward him. "I need more scotch."

"Yes, I think you do," he says with a half smile, and

promptly pours some into my glass before topping up his as well.

I take a sip, coughing a bit but still finishing at least half the glass. His eyes light up, impressed. "Anyway," I go on, "I found out afterward that they were hiring unpaid interns for my position. That's the problem now: Everyone goes to college and spends all their money getting their degrees and when they come out it's almost impossible to find a job in their chosen field, one that makes them feel useful, like their degree was worth it, let alone finding just any damn job. And then most of the fucking places won't even pay them. They want you to work for free to build up 'experience.'" I use air quotes around the word. "My friend Angela went to school for psychology. Psychology! And she spent two years working at clinics and hospitals and health care centers, all for free, all to build up experience, and she still couldn't get a paying job. Now she works in construction. She's one of those road people who holds up the signs. She likes that she's outdoors all day and the pay is actually really good, but holy hell, talk about being underused and undervalued."

I realize I've been talking a mile a minute. The scotch has really lubricated my vocal cords. Also, it's rare to have someone ask about your life and actually be invested and interested in what you have to say. Derio is both those things. He's staring at me as if I'm absolutely fascinating and not boring and mundane.

"Do you feel underused and undervalued now?" he asks quietly.

"No," I automatically say. "I feel overused," I add, jokingly.

"What about undervalued?"

I press my lips together in thought. "No. Actually, for the first time in a long time . . . maybe even ever . . . I feel worthy.

Like I'm worth something. The kids depend on me, which is annoying and nerve-racking and scary but it makes me feel like I'm doing something important. And teaching them English . . . well, it finally feels like my degree is being put to good use. You know, when I first started traveling, I had a little dream that maybe I would end up in a small village on the Mediterranean teaching English. I guess it kind of came true."

He's watching me carefully, silently.

"What is it?" I ask.

"How is it that someone like you hasn't felt worthy until now?"

I shrug and finish the rest of the scotch. The darkness of the room is starting to feel a bit heavy. "I don't know."

"Do you have any brothers and sisters?"

"Only child."

"And your parents, how are they?"

I glance at him shrewdly. "If I tell you about my parents, will you tell me about your parents?"

He nods, conceding. "Yes. But not tonight. It is getting late."

"There is no *getting*, it *is* late," I tell him. "And I'm seconds from crawling into my bed and passing out. *You* don't have to be up early tomorrow, but I do."

"Later today we can talk." He finishes his glass and sits back in his chair, his fingers resting on his lips. "Would you like to go for a ride? While the twins are at school?"

"On your bike?"

He nods. "Yes. I can show you the rest of the island."

There go those butterflies again, wings tangled with my nerves. I've never been on a motorbike before and just the image of hanging on to Derio is making me feel flushed from head to toe.

"All right," I tell him, getting up before I say something drunk and stupid. "I would like that."

"Be ready by ten a.m."

"I'll be ready at six thirty, remember?"

He smiles at that, as if laughing at the fact I have to get up so early now. Jerk.

"Thanks for the scotch," I tell him and then I go upstairs, the moonlight guiding my way through the dark. I get into bed and close my eyes. Even though I have to get up in a few hours, I've never been so excited to start a new day.

"Um, don't I need a helmet?" I ask Derio as we stand just outside of the shed where he keeps his bike. It's a big, dangerous-looking Ducati. Definitely sexy but still a bit scary for a bike noob like me.

He grins at me, his eyes squinting. "You'll be safe with me, don't worry."

"We better not go fast."

"No, no, I will go *very* slow."

"I don't believe you."

He steps into the shed and starts to bring the bike out. He's back to looking like an Italian James Dean with the leather jacket, jeans, boots, white tee. I'm sure he's about to slip on his shades and pop a cigarette in his mouth at any moment. "I will go slow with you," he says. "If you want to go fast, I will go fast. I'm very good at taking directions from pretty girls."

Is that sexual innuendo? I study him. He's got a self-satisfied smirk going on, which I've been seeing a lot more of lately. It's hard to tell. But hell . . . he just called me pretty. I'll pretend my cheeks aren't turning pink over that.

"Besides," he says as he straightens the bike out. He brings a cigarette out of his jacket pocket and sticks it in his mouth, nodding at my head. "A helmet would hide that beautiful lion's mane."

I pat my hands on my head. "I guess I should probably tie this crazy thing back." I reach into my pockets for a hair tie but he grabs my forearm, his grip soft but firm.

"No, don't," he says. "I love it when you have your hair down."

My heart skips a beat. He *loves* it? "Oh. Well, you know, it has a mind of its own. It will probably obscure your vision and you'll be riding blind."

"I know what I'm getting into," he says, still holding my arm. His eyes are glimmering teak and mahogany in the morning light.

I clear my throat. "Okay, I'll leave it down."

My hair has always been one of my defining features. So much so that my mother would often insist I wear it up so people would focus on me more than the hair. She also said it added too much weight to my face. I actually thought an abundance of hair made everything else look slimmer in comparison. Regardless, though, Derio likes it in all its wild, frizzy, curly glory. No, he *loves* it.

He smiles at me, looking so satisfied that I can't help smiling back. Something is going on between us, the air thick with something other than sunshine and the heady promise of a hot day. It both thrills and terrifies me.

But not as much as the bike.

"Come on," he says and pushes it up the short path. I run up and hold open the small gate so he can get through. He brings the bike around onto Via Tragara and gets on, starting it. The engine roars beneath him and the bike shudders to life.

Luckily it's not as deafening as a Harley but it's still strong and powerful enough to make the air vibrate.

And he's sitting on it like a prince on a steed. His entire body relaxes and conforms to it, yet remains completely confident and in control. This is where he belongs. I am hit with the feeling of disappointment that he had to give up racing. It seems like second nature to him.

"Get on," he says with a pearly grin, cocking his head.

I take in a deep breath, preparing myself for all the awkward, and try to get on. I'm short, though, so the awkward comes quicker than I thought it would. I can't seem to get my leg over the body.

He tilts the bike over to the side more so I don't have to lift my leg so high and says, "Just grab on to me and pull yourself up. I've got you. I'm not going anywhere."

The look in his eyes is so sincere that I can't help trusting him. I grab ahold of his arms and shoulders for dear life, like he's a tree I'm trying to climb. He remains firm and unyielding under my monkey grasp and I somehow manage to swing my leg over and position myself until I'm sitting comfortably, my crotch pressed flush to his ass.

"You okay?" he asks.

I nod.

"You can hold on to me as we ride, okay?"

I take my hands off his shoulders. My fingers had been digging into his jacket hard enough to leave marks, and I wrap my arms around him, just underneath his chest.

"Where are we going?" I ask him. His hair is practically in my mouth as I talk. He smells so fucking good it takes a lot of control to not bury my nose in it and take a deep breath.

"All over."

"Please tell me we aren't heading to Anacapri."

He glances at me from the side. "No?"

"No," I say adamantly. "I had fears I was going to throw myself out of a taxi; there's no way I would survive that crazy zigzag road on the back of a bike. I'm barely surviving just sitting here."

"But there's a beautiful garden over there," he protests.

"No," I say firmly. "Or I'm getting off this bike right now."

"Okay, okay," he concedes, raising his hand in defeat. "I will stick to this side of the island. *Capisci*?"

"*Capisco*."

And then we're off. To his credit he drives really slowly, so much so that he's kneading the handles as if he's trying to stop himself from going faster. Regardless, I'm hanging on to him for dear life, afraid that if I move even an inch I'll fall off the bike. I can feel his steady heartbeat under my hands and I bury my face into his neck. His stubble is rough but his skin is soft and warm and intoxicating. I so badly want to taste him with my lips, and when I breathe into him I can feel his heart beat faster.

"Don't you want to see where you're going?" he asks me, his voice throaty.

"Later," I mumble into him and now my lips graze his skin. Hot citrus.

I hear his breath hitch and then he revs the bike a bit faster. We zoom somewhere to the right and start heading up an incline. Eventually I find the nerve to raise my head and look around. We're still not going that fast, which helps, and we're passing white villa after white villa as we climb past eucalyptus, lime, and palm trees.

"Where are we going?" I ask him, relieved that we're heading in the opposite direction of Anacapri.

"Roman ruins," he answers. "*Villa Jovis*. You'll like it."

It's not long before we're pulling to a stop outside what looks to be a crumbling old fortress. Derio pays for our two-euro entrance fee at the ticket office. We walk unhurriedly among the ruins as Derio explains about the history of the place. Apparently it was built by the great Roman emperor Tiberius when he came here to escape all the warring and shit going down in Rome at the time, whenever that was.

Listening to Derio talk is far more interesting than actually looking at the ruins. While history has always fascinated me, the ruins are basically just a skeleton of the palace it once was. The rest you have to fill in with your imagination. Lucky for me, Derio really seems to have one as he tells me elaborate stories of the emperor's debauchery. I can see that creativity runs in the family.

"And this was the room where he would have his orgies," he says, gesturing to a large stretch of dry earth and crumbled stone that overlooks the sea.

"Orgies?"

He grins at me, taking off his jacket. The muscles in his arms flex as he folds it, his skin so bronze against the white of his T-shirt. It really is getting hot out and I'm sorry I wore skinny jeans, even though they made the most sense on the bike.

"Yes, orgies. You know, many people having sex together."

I give him a look. "I know what an orgy is, smart-ass."

"From personal experience?"

I bite my lip and reach out, punching him in the shoulder. "Hey, you watch it."

"I'm watching," he says, and his eyes lock on my body. "Very closely." His voice drops.

I am so close to opening my mouth and teasing him along the lines of, *Don't you know you're being inappropriate in the workplace?* to laugh off his comments but I don't want to call attention to them in case they really are inappropriate. In fact, I just want him to keep saying things.

But of course I don't know how to keep the banter going so I turn away and pretend to busy myself with the view.

"Have I embarrassed you?" he asks, stepping in front of me, close to me, so I have to look at him.

Oh God. This damn heat is getting to me. How many times in one day can a girl blush?

"No," I tell him, lying through my teeth.

"That's too bad," he says. "I like it when you blush. You look like a tomato. With hair." He reaches out and puffs up a few strands. Then he whistles, hands in his pockets, and walks away.

This playful side of him is new but I like it. It just proves that there's more to this man than distance and moodiness. I wonder what other sides I will uncover in time.

And then I realize I don't really have that much time left. A month has passed already. Suddenly, the last thing I want to do is leave. I feel like I've only just gotten started here, just gotten past the first barriers with Derio and the children. I can't imagine having to go in a month, back home to the mundane, where no thinks I'm worth anything.

There has to be a way to stay without risking deportation, but I don't know what it is.

As if sensing my mood change, Derio stops and looks at me curiously. "What is it?"

I blink my eyes a few times, trying to snap out of it. "Nothing."

He frowns and motions for me to come join him. He's heading toward a lookout where a few tourists are standing, snapping pictures of the bright blue sea.

I stand beside him, ever cautious about the railing of the lookout. I stand back and try to peer over without committing myself. The drop doesn't seem too steep, and I can see that the mountainside is terraced with thick tree canopies. The view is stupendous.

"Let me take a photo of you," he says. He holds out his hand and wiggles his fingers, gesturing for my phone. "I haven't seen you take many aside from selfies with the kids."

He's right. It's been all selfies, all the time. I even tried to get Alfonso to take a few pics but he didn't know the first thing about flattering angles. As I hand my phone over to Derio, I wonder if he'll do the same thing.

"Smile," he says and I do. "No, no," he says, even though he's still taking pictures. "That is not a real smile. I've seen your real smile."

"You have not," I tell him, even though I do feel that real smile creeping across my face now.

"That is better," he says, coming forward with such intense focus that he reminds me of the paparazzi. "But not quite there. Think of something funny. Perhaps me, in my underwear, being attacked by a cat."

And now I am thinking about him in his underwear. But not being attacked by my cat, although I can think of a few double entendres about pussy to throw back at him.

"Ah, the tomato face," he says. "*Bellissima*."

I roll my eyes and try to hide my face behind my hair. "All right, that's enough, give me my camera."

"One more," he says, bringing out his phone now. "For me."

And then he snaps a photo just as I'm making a face . . . I don't know what face I'm making. I feel put on the spot, annoyed but also sincerely flattered that he wants a photo of me on his phone. He nods at my hair. "With the sun behind you like so, you look like an angel."

"Not a lion?"

"You are definitely both, *la mia angelo e leonessa.*"

Now I'm really smiling, like a damn schoolgirl.

Another one of those heady moments passes between us and his eyes crinkle at the corners, softening. It could be from the glare of the sun but maybe it's something else.

He clears his throat and looks unsure of himself for a moment. Then he says, "Would you like to get a drink somewhere? At a bar?"

I nod, feeling absolutely parched. Lubrication is needed pronto, though definitely not between my legs. I don't think I've stopped being turned on by him yet.

"I know just the place."

CHAPTER ELEVEN

Fifteen minutes later, Derio pulls the motorbike up to the side of the Irish bar where Shay works. It's one in the afternoon so she should be on duty, or at least I hope she is. I've been wanting her to meet Derio so she can get to know him and see how handsome he is. I want her to look past all the terrible things that Lenora said about him. Even though I know now that some of those things are true, she didn't know the circumstances.

"You've been here before?" Derio asks as we stand outside of the building.

"You haven't?" He gives me a look that says I should know he does most of his drinking at home.

Inside the bar, it's delightfully cool and dark and a bit busier than the last time I was here. The tourists—particularly the day-trippers from the mainland—are flocking in droves to Capri each day. Shay is behind the bar pouring wine for a pair of fleshy, pale women with sun visors and nylon vests but it doesn't take her long to spot me. She waves enthusiastically, indicating that she'll be over in a minute.

"Do you know her?" he asks me as we sit down in a booth by the door.

"Yeah, her name's Shay. She's from New York. She and her boyfriend are like the only Americans on this island."

He nods, perhaps considering for the first time that I

might have a life outside of his villa. Although the term *life* is kind of stretching it.

Shay comes by, beaming at us. "Nice to see you here, Amber." She looks at Derio and flashes her supermodel grin at him. "And you must be her boss."

I groan inwardly, hoping she would avoid the B-word. Derio doesn't seem to be too bothered by it. He sticks his hand out for her to shake. "The boss. I like that very much. Makes me seem Sicilian, part of the Mafia."

"Even better," Shay says, shaking his hand. A little flare of jealousy rises in my stomach but I swallow it down. It doesn't help that I'm a sweaty mess and my hair is a rat's nest at this point while she's all smooth-limbed and glossy-maned. If I'm a lion, she's definitely a panther.

"So what can I get you?" she asks. "It's on me again, by the way."

"No, no," Derio says. "I'm buying the lady a drink."

I snicker. "Thank you, but since when am I a lady?"

He looks me up and down with a discerning raise of his brow. "Even ladies can get messy once in a while."

Shay has an impish look in her eyes as she looks back and forth between us. "So, what can I get you?"

"I'll have a beer," he says. He nods at me. "The messy lady can choose what she wants."

"Better than tomato face," I say under my breath. I give her a smile. "Glass of white wine please, whatever is coldest."

"You got it," she says.

"She seems very nice," he says as he watches her go. I'm studying his face closely to see if he likes what he sees. It's so hard to tell with him.

"She is very nice," I say. "I've been meaning to hang out with her more but, you know, life duties and all."

He licks his lips and it makes me want to do the same. "That would be my fault."

"It's not your fault Felisa left," I tell him.

He doesn't look convinced. He knows all the reasons, and most *do* involve him.

Luckily, Shay is fast and comes back with our drinks before we get too depressed over the circumstances. "What are you doing tonight?" she asks us, though I'm pretty sure she just means me. It's not like Derio and I ever do anything together—well, other than today. And the little swimming trip to the lighthouse.

"Taking care of the kids," I tell her.

"No," Derio says. "You're not. Have a night off; you deserve it. I'll take care of them."

I'm surprised at this. "Are you sure?"

He nods. "Yes. Please, you are young, you need to have fun."

"You're not too old yourself," Shay says to him with swagger.

"That's what I keep telling him," I say.

Derio eyes me and then looks patiently at Shay. "Please, Amber would love to come with you and do whatever it is that you wish to do."

"We're just having a little party tonight, live band and everything," she explains. She fishes a flyer out of her apron and puts it on the table. "It starts at eight. Anyway, see you there. *Ciao!*" She turns and runs back to the bar where a line has formed.

"I really don't have to go to this," I tell him.

"You are free to do what you want," he says. "I can take care of Alfonso and Annabella. I probably should do that more anyway."

"Do you think you'll be more involved with them when you hire the new nanny?"

He looks at me sharply, like I've said the wrong thing. Maybe I have. "I am already as involved as I can be. I am their guardian." There is an edge to his words.

That's not what I meant, I think, but I nod anyway and gulp my wine. It's so tempting to just finish it off and have another. All the white wines I've had in southern Italy so far have been so refreshing, it's like drinking juice.

Derio sips his beer and sits back in his chair, his attention now on the bar. He taps his fingers on the table, seemingly agitated. Funny how fast he can switch between moods.

"Thank you for bringing me here," I tell him, hoping to coax an easygoing smile and some banter out of him. "I mean, on the motorbike ride. It was fun."

His shoulders relax a bit. "You're welcome. Anytime you want to go for a ride, you just tell me and I'll take you."

Of course, it has to be at a time when the twins are in school. God, it's almost like dating a single dad. Except he's not a dad. And I'm not dating him. So maybe it's not like that at all.

I'm about to mention maybe going down to Marina Piccola sometime because it looks really pretty in the pictures when my eyes zip over to the entrance. Lenora and Utavia walk into the bar, looking for a place to sit to enjoy their weekly Guinness.

I freeze, afraid to look away, afraid they'll see us. But Derio follows my gaze and looks behind him just as Lenora and Utavia spot us.

Oh shit. My awkward-meter goes to eleven.

They both look fabulously put together—one in silk harem pants, the other in a python miniskirt, both in heels the size of my head. But I'm not so much intimidated by how they look as how they'll act. Lenora is frowning, already seeming a bit bothered at the sight of us together. Never mind the fact that I really am working for him and she knows this. I guess just being at a bar is making it seem like something more than a working relationship, something more than it actually is.

"Hello, Amber, is it?" Lenora says, wiggling her manicured nails at me. I instantly think of the horribly chipped green polish I'm wearing at the moment.

I can only nod and I can feel Derio staring at me in shock, wondering how on earth I know this person.

"*Ciao*, Derio," she says to him, pursing her lips together into an angry little pout. "I haven't seen you for a very long time."

"*Buongiorno*, Lenora," he says to her—rather graciously, I might add. He bows his head. "Utavia."

"Mind if we join you?" Lenora asks us, gesturing to the booth. I curse the fact that we didn't get a two-seater.

"No, please, sit down," Derio says so politely, warmly even, that I wonder if maybe there was more to their little date than I had assumed.

Lenora smiles like the cat that's got the canary and then says something to Utavia. Utavia runs over to the bar, leaving Lenora with us. She drums her nails on the table and smiles prettily.

"So, Amber," she says to me. "Are you still teaching English to Derio's siblings?"

"How did you know that?" Derio cuts in before I can answer.

"She was here one day in the bar. We had a nice chat. It was good to practice my English. I've gotten very good, you see." She bats her eyelashes at him. "She told me she was teaching them . . . What are their names again?"

"Alfonso and Annabella," Derio says somewhat quietly.

"Yes, of course," she says. "And how are they?" She looks at me with false sympathy. "They've been through so much, it must be so hard to teach them, yes?"

"They're great," I tell her, not willing to admit any of the children's faults.

"But of course they have that old woman."

"No, she's gone," I say, and from the daggers that Derio shoots me I know I wasn't supposed to say anything. Too late now.

"She died?"

"No, she just left. I'm the nanny for now."

"You are the nanny?" she asks incredulously. She looks at Derio. "And you are on a date with her?"

"We're not on a date," I say quickly.

"We're just having a drink," Derio explains, his voice hard.

"Well, we all know what that means with you," Lenora says with a sour laugh. "Of course, it did not turn into much of anything."

Derio finishes the rest of his beer in one gulp, obviously wanting to leave. I'm pretty much done with my wine as it is.

"He hasn't left the island for a very long time," Lenora says, jerking her thumb at him while looking at me. "I hope you don't fall in love with him or you will be stuck, too." She smirks at him and then says, "But then Amber already knows this about you."

Now Derio really wants to kill me. Actually, it's more than that. Though his jaw is twitching in anger, his dark eyes are filled with hurt. The way she said it makes it seem much worse than it is.

He gets up just as Utavia gets back to the table with their

Guinnesses. "*Scusate*," he says. "I must attend to some matters." He flings some money down on the table and leaves.

I spring to my feet, grabbing my purse, and run after him just as I hear Lenora calling out, "No use running, he doesn't like women!"

Derio is getting on the bike and seems like he's about to pull away from me. I grab on to his arm and pull at him.

"Wait!" I cry out.

He glares at me. "She told you things about me? That I won't leave the island? What else did she tell you?"

"I'll tell you," I say, "but it's not a big deal. Let's just go back to the house and away from here. She's bitter."

"She is a bitch, that is what she is," he says but he tips the bike over to the left so that I can properly get on.

"I figured that much," I say, grabbing hold of him.

We quickly zoom down the crowded streets past the cafés and fancy shops and soon we're back at the villa and he's putting the bike in the shed.

Unfortunately, now he doesn't seem to want to talk at all.

"Everything she said I took with a grain of salt," I explain.

"It doesn't matter."

"I would have told you but I met her on my first day on the island, weeks ago, and you and I weren't really talking like we do now. And I knew it was hearsay anyway."

"It's fine."

"I could tell that she was hurt because you weren't interested in her."

"That is true," he says, practically slamming the shed door shut. "Because she's not a very nice person. She was asking me for weeks to go out with her so I finally did. I used to know her brother."

"She thinks you're gay and that's why you don't like her."

He stops in his tracks and his eyes nearly fall out of his head. "She thinks I'm gay?"

I nod. "Yeah, she seemed quite adamant about that. I guess she was throwing herself at you and you weren't interested." I don't add the part about him being too drunk because that does hit too close to home. "She's really pretty and probably has lots of guys into her, so . . ."

"She was throwing herself at me," he says, shaking his head and staring at the ground. "But being beautiful has nothing to do with sex. You have to be beautiful in here, too," he says, pressing his fist against his heart and then his head.

That was actually really sweet, though I did use the term *pretty*, not *beautiful*.

"So she's feeling rejected," I tell him. "And rejected people do crazy things. I should know. I once turned down this guy at my old job, citing the whole office-romance thing, and he started hiding my lunch every single day. No matter what I put in the fridge, it would be gone before lunchtime. Then my stapler started going missing. It was like watching *Office Space*, except it wasn't funny at all."

He stares at me for a beat. "Do you think I'm gay?"

I blink. "Uh."

He steps toward me until he's just a few inches away. I can feel his body heat radiating off of him, intensified by the sun. That citrus smell teases me again.

"If I kissed you, you wouldn't think that."

Whoa.

Hold up.

"I don't think you're gay," I manage to say, my voice more like a squeak. "You were married."

He nodded. "I was. We divorced because I changed and

she could not accept that. She fell in love with someone else but I was still in love with her."

Oh, here come *all* the things.

"Are you still in love with her?" I ask, even though it's totally none of my business and shouldn't matter.

He rubs his lips together and shakes his head. "No. I am not. She wasn't right for me in the end. And I knew Lenora wasn't right for me from the beginning."

So, who are you right for?

"I am not gay," he continues, "but she can think that if she wants. I'm just very . . . selective. Especially over who I allow into my life."

"It takes time to get over the end of a marriage," I say softly.

"Yes, you are right. But how much time is too much? When do you know when the time is right?"

I shrug, looking away at the lemon trees. "I guess you just know. You go on gut feeling."

"And what if you can't feel anything at all?"

I look at him curiously. "You can't stay numb forever."

But you can sure as hell try.

He exhales and fishes out a cigarette. He nods at the front door. "You go inside. Maybe see what we can have for lunch. I'm not sure what you have planned for dinner either but let me know if you need money for the grocery store. I'm going to go for a walk to end of the road, clear my head a little."

And just like that, fun time between Derio and Amber is over and we're back to the employer-and-employee relationship, master of the house and the help.

I sigh but agree and go inside. I glance over my shoulder at him as I shut the door and see him staring forlornly up at the sky, as if asking for guidance.

....

Obviously I never end up going to the bar to see the band that Shay was talking about. Instead, I stay at home, looking after Annabella and Alfonso while Derio locks himself away in his office again, doing whatever it is that he won't tell me about. At this point I hope it's something really weird and twisted, like five-hour masturbation marathons to some weird goldfish fetish or a bizarre obsession with bidding on flowery tea sets on eBay. I would take anything aside from what he's really doing: brooding and drinking.

So I make dinner—a nice eggplant parmigiana that turns out better than I expected—and then I read to the twins a bit from one of the Harry Potter books, even though they know the Italian versions by heart. Derio never comes to the door when I knock, though he did once yell at me to go away, so at least I know he's alive.

After I put the kids to bed, I gather some of the leftovers from dinner onto a plate, pour a glass of water, and put it on a tray. I carry it over to the office and knock loudly.

"Derio, I have dinner here for you," I say quickly before he can tell me to get lost. "You should really eat something. The kids actually liked it so I think you should witness the fact that I finally made something appetizing. It might never happen again."

I wait a few seconds and then put the tray on the ground outside the door. I'm about to walk away when—lo and behold—it actually opens and he peers at me with a cocked brow.

"*Buonasera*," he says, his voice sounding extra throaty tonight, which equals extra sexy—and he's speaking in Italian to boot.

"*Buonasera*," I tell him, trying to peek inside. "You're not in your underwear again, are you?"

He gives me a lopsided smile. "I can be. Would you like to come in?"

"Are we going to drink scotch again? Because something tells me you've probably had enough."

"Come." He steps back, disappearing into the office. "Bring the food."

I give him a look that says I'm not his servant 24/7 but bring the tray in anyway and set it on the desk. He goes to the door and closes it. "Would you like a drink?"

I should say no. I sigh. "Yes."

"*Buono*," he says. He goes and pours me a glass. He hands it to me, his eyes focused on mine the whole time, as if holding me in place. Because he's drunk I can't read them for the life of me. He seems to be in a playful mood again but I'm not putting stock in anything Derio-related anymore.

I stare down at the glass. "Did you drug this?"

He smiles. "No."

I squint at him. "Why are you smiling, then?"

"I like to smile at you," he says.

I let out a dry laugh. "Right. No, Signor Larosa, you like to frown at me. Glower at me. Glare at me. Or just stare blankly at me like I'm not even there. But smiling at me? Not so much."

The smile slides right off his face. I raise my glass at him. "See, right there. Back to Mr. Angry Face."

"You really don't think much of me, do you?" he asks. His voice is strained and a little rough around the edges.

I take a small sip and suck on my top lip for a moment as it burns. "Actually, I think a lot of you."

"All bad."

"Didn't you say the bad things were the good things?" I ask him.

"Are you comparing me to a bad habit?"

I cock my head, considering that. "Maybe I am. But I happen to like a lot of my bad habits."

"Like the drinking."

"Yes."

"The eating."

"Yes."

"The sex."

A small shiver runs through me as my lips twist into a smile. Even the word *sex* sounds amazing coming from his mouth. "Especially the sex. It's the best bad habit of all."

He doesn't smile at that—no surprise—but the intensity in his gaze deepens. His eyes burn me, and his look becomes smoldering. He's making me feel like I'm standing in his office completely naked, not wearing the same billowy tank top and skinny jeans I was wearing earlier.

"Stay right there," he commands me in a hushed tone.

My heart does a few solid thuds in my throat. I swallow uneasily. "Okay."

I know I'm staring at him with wide Bambi eyes, I can't help it. I follow his every movement as he comes around the desk and walks toward me.

He stops in front of me, so tall and large. I can see his pulse tick along his throat and the dark danger in his eyes as they peer at me through black lashes.

I grip the glass of scotch hard, afraid of what's going to happen next.

Because something has to happen; something *is* happening.

I've never been looked at this way before—stripped bare

by a carnal gaze—and it would be a shame to let it go to waste.

He places both hands on either side of my face and I feel so small, so conquered, so . . . coveted. His skin is hot and rough to the touch and alights my entire body until I'm buzzing with fiery anticipation.

"I need to kiss you," he says, and it's the smartest thing he's said all day. "Please."

I try and say *okay* but it catches in my throat. I saw this coming—a man can't stare at a woman like that without kissing her—but it still unwinds me like a spool of thread.

He's still staring at me, his brow furrowing, casting shadows down his perfect face. His lips are just out of reach. "I need to know if I can feel anything. I want to feel something."

There's a quiet desperation in his voice. It makes me ache for him.

Then he leans in and kisses me. His lips are soft, perhaps a little unsure as they press against mine, but then the pressure increases, our mouths yielding in unison and it feels like drinking and breathing and living. He tastes like the honey tones of scotch and of faded smoke and mint. It's an elixir that flows down my throat and right between my legs, and his probing tongue stirs it further.

My tongue teases his back as it slides into my mouth, stoking the wildfires. Our kiss deepens and his hands find their way into my hair. He lets out a low moan that reverberates through me and I gasp in response, the glass almost slipping from my hands. I want to pull him into me. I want more of this, all the time. My free hand slips around his back and presses into his firm, hard muscles. I'm so incredibly turned on that I'm seconds from just throwing the scotch across the room and dropping to my knees. I want to take him in my mouth and make him moan again—I want to make him feel something. I want to make him feel me. I want to know what he looks like when he comes, if it brings him some kind of peace.

I want so much more than the hunger and desire he's already giving me, our lips, tongue, mouth heating up, our kiss fueling our needs and our needs threatening to take over. I wonder if he's afraid of this kiss because to me it feels a bit like drowning. But we're not drowning alone. We're clinging on to each other like a life raft.

I'm so insatiable now, so greedy, that I almost whimper when he pulls away. He holds me, fisting my hair, and presses his forehead against mine, eyes pinched shut and breathing hard. I gulp in the air, unsure if we're going to stop or if I need to refuel to go further. I could go all night and every night after that.

My lips tingle now and a few beats pass.

"Did you feel anything?" I ask softly, hopefully.

He shakes his head ever so slightly, his forehead damp against mine. "No," he murmurs. "I felt everything."

Suddenly, there's a knock at the door and we both jump, breaking apart.

"Derio?" Alfonso calls out from the outside. "*Dove si trova Amber?*"

We exchange a look. Derio is flushed and has a rather obvious erection straining against his jeans. I know I look properly messed up.

"I'm in here," I yell through the door. "Be there in a second."

I look back at Derio but he's walking slowly over to the windows, running a hand through his hair.

"I'll go see what he needs," I tell him, going for the door.

"Yes," he says thickly. He clears his throat. "I will see you tomorrow."

All right, then. So I guess that's the end of that.

I'm too overwhelmed to even get riled up over it. I take in a deep breath and smooth down my hair before leaving the office.

Alfonso is standing in his pajamas in the hall and the sight of him looking so small and vulnerable brings reality crashing down around me. I have to take care of these kids. Kissing their older brother isn't part of the job.

"What's wrong?" I ask him.

"I had a bad dream. I can't sleep," he mumbles.

"Bad dreams are just your mind trying to tell you bad stories. They can't hurt you." I take his hand and lead him up the stairs to his bed, where I read to him for half an hour—but no Harry Potter this time since he confessed that his bad dream included Professor Snape. Instead, I read to him from an Italian children's book, and though he giggles at my pronunciation through most of it, soon he's fast asleep.

I leave his room and as I head to my own, I catch a glimpse through the windows of Derio standing on the patio, watching the black sea, smoking his cigarette. Alone.

I don't have any bad dreams that night. In fact, I barely sleep at all. I keep reliving that kiss over and over again until it's more than just a memory.

Drunk or not, Derio kissed me. He felt something. *I* felt something.

And I have no idea what any of this means.

CHAPTER TWELVE

Saturday mornings usually mean you get to sleep in, but not in this household. I'm up at the crack of dawn and running around the house trying to get ready for the day. I tackle the kitchen first, cleaning and scrubbing it from top to bottom, then prepare an American-style feast for the kids with what I have on hand. They don't have bacon in the house so I fry up the cold cuts and slices of pork instead, then fry eggs with some salsa type of sauce. Sliced-up sweet potatoes go in the oven in place of hash browns.

The twins seem especially excited about this when they wake up—I think it makes them feel all exotic and grown-up to experience something different. The truth is I'm taking on the extra work because I want to keep busy. I haven't seen Derio yet and I'm afraid of what will happen when I do. What if he tells me it was all a mistake, that he shouldn't be doing this with me, that he shouldn't be romantically or physically involved with a woman on his payroll? What if it doesn't mean anything to him in the stark light of day?

As it turns out, I don't see Derio at all that morning. I ask the kids what they want to do and they tell me it's too hot to play outside—it's well into the high eighties—so I tell them to do what they like around the house, and if they're bored and dying by the end of the day, I'll take them to the free beach by Marina Grande. It's days like these that I wish they had some good friends they could go play with, but both of them seem to be quiet loners. I know a lot of twins are like that but I think Annabella and Alfonso are even more closed off because of the accident. I make a mental note to hang around after I drop them off at school sometime and get to know the other parents. Perhaps if they knew what was going on, they would encourage their own kids to be more inclusive.

I laugh a little at those thoughts. I'm starting to sound an awful lot like a parent. I have to remind myself that I'm not the kids' real nanny. Any day now we'll find one and then I'll be off the hook. I can go back to having a little bit of a life again, although the longer I'm a nanny, the faster I can earn the money to get home.

If I even want to go home anymore.

I sigh and then finish cleaning up the kitchen after the kids scatter throughout the house. I make myself a latte from the espresso machine and take it and an English mystery novel I found in town out onto the patio. I'm only out there for a few minutes before I start to roast and sweat pours down the back of my strapless sundress. I stare longingly at the indigo sea and the boats that ply through the intensely gorgeous waters. Every day there are more boats and less sea visible from the patio. I have to wonder how many tourists Capri can handle; it's starting to feel at capacity. I can understand now why Derio prefers the winters here. I wonder if I'll ever get the chance to experience it myself.

Finally, I've had enough of the heat. I take the remains of my latte and book and go to the shady side patio outside of Derio's office. It's cooler here and I make myself comfortable at the small iron table next to the disused fountain. It would be beautiful if it were repainted and turned on; the charming antique, with its intricate carvings, looks too valuable to go to waste. I wonder if I can turn that into a side project of sorts.

Then I notice that the French door leading into Derio's office is open a touch. I sit there, wondering if he's inside—it's hard to tell from this angle and I can only see a reflection of myself in the glass.

Out of the corner of my eye I see a black shape slinking over the sun-bleached gravel—Nero. The cat pauses at the door, tail twitching, and without a glance in my direction he goes into Derio's office.

Oh no you don't. If Derio's not in there, he's going to lose his mind. If I'm not allowed in there, the damn feral feline isn't allowed in there either.

"Hey," I whisper harshly to it but it's already inside. I get out of my chair and hurry over to the door.

The office is empty. I see the cat has jumped up onto the desk.

"Get away from there!" I yell at the cat, trying to shoo him away. The cat looks at me with disdain and then jumps off, knocking over a stack of papers that were lying on the desk. They scatter across the tiles and the cat runs for the bookshelves.

I swear under my breath and am about to pick up the papers when something on the desk catches my eye. It's a printed manuscript, about two inches thick and held together in the corner by a heavy-duty binder clip. The typewritten pages are marked up with red pencil; I can see scrawled handwriting in the margins and between the double-spaced sentences. The header says *Correre il Sole—Sophie Larosa.*

Don't snoop, I tell myself, though it seems to me like Derio is editing something of his late mother's, or at least reading something she may have edited herself.

I tear my eyes away from it, putting a stop to my curiosity, and then stoop down to pick up the papers. I try not to look at them either to protect his privacy.

But these aren't related to his mother's books.

They're résumés. All in Italian. All dated within the last few weeks. I see the words *bambini* and *bambinaia* in bold letters. I flip through them and then realize there are a lot more in the trash can beside his desk.

I start picking them out, poring over them. Even with my limited Italian, it's pretty obvious what they're all applying for.

"What are you doing?"

I jerk my head up to see Derio standing in the doorway, shock and anger rippling across his features. But I don't even remember that I shouldn't be in here.

I stand up and wave the papers at him as he strides toward me. "What are these? Résumés? Are these résumés for the nanny position?"

"I told you not to come in here," he spits out, looming over me.

"No," I tell him, shoving the résumés into his chest. "Felisa told me to never come in here. You know, the woman you said you can't replace for a job you said no one has applied for. Well, what the fuck is all of this? You lied to me!"

His nostrils flare and he closes his eyes. "It's not like that."

"Then explain it."

He tears the résumés from my hand and flings them into the garbage. "They are no good."

"You said no one applied. Why did you lie?"

"Because what is the point? They are not good enough for the position."

"How do you know?"

"Because you're good enough. And they aren't as good as you."

My mouth drops open. "What? What are you saying?"

"I'm saying . . ." he says and then growls in frustration, turning away. But I don't want him to turn away anymore. I'm sick of him disappearing when things get rough.

I reach out and grab his arm, my fingers digging into his flesh. I'm surprised at how angry I am. I pull him toward me, not afraid.

"What are you saying?" I repeat. "You know this isn't my job. This wasn't what I was hired for."

"I know," he says through gritted teeth. "You make that perfectly clear."

"Because it isn't!" I yell. "I'm not cut out for this. I came here to teach the kids English, not become a substitute mother."

"Even though they need you?" he asks, his voice lowering. He's breathing hard, his jaw set in a stubborn line.

"They don't need me," I tell him. "They need someone who can really take care of them, someone who knows what they're doing."

His Adam's apple bobs as he swallows hard. He licks his lips and a look of sincerity washes across his face. "What if *I* need you?"

I blink at him, afraid to think about what he means. "You can easily find someone who will fill those needs."

"Those aren't the needs I'm talking about," he says, turning in to me and sliding an arm around my waist. He cups my face with the other hand and runs his rough thumb across my lips. He gazes down at me through hooded lids, simmering with lust. "*Mia leonessa. Te voglio, voglio te far l'amore, voglio la tua dolce bocca. Baciami.*"

He kisses me hard, hurriedly. I have no idea what he just said but I'm agreeing to all of it and melting in his hands.

I'm still angry at being somewhat deceived but a different fire burns brighter now, hotter, stoked by his desperate tongue and greedy lips.

He pushes me back until my ass is pressed up against the edge of the desk and I can feel his urgency. His mouth is on my neck, on my shoulder, his lips wanting and searching, and I'm not sure what to do with my hands. I want to grab him, feel him, every beautiful inch. I want to do more than we did last night.

Of course, somewhere in the back of my head, amid the heat from his body and the haze of summer and the dreamy lust, I wonder if this is a good idea. I'm the nanny. More than that, it seems like he's intent on keeping me as his nanny. I should be mad about that. I should be cautious. I should realize that having sex with Derio is a big, big step, and I'm not sure if I'm ready for it.

But he's beginning to make animalistic sounds against my skin and I'm starting to crave his body, his masculine power, his raw desire for me. I want him. On this desk, if need be, in this room that has been as forbidden to me as he has.

He brings his face up to mine, his breath heavy. He teases my lips with his and runs his hands through my hair.

"I need you," he says, his voice low and gruff.

The passion in his eyes burns and I am swept up in it, untethered. I place my hands behind his neck. I am more than ready.

"Then have me."

He grins and reaches down beneath my thighs and lifts me up, placing me on the desk. He hikes my dress up around my waist and I wrap my legs around him. He tugs down the front of my dress, exposing my breasts, and runs his tongue over the soft swells. I can't help throwing my head back, trying to give him greater access. His mouth and hands ravage me like I'm a cold drink on this hot, hot day.

"Are you . . . on . . . a pill?" he asks, pausing between biting my nipples.

I nod. "Yes."

"I haven't been with anyone since my wife," he says huskily. "I am clean."

I tell him I am, too, which is true—tested and clean—and I have no reason not to believe him. And then it hits me. Derio hasn't had sex in a year. Suddenly, I feel a lot of pressure to make this memorable for him.

But from the way he's touching me, kissing me, staring at me, I think I'm already halfway there. With his tongue on my breasts, he slips one hand between my legs, where I'm wet, and strokes me softly. I let out a breathless moan, overcome by his touch, and he slips my underwear to the side while he quickly unzips his fly. The sound of his zipper cuts through the room and it revs another part of me, turning me on and on and on.

Now his mouth is back on mine and my hands grip his waist as he guides his cock into me. I can't help sneaking a glance and my eyes widen at the sight as he pushes his hard, thick length in one slow stroke. It's a fucking hot sight and an even better feeling, even though I do experience the initial pinch as he slides inside of me. I take a deep breath.

"Are you all right?" he murmurs into my neck, sucking my soft skin. "I can take this slow."

I wrap my legs around him tighter and press my nails into the small of his back. "Please don't."

He groans and looks at me through heavy lids. "You feel beautiful." He places a slow, teasing kiss on my lips. "You are beautiful. *Bellissima.*"

We stare at each other for a moment in a long, lust-induced haze and he slowly pulls back. I can feel every inch of him as he slides out and I'm almost bereft at the absence. Then he pushes back in to the hilt and I gasp, stretching around him, feeling him so damn deep.

In and out. In and out. So wet, so slow. Maddening.

He's looking at me now like a wild animal, his mouth parted almost in a sneer and his eyes, so dark and desirous, reach right into me. He begins to thrust in and out, harder, faster, as he holds me on the desk and I clutch him to me, keeping him as deep inside as possible. Sweat forms on his brow and drips between my breasts and everything about the moment, about us, about the air, is too damn hot. I've never felt so wanted, so thoroughly fucked before. Every time he sinks in farther it awakens another part of me.

I want to come so badly, my body is straining, begging for release, but my G-spot isn't being hit at this angle. I slip my hand to my clit but he immediately pushes my fingers aside and places his own there. The pressure is so firm, so all-encompassing of my swollen flesh, that my body jerks into him further.

"My job," he growls. "I'm the one who makes you come."

He's fucking hired.

It only takes one thick swipe of his fingers just as he thrusts into me to the hilt to send me over the edge. The tension unleashes like a dam and I go from wound-up as all fuck to flowing freely, lost in a million colors. My limbs spasm and my fingers dig into his back and the round thickness of his ass and I'm holding on while letting go and succumbing to a feeling of freedom I've never experienced before. It's just me and it's just him and he's coming now, too, with ragged breath and a pained cry. I stare up at him, wanting to see that peace on his face. He closes his eyes tightly, his features contorted as he pours into me. Then he relaxes, catching his breath, and when he opens his eyes and gazes at me, I see total softness in him, like looking into a deep, cool pool, an oasis of calm.

I can't help smiling lazily at him as I brush back a strand of thick hair from his forehead. "So, was that your way of convincing me to keep the job?"

He grins, biting his lip, and then kisses me softly. "Yes. Did it work?"

I nod, my heart still going a mile a minute against my ribs. "We can make this part of the benefits."

"Health benefits," he murmurs, nuzzling his lips into my neck. He groans. "Your taste is so sweet. *Dolce.* Just as I thought." He licks a path up to under my ear and bites me there. He hasn't even pulled out yet but it feels like he's growing hard again. I guess all the stereotypes of Italian lovers are true. I can definitely work with that.

Meow.

What the hell? We both look over to see Nero, that damn black cat, slinking along a bookshelf.

"*Basta!*" Derio mutters and then slowly pulls out of me. It's only then that I'm aware of how exposed we are, even in Derio's office. The twins could have seen us easily from the patio; after all, Nero got in through the open French doors. That would traumatize them for life, even though Alfonso did wish for me to be Derio's girlfriend.

While Derio pulls up his shorts and runs over to the cat, waving his arms, I tuck my breasts back into my top and hop off the desk. Everything throbs—in the best way possible. I'll be sore tomorrow, I can tell already, but it will totally be worth it.

Derio manages to get Nero out of the office and locks the

door behind the disgruntled cat. He turns to me, looking rather shy. "I hope that was okay."

I raise my brows. "The sex?"

He nods, walking over to me. He tucks a piece of hair behind my ears and gives me a timid smile. "Yes. The sex. And the job. I understand if you don't want to be their nanny. I just thought maybe if you gave it time, it would grow on you."

My resolve liquefies. "It has grown on me," I tell him honestly. "Really. But it's just a lot of work. I can't do it all by myself. I'm sure—no, I know—that Felisa was a superwoman, but she had a lifetime of experience. I only have a few weeks'."

He lowers his chin. "I understand. I will go through the résumés and start calling a few candidates in for interviews."

"No," I tell him, reaching for his hand. "You don't have to do that. I just need help—*your* help." I pause, my eyes flitting to the manuscript on the desk. He follows my gaze, worry coloring his face. "Don't worry," I implore him. "I don't know what you're doing in here all day long, and as long as it's important to you, I don't care either. But if you can just find some moments to help me, to help Alfonso and Annabella, to step up and be their brother, then I can do this. *We* can do this. But I need your help. I can't do it alone."

He licks his lips and then nods. "Okay. You are right."

"You're not their father, Derio," I tell him quietly. "You don't need to live up to him, you don't need that added pressure. You're just their brother who has sworn to look out for them. You can still be their brother, and only their brother, despite everything. I know that's something you know how to do. And I know you do it really well."

He blinks a few times and looks away from me. He nods once but doesn't say anything else. I know part of his problem has been the insane amount of responsibility that comes with being a guardian to two young children. I know it gets even more complicated when you're used to a different role with them. I imagine when the twins were born, Derio was long out of the house and in the middle of a budding career. He probably never saw them as much as he would have liked. It wouldn't have been the same kind of relationship had he been raised in the house with them, had they been closer in age. He probably never really knew them until his whole world changed and they were thrust into his care.

"You will stay, then," he says, glancing warily at me, "if I promise to be better?"

I give him a gentle smile and place my hand on his cheek. "I will stay if we do this together."

He nods and leans in, his lips just inches from mine. "I am so lucky to have found you. You are worth your weight in gold. You are gold." He runs his fingers through my hair. "*Sono ricco*. You know what that means?"

I shake my head. "It doesn't matter. It sounds beautiful."

"It means 'I am rich,'" he says. "Because of you."

My heart is swooning a little, like it's about to faint. I'm drowning in his sweet talk.

"And," he says, kissing along my jaw, "this is not just a fling." He pulls away and peers at me intently. "I am not that kind of man. You make me richer; you matter to me. I want us to be together."

"Even though I'm the nanny?"

His lips twitch. "Maybe especially because you are. You don't find that a bit sexy?"

I don't want to admit that I do. "I find you sexy," I tell him. "Is that so?"

"Well, I just fucked you on the desk."

He grins. "I was fucking *you*."

"Oh, I forgot, that's your job."

"Yes," he says, kissing me sweetly. "You do your job and I will do mine."

"It sounds like everyone wins."

"Everyone does."

"Except the kids who are probably dying of boredom out there."

He nods. "Yes. Well, what shall we do with them?"

We? Maybe he's changing already.

I tell him about my idea of taking them to Marina Grande.

"Sounds good," he says. "It's too hot now and the beach will be very crowded, but the water is cool. It will be worth it."

He grabs my hand and leads me to the door.

I pull back, just a little, and raise our joined hands in the air. "What about this?" I ask. "I don't know if the children are ready to see us . . . well, *together*. Even though Alfonso did ask me if I was in love with you."

This gets his attention. "Oh?" he says, his eyes wide. "And what did you say?"

"I told him I thought you were gross. Ew, boys, yucky."

"Ah yes," he says, seeming satisfied with that. "And probably true. *Allora*, let us take this slowly then."

"I don't think we can take it much slower given what we just did on your desk. By the way, I think you might have to wipe that down."

He lets out a small laugh that lights up his whole face. He looks positively angelic. "Yes, yes." He pulls me into him and kisses me, then lets go of my hand. "We will take it slowly in front of them. How about that?"

"And take it fast in private?" I ask with a bat of my eyelashes.

"And hard and long and rough." He punctuates this by

biting my neck and letting out a low, primal groan. "*Bella, bella, bella.*"

I ignore the heat flaring between my legs again, obviously ready for another round. This situation might be harder to juggle than I thought.

Still, sex with Derio has got to be worth any complication.

At least, as we walk out into the hall, back to the way we were before, that's what I have to tell myself.

CHAPTER THIRTEEN

Even though I had the best intentions when I told the twins that I—well, we—would take them to the beach, I regretted it the moment we stepped foot on the hot, smooth pebbles.

Yes, walking from the villa all the way to the funicular and then waiting in line with throngs of tourists and then nearly getting hit by errant taxi cabs at Marina Grande and then trying to find a spot on a beach packed with bodies was annoying, albeit totally expected. But what I didn't see coming was how hard it was to keep my hands off of Derio now, especially when he stripped down to that goddamn Speedo again.

It wasn't just *my* eyes that were constantly roving all over his body but the eyes of all the women on the beach. I felt proud, not threatened, that he had fucked me earlier on his desk and fucked me good, but it really didn't help that I just wanted to run my hands all over his tight body. He was more naked now than he had been in the office.

"You are good?" he asks me as he settles on his towel. We're both lying on our sides, facing each other. The twins gathered a few water toys and are splashing in the clear shallows near a bunch of other kids. I hope that maybe they'll hit it off and play together.

"I'm good," I tell him. "I can't stop staring at you, though."

He gives me a cocky grin and looks down at his body. He places his hand on his bulge and momentarily rubs it. I immediately get a lady boner from the sight, wishing I were the one rubbing him.

"That's not fair," I whisper.

He does it again and closes his eyes briefly, his lips parted. Holy fucking shit, can he not touch himself in public? I'm going to fucking die.

I look around me. So far no one is paying attention, as most people are succumbing to the heat and lying on the ground like limp noodles.

But Derio, of course, is the opposite of limp. He now has a full-blown hard-on inside that Speedo and it's barely being contained.

"My God, what did I awaken in you?" I say, leaning in closer to him and almost shielding his body in case someone walks by close to us.

"What did I awaken in *you*?" he asks and reaches over, slipping his fingers down the front of my bikini until they sink between my cleft. "You seem ready to go." He edges closer to me, his finger sinking in deeper. "*Bravissima*," he says through a ragged breath.

With the sun searing my shoulders and my body drowsy with heat, his fingers feel impossibly good. I want nothing more than to close my eyes and give in to him. But at any moment, if anyone at all walked past us, they would see something entirely inappropriate. I know Italy is really relaxed and all—there are topless breasts on every beach—but I'm pretty sure public hand jobs are frowned upon.

"Relax," he hisses softly. "No one is coming. Except you."

I laugh then gasp as he comes even closer, his finger finding purchase deep inside. We're close to each other now but he continues to stare at me, his head propped up on his hand while his other one goes to work.

"Keep looking at me," he says as my head wants to flop backward. "Pretend nothing is going on." He leans in closer, his gaze on my lips. "I wish my tongue were my fingers. I wish I could taste you from the inside."

Oh God. Where did this man come from? What happened to the brooding, sulking, silent guy? Not that I'm complaining. *At all.* No, I might never complain again.

I suck in my breath as he draws his fingers out and then starts rubbing my clit in small concentric circles. He's barely moving at all but I'm feeling everything.

"Look at me," he whispers again and I'm forced to meet his eyes. They are glittering in the sunlight, burning with intensity. I'm not sure how much longer I can hold on. I want to come but I also want to wrap my hands around that long dick of his and make him come, too.

He must have followed my gaze because he suddenly applies firmer pressure and just like that it's a trigger and I'm the bomb.

The orgasm rocks through me, but he's grabbing my face with his other hand. "Look at me," he says and I'm forced to meet his eyes. The cry strangles in my throat and my mouth drops open as I ride the wave. It takes everything I have to keep my body as still and quiet as possible—my pulse feels like it's trying to rip out of my skin, and my muscles cramp up to keep my limbs from jerking, but through it all I stare into his brown eyes, lost in the flecks of gold and black that make them rich and bright.

"You are like the sunrise when you come," he whispers to me when I begin to calm down. "All this light, chasing away the dark." He slowly, deliberately removes his hand and then sticks his finger in his mouth, drawing it out leisurely. "*Dolce.*"

I blink at him, taking in a deep breath, and slowly look

over my shoulder. No one is staring at us. We weren't caught. Derio looks down at his erection and then grins at me. "Unfortunately, this can't be dealt with out here," he says. He's right about that. Even the water is crowded with people.

"I'll fix you up tonight," I tell him, relaxing back against the stones as the endorphins flood my body. Holy hell. Did that really just happen? Especially after all the talk about taking it fast—in *private*. But his twin siblings are still playing by the shore, trying to do handstands in the water, and no one else saw him getting me off. It's just that I've never been open and vulnerable with someone like that, especially in public, and so soon. It worries me just a little bit. I've been known to fall hard and fast for all the wrong guys and I don't want to do that with Derio. And I don't want him to be the wrong guy.

He trails his fingers over my neck, my collarbone, my breastbone, soft and gentle, like I'm written in braille and he's trying to read me. I glance up at him and my heart flips at the tenderness in his eyes. I should have known from the start that this man was going to give me a reason to stay.

....

The rest of the weekend flies by. After the beach, the four of us had dinner at one of the tourist joints at the Marina Grande. They're not the best on the island but the twins were happy with their "Americanized" meals, even though I wasn't too happy with them eating French fries, especially after the breakfast I had served them. I think Derio found it quite amusing when I went into "mom" mode, which I just found more scary than anything else.

The next morning, I took the twins—and Derio, though he needed a lot of convincing—to church. I'm not a religious person, though I'm definitely spiritual, but I had heard there was a Sunday school after the sermon, with cookies, juice, toys, and, most importantly, other children Annabella and Alfonso could play with. Once Sunday school was over, the priest told us we could drop them off again just before dinnertime for an activities program.

Naturally, we had to say yes. Not just to give Alfonso and Annabella the chance to socialize with kids in a new setting, but for our own budding relationship as well.

As we walk back to the villa after dropping off the kids, the Via Tragara now busier than ever, Derio asks, "Want to go on a ride with me?"

"Sure," I say with a smile. He grabs on to my hand, holding it firmly, and we pass through crowds of people. I feel extremely giddy being led by this man. I can't help smiling at everyone, tourists and locals alike. I don't feel the heat that's steadily building, nor the loud chatter in a million different languages. Though Capri doesn't feel like it belongs to us at the moment, I feel like I belong with him.

Once back at the villa, we waste no time in bringing out the bike. We only have about three hours or so to ourselves so we have to make the most of it. What I really want is to drag Derio into the house and spend those precious hours in his bedroom—that would indeed be time spent wisely—but Derio is happier than I've ever seen him, all squinty eyes, handsome smiles, and tanned skin, and for once I find myself craving the freedom of the open road. The roads on Capri aren't very open but I want his body pressed to mine and the wind in my hair and that wild feeling of nothing but time. Even if time is only a lie.

I hop on the back of his bike, easier now that I'm comfortable hanging on to him like a monkey on a tree, and we jet off, trying to make our way down the street without running people over. It's not easy, so I start yelling *"Permetti!"* at the top of my lungs, which eventually gets people out of the way.

Once we've somehow made it through the maze of Capri town, I want to ask him where we are headed but it's already pretty obvious. There's not much else to see on this side of the island—everything else resides on the other side of hell's highway.

He pauses the bike near the main traffic circle, already crammed full of mini blue trucks and orange short buses and tourists wobbling on Vespas, and glances at me over his shoulder. "Are you okay if we go to Anacapri?"

I nod.

"Just hold tight, okay?" he says. "Don't worry, you won't fall off. I've got you. Close your eyes and I'll get us there safely, okay? I use this route all the time. Piece of cake. *Capisci?*"

"Capisco."

He shoots me a grin and guns the bike. I wrap my arms around him tighter and bury my head into his neck, making sure my face is on the left side, a.k.a. not the side that has the precipitous drop. I trust Derio completely to get us there in one piece, but I don't trust my panic attacks.

At first I'm okay with it. I can feel the air whizzing past us, the cars and the traffic, the few times that Derio has to weave around vehicles. Then the incline gets higher and higher and we zig and zag, climbing, climbing, climbing. The switchbacks stop and that's when I know where we are: the part at the top.

And that's when I decide to raise my head. Because I'm an idiot. We're actually in the midst of passing a bus on the right, which means we are hugging the edge of the road and only a short metal fence, like the kind someone would put around their yard, is between us and falling through weightless air to an imminent death.

I can already feel myself falling, feel myself going over the edge, and there's nothing to stop me from hitting the hard ground, nothing left but the short time allowed to look back on my life before it's all over. That's the worst thing about vertigo, about these specific panic attacks; the actual fall doesn't have to happen for it to feel like it's happening.

"I've got you!" Derio yells, knowing I'm looking up, knowing I'm panicking. I guess the death grip I have around his chest is a sure sign. "It will be over soon."

I close my eyes and try to breathe through it. In and out. It's hard. It's always hard. It's even harder with the sounds all around me—the wind in my ears, the roar of the motorbike, the honks and gear changes and squeaky brakes of all the cars.

But eventually, like last time, I survive. I look up and see the green foliage and hidden houses of the Anacapri area and I immediately feel a million times lighter. Adrenaline is rushing through me and I feel like laughing for being such a fool. The girl who was scared, hiding from her fears, that wasn't me, that was someone else. It's always someone else.

Derio guides the bike up into town, snaking up the white-washed streets past stone and stucco houses, the smells of garlic and basil and fried anchovies wafting past us, and stops in front of a mural of Mount Solaro.

He turns off the bike and twists in his seat to get a better look at me. His brow furrows in concern. "You are okay?"

"Yeah," I tell him, feeling a bit stupid. "I don't know what comes over me in those moments."

"Fear," he says gravely.

"Well, yes."

"Fear is the most powerful force of destruction. Fear is the devil's greatest illusion."

I frown at him. "I don't remember learning that in church today."

"I can help you, you know," he says so sincerely I feel I have no choice but to believe him.

"What are you talking about?"

"Facing your fears. Even the little ones can cripple us."

That's all fine and dandy but I'm talking to a man who fears the open ocean so much, he hasn't left the island in a year.

"Trust me," he says, his voice low as he reads my face. "I have many fears, but I'm working on them. I am exposing myself to one as we speak."

"What fear is that?" I ask.

He holds me in his steady gaze. "The fear of letting go. Of opening up. Of trusting. Of falling."

"You have a fear of falling, too?"

"In a way . . ." He pauses. "Yes."

I'm not quite sure what he's saying but from his direct gaze I know he's being honest.

"I guess we have to go back the way we came up."

"And what about there?" He gestures to the mural of Mount Solaro and the happy painted people on the chairlift, soaring above faded wildflowers. "Will you come with me?"

"Are you kidding me?" My blood freezes up at the thought of being stuck on that skinny chairlift.

He starts to get off the bike but I'm trying my best not to move.

"I promise you it's not so bad," he says. "I'm serious."

"How can it not be bad? I've seen the chairlifts. They fit one person at a time. Barely!"

"It is not as bad as you think. Please trust me."

"You don't understand," I say, almost whining.

He tips my chin with a finger so I can meet his eyes. "I do understand, Amber. It is scary but worth it. You have to trust me and you have to trust yourself. You must trust that nothing bad is going to happen." He swallows. "If I see you be brave, I can be brave, too."

My heart sinks like a stone at those words and in his eyes I can see how serious he is. This lost, damaged, broken man is asking me to guide him, to show him what is possible.

I take in a deep breath and find myself nodding. "Okay," I say in a small voice.

He takes my hand and helps me off the bike. He doesn't let go.

CHAPTER FOURTEEN

Minutes later, after purchasing our tickets, we stand in line for the chairlifts up to Mount Solaro. To be honest, even though the mountain is a jagged piece of rock looming over the earth, it doesn't look so imposing when you're at Anacapri, which is already pretty high off the water. I can see the way the chairlifts dip up and down over the scenery, disappearing and reappearing as the little chairs coast over small hills, and it doesn't look that high—not until you get to the last part of the lift anyway. But even then, the fact that I will have to do this alone terrifies me.

I look behind me at Derio, who seems the epitome of cool, quickly puffing on his cigarette until he has to put it out. "Do you want to go first? Or should I go first?"

"You go," he tells me just as the empty swing comes toward me. "I have your back."

Just then the chairlift worker leads me quickly to the seat. I sit down and the bar is lowered over me and then I'm whisked forward. I let out a little yelp, gripping the bars for dear life as the chairlift swoops over a crop of trees. Then the yelp of fear slowly turns to one of laughter as my mind begins to register that I'm secure behind the bars, that I'm moving forward, not down. I swing my legs beneath me, feeling like a child again. In a way it's like flying, not falling.

"Hey!" I hear a jubilant voice and crane my neck to see Derio behind me. He waves at me and looks absolutely adorable in the chair, like an overgrown kid, though somehow he still manages to exude sex appeal. I don't know how he does it.

"This isn't so bad, is it?" he yells at me.

"Not yet!" I yell back and then turn around before I get motion sickness. I stare at my feet, glad I wore sandals with secure ankle straps, and watch as we soar over neat squares of bright green vineyards and silver-leafed olive groves clinging to the hillside. Flowers of all different colors bloom among the sun-scorched grass and yellow bursts of broom dot the slopes. I want to take my phone out and snap a million pictures but I'm not brave enough to let go of the bars so I take mental snapshots I hope I'll be able to draw upon later.

The scariest moment is the one I predicted, when the chairs rise above the hills and the peaks of limestone cliffs, and my mind tells me we're going to crash. But before I know it the chair turns into the roundabout and suddenly I'm on solid ground again, my legs feeling a bit like jelly. In seconds, Derio gets off, too, and joins me by my side.

"You did it," he says, holding my face in his hands. "I am proud of you, *mia leonessa*."

I laugh as he kisses me. He puts his arm around my waist and guides me toward the viewpoints.

"It wasn't so scary," I admit as we walk. "It was more thrilling than anything else. In a good way."

"*Brava*," he says, "but don't get too attached. I thought maybe we could walk back down. It only takes about forty minutes but it takes you past a tiny church that many people never see."

"Sure," I tell him. "And if I get too tired, you can carry me like a pack mule."

He squeezes my hand and we start walking up a short

staircase until we're at the top. Suddenly, I stop dead in my tracks.

We've come through a stand of pine to the guardrails that mark the viewpoints. Beyond the people gathered at the edge of the guardrail is the most stunning, dizzying, terrifying view I've ever seen.

"Holy shit." I breathe out. "This is beautiful."

Derio takes out his phone with his other hand. "This time I will take all the photos. You just enjoy the view, the moment. Do you want to go closer?"

Normally, I would say no and stay as far back from the edge as possible but the whole motorbike ride plus the chairlift has left me with a sense of fearlessness. I'm not about to run to the edge but the terror no longer feels quite as real. Maybe it's the man whose hand I'm holding.

"Yes," I tell him. "Let's go closer."

We make our way through the people and then it's all there in front of me. Unlike the stunning views I've seen before, this one makes you think you're God himself with the whole world at your feet. From here, Capri town and the Faraglioni Rocks lay beneath you like a postcard, like something you can hold in your hand and hang on your wall. The water and sky meld together into a smooth plane of cerulean blue, and white clouds hang like accents. The island itself is sharp and distinct, even in the summer haze, and you can almost count every white house, every green tree, every ecru-colored slab of rock.

It's sobering. Not just the fact that I'm able to stand near the edge and not feel sick but because this view makes me realize how small the island is. Somewhere down there, Alfonso and Annabella are with their new church group. Somewhere down there—and if I had binoculars I could probably see

where—the house of the sad lemons sits along the prome-
nade. So many sorrows and tragedies and small triumphs contained in the history of one place, hidden from most people's
eyes. I wonder how many other stories of heartbreak and hope
are attached to each of these houses.

"No wonder your mother was a writer," I blurt out.

Derio looks at me sharply. "What do you mean?" Though
he looks wary, as he always does when the subject of his parents comes up, his voice is gentle. I know he's not going to fly
off the handle this time.

I gesture to the miniature island below us. "Look at that.
Look at all those people, all those lives containing all those
stories that we have no idea about. Your mother, she must
have come here sometimes and wondered these same things.
She gave those people the lives she imagined for them."

He nods slowly, chewing on his lip for a moment. "Yes,
she came here sometimes." He glances at me. "But, you know,
not all of her books were set on Capri. Only one was. Well,
two, technically."

"*House of the Sad Lemons*," I say and then catch myself. "I
mean *Villa dei Limoni Tristi*."

"Correct."

"And what is the other?"

He looks around us at all the sunburned, baseball-cap-wearing
tourists clamoring for the best shot and then guides me away from
the viewpoint. When we're far enough away, he says, "*Correre il
Sole*. Racing the Sun."

"That's the book I saw on your desk." He flinches at that.
I stop walking and look up at him, holding on to his arm. "I
told you I didn't read it and I meant it. I just saw the title and
your mother's name. You know I can't read a lick of Italian
anyway."

"Yes," he says carefully. "Well, the book was never published. She . . . died before she could finish it."

"Is that what you're doing in the library all day? Are you reading it?"

He exhales sharply out of his nose and looks at the ground before straightening his shoulders. "I was reading it. For a year, it's all I would read. I thought that if I kept reading it, I would know how it would end. If I knew how it ended, she wouldn't really be gone. I wanted answers, any kind." I hold on to him tighter, my heart bleeding for him. He goes on, though I can tell it's difficult for him. "But there never were any answers. Not in the book. So I started reading all of her books. She has so many, you know, over thirty. And in my whole life I had only read one of them, *Villa dei Limoni Tristi*, the one that made her famous, successful. I wanted to keep her alive by reading her work. She would often say that immortality was the writer's gift and the writer's curse. I believe her now. She's always haunting me but she's never here."

I pull him over to a low, flat stone beneath a cypress tree and we sit down. "You were close with her, I gather."

He smiles to himself, scratching at his sideburns. "All Italian boys love their mamas, or at least that's what they say. And it is true. But I really did love her. She sacrificed so much for me. When I said I wanted to race, she was the one who convinced my father that it was something I had to do, something I would be good at. Of course, I loved my father, too. He was a good man, very smart, and he worked very hard. But he wasn't as open as she was. His love was harder to earn. Her love was so free." He pauses and places his hand on top of mine, bronze against white. "You remind me of her in a way. You're both free and looking for something. My mother was always looking for it in her books. I don't know if she ever found it."

He blinks and his eyes are wet. My insides feel like they're being shredded by what he has lost. "I like to think that she did but maybe it was always out of reach," he says. "All those days she would spend in that office, hours, living in her own world and giving so much to that. Then she would come into my world and give so much to me and my father. She never stopped giving. I don't know how she never ran out of love. God chose to end it all before we had a chance to find out."

I run my fingers over his cheek, feeling his permanent stubble. "I am so sorry," I whisper.

He nods. "I know. I know you can feel it, that you are not just saying it. That is why I . . . You are good for me, Amber. You bring things to the surface but you do not run away. I have not had someone care for me the way you do in a very long time."

I kiss him softly on his cheek and am surprised to feel a tear escape from me. He brushes it away with his fingers, smiling beautifully with those perfect teeth. "See. You feel everything. You make me feel everything."

I do feel everything. I feel so damn much for this man that I'm not sure what my heart is going to do. It wants to hold me hostage but it also wants to be a protective shield.

"So," he says, clasping his hands together, "I've decided to try to help my mother the way she would have helped me. I knew she was working on this last book but had not talked too much about it. I knew it was set on Capri and she said she hoped her publishers would want it but she was not sure. She thought it was her best work and it just flowed out of her fingers. That's how she would describe it on good days. So I decided to read it. Then, after I couldn't figure out the ending anymore, I decided to edit it. Such a simple thing, just making sure it was the best it could be. I know nothing about editing but she had said she never even went back once to read it. She was too much involved. I started cleaning up the misspelled words, strange sentences. It gives me a sense of purpose, and at the same time it makes me feel connected to her. I know it's something I will have to let go of one day but . . . I cannot yet." He gives me a shy look. "It's one of those fears I am trying to face."

I want to sit on the top of Mount Solaro and talk to him forever. I want him to keep opening up to me, not just for my own curiosity or to stroke my ego, but because it's making him stronger. I want to help him. I want to talk about what happened the night they died and he survived, I want to get him on a boat, I want to find out why he quit racing when it was supposed to be something he lived for. I want to know so much more but I'm too afraid to uncover more than one rock at a time.

"We should go, it's getting late," he says, glancing at his phone.

"Wait," I say, putting my hand on his arm. "Take a picture. Of us."

He sticks his arm out—long and strong, perfect selfie material—and takes the picture. When we look at the result, I'm absolutely smitten with it. I look happy. He looks happy. And damn if we don't look good together. Beauty and one sexy Beast.

"E-mail that to me," I tell him.

He scoffs. "E-mail? I will print it out and frame it. We are a work of art."

I beam at him, feeling absolutely girlish, like what he said means that we're "official" and serious. As silly as it is, I won't be faulted for feeling giddy over a boy. It's one of the best feelings in the world.

We follow a dirt path that leads away from the tourists and heads down the slope past yellow-flowered broom, graceful pines, and fragrant shrubs. The sun is more potent up here but the heat is tempered by the constant breeze. We walk for a while in silence, just enjoying being outside in this beautiful place, alone as we make our descent.

"So," he says as he finishes the cigarette he was smoking, "now you know about my parents. Time to tell me about yours. Wasn't that the deal?"

"Was that the deal?" I ask, feigning ignorance. "It was so long ago, I don't remember."

"Yes it was, and you know it. Tell me about your mother."

I sigh. This is the absolute last thing I want to talk about. "I don't want to spoil our day."

He takes out his phone again and shows me the timer. "I'm counting down five minutes. In five minutes we will come to the church and the Cetrella Valley and you can stop talking and I will make you smile again."

"You promise?"

"You know I will deliver," he says with a wink and there's just enough suggestion in his voice that solidifies the deal.

"The CliffsNotes version is—"

"What is CliffsNotes?"

I smile. Sometimes I forget that we're from two different worlds. "Just a shortened, condensed version of things. Basically my mother is a very nice woman but she's everything that I don't want to be. She married for security, not love, and she gave up her dreams of interior design to become a mother. Now she spends her days taking on part-time work, mostly for direct sales companies, even though she's fully capable of getting a real job. When I was little, she sold Avon products but then ditched that for sex-toy parties, then she ditched that to sell freaking Tupperware, then she ditched that to sell skin cream and magazine subscriptions. Now she sells stick-on nails. If there's any wonder why I'm trying to find myself, it's because I don't want to be finding myself like that when I'm older."

"But that doesn't sound so bad," he says.

"It wouldn't be if she were happy," I tell him. "But she's not. And she deals with it by going from temporary thing to temporary thing. That, and by stuffing her face. She overeats. A lot. And I'm not being mean because I don't care if my mom is overweight or not, but it's impacting her health. I worry about her, and my dad does, too. And I know she's aware of it. She spends a lot of time trying out the newest fad diets and supplements and shakes while lecturing me about my own body. I know she's afraid I'm going to turn into her in more ways than one. And I can't deny that I'm afraid of that, too."

Derio stops walking and holds me at arm's length from him, looking me up and down. "And what could she lecture you about?"

I give him an incredulous look. "Well, it's not like I have the best body. My ass is too big, my thighs don't have a gap, my stomach is round and pudgy, and my boobs are annoying."

"Your boobs are annoying?" he repeats, and now he's the one sounding dubious. He reaches out and cups them with both hands. "Your boobs are a gift."

I almost laugh at the sincerity on his face. "They aren't big enough to balance the rest of me but they're big enough to get in the way."

"No," he says. "They are never in the way. They are perfect." He leans down and pushes them up through my scoop-necked shirt to kiss the swell of each one. Then his hands glide down my sides. "All of you is perfect."

"I'm not, I'm—"

"Amber," he says, his voice authoritative. "Your body, every part of you, is perfect to *me*. What does it matter what anyone else thinks?"

I bite my lip shyly, not used to compliments of that nature. I guess it wouldn't matter much if Derio were going to be a permanent fixture in my life. I hate to think that one day I'll be back at home, dreaming of the man who liked me just the way I am.

"And thigh gap?" he mutters to himself. "I hear that phrase all the time. I don't understand it. Your thighs part well enough for my cock and hands and face. That's a big enough gap for me."

I had to give him that. If they could part for *his* cock then I was doing okay.

"*Allora*," he says and we continue walking down the dusty path, "that is your mother."

"Yeah. I know I've painted a not-so-nice picture of her but she is a good mom. She just has issues with herself and passes them on to me."

"Have you told her this?"

What is this, therapy?

"It can be hard to get through to her." And that's true. She's so hung up on her own shit and battles that she rarely listens to me. But maybe I just need to try harder. Half the battle is just trying to get my parents to listen to me.

"And your father? What is he like?"

Another long breath escapes my lips and I wipe the sweat from my brow. The more we descend, the hotter it gets. The air is starting to warp and bend around us in shimmering waves, like in an oven.

"My father is . . . practical. He's a loving guy and he's good at being the voice of reason when it comes to my mother. He often brings her down to earth better than I do. But the older he gets, the more rigid he becomes. He's a psychologist . . ."

"Oh," Derio says, as if that explains everything. In fact, I think it might explain everything.

"Yeah, so growing up with a shrink wasn't much fun. And he used to be prolific, you know, like he was well known in his field and did a lot of lectures at colleges and universities—that sort of thing. He seems to think I suffer from some kind of Peter Pan syndrome. Always has. They spoiled me a lot since I was an only child, so maybe that didn't help. It's not like I acted like I was spoiled, I was just used to having things handed to me. You know?"

He nods. I go on. "So on the one hand he would indulge me with whatever I wanted and on the other he would resent himself for doing so. I went to college, which they paid for, and I guess he thought that once I was in the real world I would smarten up. And I did, I mean I really fucking tried to get a job. But to him, I didn't try hard enough. When I finally got hired and then fired, it was a major blow, to them as well as me. It made it seem like I couldn't even hold down a simple job when that was far from the truth . . . though looking back, maybe I could have tried harder. I could have worked harder and longer. Maybe I could have moved up sooner. I wouldn't have been so expendable."

"But if you had tried harder, for the wrong job, maybe you would still be stuck there. And you wouldn't be here, with me."

I smile gratefully at him. "You're right. And that's what I

told myself. After that, I decided to just go out into the world and find myself, find something. Maybe then when I came back home, things would be better. And my parents, surprisingly, were on board with this idea. I think my dad thought it was either a last hurrah or a way to teach me responsibility. I had some money saved for the trip, but when I ran out of that they started to pay my way, and then they sold my car to keep me going. Now I don't have any money at all. Well, aside from the money you're giving me. That's why I've been in Italy for so long."

He grins. "That makes me sound like a *pimp*."

I can't help giggling at the way he pronounces *pimp*. "Yes, my Italian *pimp*."

He grabs my hand and his features suddenly turn grave. "But the other day you said your father called you names, like 'useless.'" He lowers his voice and looks ashamed. "Just as I did. I am so sorry about that."

"I know you didn't mean it," I reassure him. "And maybe my father never meant it either. He's got a temper and he's prone to saying the wrong things all the time, though God forbid you ever call him out on it. I think I just frustrate him that I'm not really shaping up to be anything great. Not like him. I'm just this useless, helpless, average little human being who will never live up to her potential."

As I say the words, I feel bereft. Once again, real life is sneaking into the one I've escaped into, reminding me of what's waiting for me at home and what I'd be leaving behind in Capri.

"Amber," Derio says softly after a beat. "You are little only in height and nothing else. If your father could see you now, how happy you make me, how happy you make the twins, the way you run this household, helping them, helping all of us, he would take back every wrong thing he's ever said about you."

"I make you happy?" I ask as my heart dances hopefully in my chest.

"You make me more than happy," he says, stopping to cup the back of my neck. He kisses me with a quiet hunger, with determination and promise, and pulls me into him. His tongue is hot and soft and it makes the heat around us intensify. The hardness of his cock digs into my hip and he smiles against my lips. "You make him more than happy, too."

Tension builds throughout my body like a tightening thread, and the mere feel of him against me makes me wet and wanting. I clench my thighs together and kiss him deeper, harder, my hands digging into his back, feeling his muscles, his strength, his everything. This man, oh how I fucking want this man.

He's breathing hard when he pulls away. He looks over my shoulder. "The church is right down there, through the trees."

"I'm not having sex in a church," I tell him, though considering I'm getting more turned on by the moment, that could soon become a possibility.

He grins, kissing me quickly. "Not in the church." He takes my hand. "Come on."

He takes me down the slope, past blooming orchids and green oak until we come across the tiny church of Santa Maria. It's adorable, with its mission-style bell tower and rustic stone wall. To the other side is nothing but air—it sits on the edge of the cliff.

"Wow," I say. "I would worship here every day."

"And I will worship you beside it," he says. "I think I know of a good place." He looks around to see if anyone else is watching. I hear voices coming from the church courtyard but I can't see the culprits. I follow him as we jog quietly through the golden knee-high grass toward the side of the church and sneak along the stone wall, which is high enough to hide both of us.

We round the corner and come to an area of dry, thick grass, shaded by an oak on one side and the wall on the other. At our feet, the rest of Capri and the sea spread before us like a banquet. Unless someone wants to peep over the wall or a paraglider flies past, no one will see us.

Derio pulls me down into the grass with him and I let out a few giggles as I fall. He presses his finger to my lips to silence me and I take his finger in my mouth instead, sucking on it. He closes his eyes, his mouth parting, and I can see the pink of his tongue, wet inside. He's so beautiful, especially when he's turned on. He's just this bronzed, dark-eyed, Italian sex machine.

"We are outside the holy grounds," he whispers when I remove my finger. His own are busy pulling my shirt over my head. "But I don't think the priest or nuns will look too kindly if we are caught."

"Would it cause a local scandal?" I whisper back.

"Knowing this town and its gossips," he says in a warning tone, "yes."

I briefly remember Lenora and the shit that she was spreading. "I'll be quiet if you'll be quick. Take off your pants."

"Take off *your* pants," he retorts and then leans over, unzipping my jeans and pulling them and my underwear down and over my sandals. He lies back on the grass and takes a firm hold of my hips and pulls me onto him so I'm straddling him.

"World's most perfect view," he says, his voice laced with lust, his gaze heavy as he watches me above him. "Better than the one out there."

I reach down and bring his dick out of his pants, hot and thick in my hands, feeling a bit shy that I have to be totally naked while he gets to keep his clothes on. I mean, broad daylight isn't exactly flattering, but from the hardness of his erection, I don't think he's too bothered by my flaws and pale skin. I have to remind myself that just moments ago he was telling me how perfect I was. I have to believe it if he believes it.

"At least take off your shirt," I tell him, tugging up the hem of his shirt.

He smiles, conceding, and then pulls it off. I get up briefly and slide his pants and briefs down below his ass. I stroke his dick slowly, up and down. He bites his lip, watching me, his hands roaming up and down my thighs and waist, before he lowers his head back to the grass. I work him for a few minutes, feeling that sun on my back, the look of ecstasy on his face.

Finally he looks up, his eyes dizzy with lust, and says breathlessly, "Come over here."

I raise my brow. Is he asking me to sit on his face? Because I'll totally do that.

"Um," I say. "How?"

"I'm ready for you but you're not ready for me," he says, lips curling into a smirk. "Come here."

Okay, so I guess that *is* what he's asking.

Continuing to straddle him, I edge myself forward until I'm pretty much sitting on his face. His hands grip my thighs.

"Perfect," he says and then proceeds to lick me inside and out.

I don't think I've ever felt so sexual and so free before in my life. The sun is bearing down on us, the air is thick with the smell of sex and sage and heat. Being out here, naked, in the wild grass and below the wavering oak, the limitless blue sea at my back, feels otherworldly, and every single sense I have is heightened. His eager mouth devours me and I lean my head back, as if I'm offering myself to him, to the sky, to the world. Never in a million years would I have felt so liberal, so decadent, so open but here and now, I feel the rest of my fears slip away. I feel everything.

Just when I'm about to come, he stops and pulls back. I look down at him, his mouth glistening.

"Now you are ready," he says, voice throaty.

I think I've always been ready.

I scoot back and then slowly lower myself onto his still-hard cock, desperate to finish. I ride him, first at a leisurely pace, then faster as I feel the urgency of the moment. My breasts bounce wildly, and with strong hips he pumps upward into me as I push down, fever taking hold of us. Soon we're on the edge, and as I look down at his face I see his head falling backward, his eyes scrunched shut, hissing my name through his teeth. Just the sight of him in such open pleasure triggers me and I come fast and hard, trying to ride out the waves of sharp and soothing orgasm while maintaining my balance.

After he comes, his nails digging into my hips, pumping himself into me, I relax and nearly collapse on him. We're both slicked with sweat, both drowsy and sated. I want to tell him that was amazing, unforgettable, that it was so much more than just sex.

Much more.

But no words come. Instead, I press my lips into his neck and trail my fingers along his warm, damp skin. We lie like that for a few moments, just soaking each other in, until we hear voices from the church. We get up and slip our clothes back on in seconds flat and then hightail it out of there before anyone can discover us, discover what we've done.

We walk back down the rest of Mount Solaro, hand in hand, and I don't know the last time I've felt so damn free and so damn happy.

CHAPTER FIFTEEN

When July slides into August, like a hot greasy egg sliding off a frying pan, Capri becomes its most unbearable. No matter where you go, you run into people. People on the Via Tragara, people in the Piazzetta, people on the funicular, on the streets, down the private lanes, on the beaches, on the cliffs, on every square inch of the sea. There are German tourists, Swedish tourists, American tourists, Australian tourists, and yes, a lot of Italian tourists. Everyone comes to the island, if not for a day then for a few until the crowds begin to get to them, too. The color of the water loses its appeal, the dry climate and lavender-scented air become cloying, the food loses flavor and remains overpriced.

And then there's the heat. Some days, it's like the sea isn't working at all, like the air is all jammed up in an invisible dam somewhere out there on the hazy horizon, and you're breathing through a furnace. It's dry, people will tell you, as if that makes a difference, but it's still hot as hell and even the most powerful fans can't break it up. Even a villa like the *Limoni Tristi*, in its lavishness, doesn't have air-conditioning.

For the weeks that Capri becomes a living hell for those who live here, I create a routine. Alfonso and Annabella are out of school now as Italy prepares for August, the month where the whole country seems to go on holiday, so they inevitably become a part of it. Thankfully, the heat makes them agreeable to hanging around the house and not going anywhere, even if they are a bit cranky.

In the mornings, after breakfast and before it gets too hot, I start doing my home improvement projects around the house. Most of the time I can enlist the kids to help if I promise they can go swimming later on. The pool is now filled with chlorinated water, something I begged Derio to do. Then came the fountain at the side of the house, freshly painted bright white, the power-washing of the bricks and tiles, the cleaning of all the outdoor furniture, and the pruning of the trees and plants. I also gathered enough lemons, limes, and pomelos to bake fruit cakes for every day of the year.

Derio helped for a lot of it—I'm not the most graceful with a power-washer hose—but now that I know what he was doing in that library, how it was almost a grieving ritual for him, I encouraged him to go back to editing or whatever else he needed to do.

Today, I'm replanting a few rosemary bushes so they're in soil with better drainage. Their browning leaves tell me they're one step away from root rot, thanks to my zealous overwatering when I first arrived here. I've picked out the dead weeds and flowers that were in a row bordering the side of the bricks stairs leading from the pool toward the house, and stuck the rosemary bushes in there. It would be a shame to lose them—I've been throwing fresh sprigs of rosemary into everything I cook these days.

Which is turning out to be a lot. Derio surprised me one evening by bringing over a chef from one of the finer local hotel's restaurants to give us private cooking lessons. I guess I should have been insulted but Derio wanted to learn a few things, too, other than the basics that most Italian boys know. The chef, Signora Bagglia, was a plump but pleasant woman with a big smile and sparkling eyes. She coaxed us through roast chicken with olives, puttanesca sauce, fresh linguini, and, yes, the infamous tiramisu. The twins watched the whole thing with big eyes, cracking the eggs whenever the moment called for it.

After that I took to buying cookbooks. I wanted the Italian versions because then I knew I was getting the real deal, and even though I couldn't read the directions properly at first, I started to get the hang of it and the language came easier to me. Of course, there was that one time I substituted *frutti di mare* for *frutti di bosco*. Let's just say I should have trusted my instincts when I thought it was weird to put shrimp in a fruit pie.

"*Buongiorno,*" Derio says to me, walking down the steps.

I stand up, wiping the dirt off my shorts. I know I look an absolute mess—no makeup; hair frizzing in all directions for miles; red, sweaty face; hands covered in dirt. But Derio stares at me like I'm the most beautiful thing he's ever seen.

"*Buongiorno,*" I greet him. He leans in for a kiss—it's become second nature now—then stops himself when he notices the twins sitting by the pool with their legs splashing in the water, just dying for me to finish up and give them the go-ahead.

I look over my shoulder at them and shrug. "I think they're starting to figure it out."

We've been careful about showing our affection for each other around them but not too careful. We're very physical, especially Derio, who is always touching me every chance he gets, like his skin is addicted to mine, but we haven't been kissing. We don't even stay the night in each other's beds yet.

He clears his throat. "How did you sleep?"

"Fine. It would have been better if you had been there."

"I know," he says. "We will sit them down and tell them soon. I think they will understand."

"I think they already know." As I say that, the twins look over at us and then Annabella whispers something to Alfonso, who makes a face while Annabella giggles. The kids have become dark brown and freckled from the summer sun, all long legs and highlighted hair.

I, too, have taken on a bit more color. I'm not as deep and dark as Derio, but I've got a golden glow going on and my hair is two shades lighter. I'm even thinning out a little and my legs and arms have more definition. It's probably from having to walk Capri's hills in this heat all the time, and the fact that I rarely get a moment to just sit around. I look more and more like *la leonessa* every day.

"What have you been doing?" I ask him. "Edits?"

He shakes his head. "Smoking. Drinking espresso. *Il dolce far niente.*" The sweetness of doing nothing.

"Sounds nice," I say with a tired sigh, gathering my hair behind my head.

"It is," he says. "And you should try it, too. I have a little surprise." He waves his hand at the kids. "Alfonso, Annabella, *venite qui.*"

They moan, reluctantly bringing their legs out of the water and staggering over to us with exaggerated effort.

"Can we go in the pool yet?" Alfonso asks me.

"Soon," I tell him. "What is it, Derio?"

"In an hour you kids are going off on an adventure."

Their eyes brighten. "*Cosa succede?*" they ask in unison while I say, "What?"

He looks at us rather smugly. "Signora Bagglia has an overnight kids' camp for children interested in cooking. I thought, perhaps, since you were so eager during our lesson, you would like to go."

The twins exchange a look, a little unsure. "Where is it?" Alfonso asks.

"It is in the hotel where she works, near Augustus Gardens. I have already arranged it, if you wish to take part. There are a lot of children there your own age. It would be a lot of fun; maybe you can even have a food fight."

They still don't look convinced. I know they're scared about being away from the house without us there but they're getting to that stage where they have to at least socialize, if not experience a real sleepover.

"But I had to promise to Signora Bagglia that you are big kids," Derio goes on in a stern voice. "That you are brave and smart and old enough to be away from us overnight. Was that right of me to say?"

Derio is smart. That's a tactic my father would have used.

Of course, the twins nod eagerly. "Yes," Alfonso says, always the showboat of the two, "of course we are old enough. We are not babies."

"We are seven years old," Annabella scoffs. I know they still look uncertain but now that they've said this, they won't back down. They are too stubborn, just like their brother.

"And maybe then you can cook with me," I put in. Alfonso scrunches up his nose at that but Annabella nods enthusiastically.

An hour later, we are dropping the children off at the Hotel Luna, located on a cliff at the end of a shady path. Signora Bagglia is waiting out front with a gaggle of over-excited children running around her, overnight packs on their shoulders, while a few parents look on. Derio had read the brochure of the program to me as we walked over and it sounds like a popular—and legit—event.

After we tell Alfonso and Annabella to behave and be brave, Signora welcomes them over with a hearty wave and a platter full of hard candies. The candy works like a charm and she attracts all the children to her like bees to a flower.

We watch until they go inside, Alfonso and Annabella already chatting with a cute, pudgy boy, then Derio puts his arm around me.

"Do you think they'll be okay?" I ask, leaning into him.

"*Tutto va bene*," he says, which pretty much means *s'all good*. He gives me a squeeze. "And now the two of us can have a well-deserved break. Let's start with a drink on the terrace."

He leads me to the tiled patio and we find two comfortable chairs with deep cushions to sit on. Cacti and magenta flowers line the railing, separating us from the sparkling sea and the sharp Faraglioni Rocks that rise out of it. It's just before noon and lunch isn't being served yet, so we have glasses of honey-colored wine and snack on bowls of bar mix. There's not many people out here enjoying the view, though I know that won't last for long.

Once we've finished our drinks, content to cuddle into each other and ignore the rising heat of the sun, a man approaches us. He's dressed well in a suit, despite the heat, with a shock of white hair, black eyebrows, and deep brackets on either side of his mouth. His eyes are kind, though, and he looks to be about my father's age.

"Desiderio?" the man asks politely.

Derio looks up at him and recognition slowly comes over his face. "Ah, Signor Vincetti!" He gets out of the chair and shakes the man's hand. The two of them converse quickly in Italian, with lots of nodding and smiles, accompanied by low voices and furrowed brows. From what I can piece together, they're probably talking about Derio's parents.

Then Derio gestures to me, shooting me an apologetic look, and says, "Where are my manners? Signor Vincetti, this is my girlfriend, Amber MacLean."

I think I'm smiling at the man but really my mind is reeling over his words. He introduced me as his girlfriend. Not a nanny, not a teacher, not a friend—*girlfriend*.

"*Incantata*," I say to him, getting up and shaking the man's hand.

"Ah," he says in his thick accent, "but I speak some English."

"*Buono*," I say, "because that's all the Italian I know."

"He is, or was, a good friend of my parents," Derio explains with a wide smile, clearly pleased to reconnect with this man. "He used to own a house down the street from us—you know, *Villa Celeste*, with the plaque of the goat near the gate? He and his wife now live in Florence."

"Oh, I wanted to go there," I say, "but I picked Rome instead."

"Bah," he waves with his hand. "Rome is too dirty. Florence is beautiful, you should both come one day. In fact, I insist. Bring the twins. How are they?"

Signor Vincetti doesn't notice how Derio stiffens considerably at the mention of travel. He must not know that Derio hasn't left the island in a year.

"The twins are very well," Derio tells him, sidestepping the question.

"And you still have Felisa?"

Derio nearly winces. "She has gone on to other things. Amber is helping."

Vincetti nods at me. "That is very kind of you."

I don't bother mentioning that I'm getting paid for it. "*Non importa*," I say with a shrug.

"But you are no longer racing?" Vincetti turns to him.

Again, clearly something that Derio doesn't want to talk about. He gives him a quick, false smile. "For now."

"You were very good," Vincetti says. He eyes me with a fat smile. "Desiderio was one of the best there was, in his"—he snaps his fingers, searching for the word—"*class*, you know. Very exciting to watch. You should convince him to start again. He is missed." He pats him on the back heartily. "You are missed, boy."

The two of them converse in Italian for a little longer, then Signor Vincetti points to his watch and waves goodbye to us.

"He was very nice," I tell Derio as we watch him walk into the hotel.

Derio makes an agreeable sound. "He was the best of my parents' friends. Always interested, always supportive." He eyes me. "Are you going to ask me to get back into racing?"

I'm taken aback. "No," I say, surprised. "I mean, if you want to, I'll support whatever you choose to do."

"You wouldn't find it exciting?"

"I would find it scary, to be honest. But if it's your passion, you have to follow that, too, even if it's scary."

He watches me closely and seems to think that over.

"He didn't ask about your ex-wife," I say, though I may be treading in dangerous water bringing up his ex at all. "I would have thought the two of us together would be questionable."

He shakes his head, smiling sourly. "Believe me, what happened between Daniella and I was very public. Who could forget the man who gave up racing when he was at the top of his game, and the woman who gave up that man for someone else? Everyone knows the story."

I try not to make a pitying face. That must have been so humiliating, especially for someone as proud as him. I feel like finding Daniella and bitch-slapping her across the face.

"So why did you give up racing?" I ask warily, unsure how he's going to answer. But this is the closest we have ever been to the subject.

He sighs and pulls me back down to our cushioned seats. He signals the waiter for two more glasses of wine and clasps his hands together. "It was a stupid accident. I made a careless mistake around a turn, a mistake I used to make all the time. I overtook another racer at a sharp turn on my weak side and spun out of control to avoid him. I hurt my leg and shoulder very badly and broke a few bones. It was not too serious, but while I was lying on the ground, half conscious, hearing the screams and the sounds of the track and the emergency horns, I thought maybe I would die. Maybe I would not walk again. When something like that happens, you have no idea how hurt you are and if you are going to be okay. That had never bothered me before, but it bothered me then."

He pauses as the waiter gives us our wine and then he takes a big gulp of it. I'm too busy hanging on to his every word to even touch mine. He licks his lips and continues. "I realized if I died, if I was seriously hurt, I could not take care of Alfonso and Annabella. They would be true orphans, with no family at all. We have an aunt who lives in Florida but the twins have never met her. They would be ruined. They would have lost too much. So as I lay there and the medics rushed toward me, I realized I had to make a choice. I could no longer be irresponsible, I could no longer think or live just for myself anymore. I had to quit." He pauses with a heavy sigh. "After that, Daniella did not want to be with me anymore. She had only been attracted to my status to begin with. It's very obvious to me now; maybe it was obvious then. But I was in love and I was young and a stupid fool. The thrills, the danger, the celebrity—that's all that she wanted. Not me. Never me. Now

I had guardianship over the twins and she did not want any part of it. She left me and moved on to someone else, a rival of mine in the racing world, of course. Isn't that always the way?"

He exhales slowly. "After that, because of the accident, because she left me . . . it stirred up bad memories. Of the night they died. Aside from the police, I had never really told anyone what happened. To relive it was too much for me. But I was reliving it somewhere deep inside after that. The thought of stepping onto a boat was paralyzing. Terrifying. I could not do it. And so I could not leave the island, no matter how badly I wanted to. I was stuck here, in this life, forever. In some ways I still am."

I put my hand on his knee and squeeze it. He glances at me, his eyes watering and his face contorted with anguish. It breaks my heart to pieces. "You know," he says, his voice choked, "I resented them. The twins. Because I did not ask for this. And then I resented myself, for being so selfish, for feeling that way toward them, my own flesh and blood. We had all lost so much and yet I felt that I had lost the most. I lost more than my parents—I lost the life I had, the love I had. I lost everything." He closes his eyes and sinks back into the chair, taking slow, heavy breaths.

"You have not lost everything," I whisper to him, putting my head on his shoulder and wrapping my arm around his waist. "You have them. You have me."

"Do I?" he whispers.

I tilt my head up to him, perplexed.

"Do I have you?" he repeats, staring down at me with dark, searching eyes. "Deeply?"

I swallow and nod, squeezing him to me. "Deeply."

He doesn't look all that convinced. "You know, sometimes

I feel so trapped. So lost and alone. And then I look at you and I feel found. Does that make sense?"

I almost want to cry. "That makes perfect sense. More than you realize."

He gives me a small smile. "Come. Finish your wine and let us find each other again."

When we go to pay for our drinks, though, the waiter informs us that Signor Vincetti has already taken care of it.

The look of quiet comfort in Derio's eyes at the old friend's gesture warms me to my soul.

CHAPTER SIXTEEN

That night, we go out for a proper dinner, just the two of us, at a small, homey restaurant off the edge of the Piazzetta. I have *spaghetti e ceci* and he has grilled fish. When we get back to the house, we make up for lost time by making love in the kitchen, the living room, underneath the lemon trees. The last one leaves me sticky with grass and lemon pulp but it's worth it to have such a man take me in such a way—fast and reckless and delirious.

Later, we sleep together in his bed, the whole night through, without fear of being caught. I assume that I'll get to sleep in as well, since there is nowhere for us to be—the twins aren't finished until noon.

But Derio shakes me awake before the sky has a chance to lighten from ink to gray.

"What is it?" I mumble into the pillow.

"Get dressed, quickly," he says.

"Why?" I'm starting to feel more awake now and slightly panicked. I roll over and look at him but he's smiling. Also completely naked, which in turn makes me smile. He pats my legs then walks over to the couch where I threw my clothes last night. Though I'm half asleep, the sight of his tight, toned ass in the dim light has my full attention. God, I'm lucky.

He tosses a strapless dress at me. "Put this on, grab your bikini, and meet me downstairs in two minutes," he says, then grabs a pair of shorts out of his dresser and leaves the room.

What the fuck? But I get out of bed and do as he says, going off of the sparkling look in his eyes and his voice, which promises danger.

Minutes later, I'm on the back of his bike and we are riding through the silent pre-dawn streets. Everything is washed in watercolor blue, like God smudged ink all over the world. A few birds sing from the flowering bushes and the air is soft and cool. The smell of a new day, all the blooms and herbs and the waking sea, is utterly intoxicating. I want to make a point to start waking up before dawn and experience Capri before the day ravages it, but who am I kidding, I cling to sleep like it's a sinking ship.

I don't ask any questions as we ascend toward Anacapri; I'm content to just hold on and watch the world go past. Even the heights of the zigzag road don't scare me like they used to. As long as I have Derio, I feel safe.

Eventually, we zoom through the center of Anacapri, the occasional chicken darting across the road, and head down a road I've never been on before.

Finally, I have to ask, "Where are we going?"

"You will see" is his totally non-helpful answer.

But then I do see. We are on Via Grotta Azzurra, which leads to the famous Blue Grotto, Capri's shining jewel and one of the places I've wanted to visit. The renowned light paints the water in the cavern electric blue, but because you have to pass through it on a small gondola, I figured Derio wouldn't want to do it. It's not quite the open seas but it doesn't help.

"Here we are," he says, parking the bike next to an empty café. We are the only people in the small parking lot overlooking the cliffs.

"What are we doing?" I ask.

"Going for a swim."

"A swim?" I repeat, looking at the water. Though it's calm, with only small waves rhythmically lapping against the rocks, it's still kind of dark. The sun is barely touching the tops of the few trees scattered about.

"Yes," he says. "I used to do this when I was a teenager. All the locals do. But I haven't done it since . . . you know . . ."

I nod and he says, "This is the first step toward facing my fears. You did it with the bike, on Mount Solaro. Now I must do the same." He pauses and gives me a serious look. "If you are with me, I know I will be okay."

He takes my hand and we walk over to a locked gate, which he helps me climb over, lifting me up like I weigh nothing at all. We walk down steps carved into the rock and stop at the end. There are no stairs leading down into the water, which seems deeper and darker than I imagined. It's one of those jump-in-or-don't-get-in-at-all situations.

Now, I'm not afraid of the sea the way Derio is, but I'm also not a fan of deep water, especially when I can't see to the bottom.

"Is this safe?" I ask him as he takes off his shorts, revealing his buck-nakedness underneath. I blink at his penis because it's such a wonderful but unexpected sight. It even seems to grow under my watchful gaze.

"It is as safe as anything," he says, gesturing to my dress for me to take it off. "Hurry, we only have so much time before the first boat shows up."

"You don't want them to catch you naked."

He gives me a cocky look. "I don't mind if they catch me naked. I might give a little old lady a thrill. But we could get in trouble and I don't want that to happen to you."

I can't argue with that. I tear my eyes off his body, not surprised that he's not the slightest bit bashful about it, and take off my dress, tucking it under his shorts on the platform. I can't even see the entrance to the grotto from here; it's just nothing but steep rock.

"I'll jump if you jump," he says, gripping my hand tighter. He smiles and his face looks so bright against the grainy light. It seals the deal.

"Okay."

"*Uno, due, tre,*" he counts down.

And then we jump.

The icy water surrounds us and my first reaction is to kick for the surface. I let out a little yelp as my head breaks through and I stare right at Derio's grinning face, his wet hair flopped over on his forehead, making him look a little like Elvis.

He lets out two hoots and pulls me close to him. We are still close to the rocks, though I'm not sure how we're going to get back on the steps since the platform seems so high above the water now that we're in it. I make the mistake of looking down between us. Beyond the pale white of our legs treading in the navy blue, the bottom remains dark and mysterious and out of reach. The cliffs must go straight down.

"Come on," he says, pulling me along. We swim toward the opposite rock face and only then do I noticed the tiny entrance to our right. The hole to the cave is even smaller than I thought. I'm surprised a boat would even be able to pass through it. I can see why in rough seas, going in there wouldn't be an option.

Once we're at the mouth of the cave, Derio leaps upward out of the water and grabs hold of a chain that threads along the roof of the cave entrance. He pulls it down and tells me to hold on. "This is meant to guide gondoliers in and out of the cave. The water is not rough so you do not need it but it might make you feel better." The fact that he's holding on tells me I should do the same.

"Are you ready?" he asks.

"Let's go for it," I tell him.

He goes first, pulling himself along, and I have the pleasure of watching his beautiful back and shoulders work above the water, mirrored by his ass and legs below the surface.

I am not as graceful. I hang there like a fat orangutan and shuffle myself along until we're just inside the cave. Then I let go of the chain, falling into the water, but Derio's arms are around me, keeping me afloat.

The cave seems so black and dark in front of us and behind us; the tiny opening only lets in so much light.

"I thought the cave would be blue," I tell Derio. By now the water is a lot warmer and my body is getting used to treading water.

"Just wait a moment," he says and swims farther in.

Now this is feeling a bit more like nightmare territory. I paddle after him and try not to think of what could be lurking beneath my feet.

"Did you know," Derio says, his voice bouncing off the unseen walls of the cave, "that in ancient times, Tiberius, the emperor who built *Villa Jovis*, used this cave? They have found sculptures and artifacts from that time period at the bottom."

"So there is a bottom," I muse, spitting out some of the salty seawater.

"It is very far down," he says, and I detect a slight tremor to his voice. He swims over to me, his features becoming lighter as he nears me and the entrance to the cave. "But I hear it is sandy, if that helps."

Normally, a nice sandy ocean floor wouldn't scare me as much as a nebulous rocky one, but in this cave everything is kind of scary.

"You know what else is special about this cave?" he asks, an arm circling my waist.

"What?"

"There were many ancient orgies in here," he says with a wag of his brows.

I burst out laughing and the sound echoes around us. "You and your ancient orgies, my God."

"It's true," he says, "they would swim in here and have sex with the witches and sea monsters."

"Your imagination both frightens and intrigues me."

He smirks and then looks between us at the water just below my chin. I swallow and follow his eyes. Our legs turn from white to black as the water around us slowly becomes a saturated blue, the color of sapphires, and we become floating silhouettes.

"The sun is hitting the water," he says with a smile. "Out there somewhere. The light comes in through the entrance, as well as an opening farther below."

It's like magic. Slowly, the cave walls begin to lighten just a little and the water lights up as if lit by blue glow sticks. The water stretches far back and the cave ends up being a lot longer and higher than I imagined. In less than a minute, it goes from something unknown and scary to something spellbinding and surreal. Our bodies in the water are black, lit from below, while neon blue reflects off the bottom of Derio's strong jaw and alights in his dark eyes.

He kisses me, his lips wet and salty. His hands slide up and down my sides as he swims forward and I glide backward until I'm pressed against the side of the cave. It's rough against my skin but not painful, and he grabs on to a ledge with one hand while he yanks down my bikini top with the other. He nips and licks at my breasts and slides my bikini bottom to the side, slipping a few fingers between my legs. Everything feels so effortless, so silky in the water, while the rough cave wall presses against me, a contrast in textures. Though it takes me a few minutes to warm up, soon I'm pulling him toward me as he guides himself inside. He pushes in slowly, his lips going to my ear.

"You erase my fears," he whispers, his breath hitching as he eases himself inside. "You give me life from all the death." He kisses me hungrily on the lips and I expand around him, greedy for his words, for his sex, for his love.

His fingers start working my clit and he pounds me harder, my back hitting the wall. I'll be scratched up later but it's worth it. Worth it to feel him so deep inside of me, to be floating so freely. In this dark cave, I feel our lovemaking is taking us to another place, somewhere that transcends lust and desire. There is hope and light and as we float in the blue glow; there is hope.

And there is a hell of a lot of pleasure. I can feel my back sting from the salt but I'm so wild for him that the pain feels good. Everything feels good. No, amazing. My legs wrap tighter around him and he works me harder, his hips swiveling at all the right moments, his dick hitting all the right places. His mouth murmurs my name and his lips kiss my salty lips and his tongue teases my skin and I am his to have, again and again.

I don't ever want this to stop, this freedom, this connection. In the blue grotto we are soaring over colors and through light and we are moving as one, feeling as one.

This man has my heart. He has every part of me.

"I am going to come," he says through a deep groan. "Come with me, *mia leonessa*. Please come with me."

I always do. The pressure I've been keeping in check lets

loose and as he drives into me with reckless abandon, and I'm thrust into the powerful throes. Behind my eyes, my world glows blue and my heart grows warm and I am swimming through waves of light, drowning in the feeling of pure ecstasy. I'm swearing and calling out his name and it echoes against the walls of the cave. Every single grunt and groan and breathless hiss he gives to me is magnified.

That isn't just sex. That is supernatural.

"Holy shit," I whisper raggedly, trying to catch my breath as I still pulse around him and we struggle to come down to earth.

"Yes," he says, licking his lips and brushing the wet hair off my face. Even my cheeks tingle from his touch. "I have no words in English."

"I have no words at all," I say quietly, my heart racing like a jackrabbit. I breathe in and out, bringing myself back down from the clouds and into the bright blue.

He kisses me softly, lingering and wet, before pulling away and gingerly pulling himself out of me.

"Your back must be sore?" he asks, placing his hand behind my shoulder blades.

I wince a little but smile. "It's a good kind of sore," I tell him. "Do you think your fears are gone?"

"For now," he admits, kissing me again. "For now, everything is gone, except for you." He pulls me away from the wall and into him, his arms encircling me. "You're all I need."

We stare at each other, our faces lit from below by that brilliant blue, and continue to float. This is heaven after heaven.

In the distance, there's the faint sound of singing. Derio seems to snap out of his daze and looks at me with big eyes. "First gondoliers of the morning. We better go."

We start swimming for the entrance, the current and the act of having sex having pushed us farther back into the cave without us knowing it. We're almost at the mouth of the cave when we see a small boat coming toward us. Derio pulls me to the side and we flatten against the wall as much as we can while staying afloat.

The boat comes in, the gondolier pulling it along by the chain and singing, his voice booming off the walls. A couple suddenly pops up at the back of the low boat after lying back to get through the low entrance. We watch as the gondolier rows the boat into the depths and the boat's passengers, now dark figures against the glowing blue, start snapping pics and oohing and aahing.

"Let's go," Derio whispers to me and we quickly swim out through the entrance before another boat comes in.

Once outside, the sky and sun are blinding and we can see a few small rowboats towed just offshore by a larger power-boat. That must be how they get here for the day. We swim for the platform and I gasp when I see a young couple come down the steps. I'm not worried about getting caught by them—they seem to be tourists here to catch the first boats before the crowds set in—but I *am* concerned that Derio is stark naked.

Of course, he sees them, too, and shoots me a grin over his shoulder. He couldn't care at all. And why should he. We just fucking had sex in the Blue Grotto. And at that thought, I realize that I don't care either.

We reach the edge of the platform and he's the first to go up. He does so like an athlete, using the pure power of his upper body, and I make a silent thank-you for the exercise room in the house. Then he bends over to help me up, absolutely mooning the couple down the stairs and probably giving them a good show of his balls as well.

I try not to laugh as he pulls me up but when I hear the girl giggling in the background, I can't help it. I scramble onto the cement, slip my dress on while he pulls on his shorts, and the two of us trot up the stairs past the couple, snickering as we go.

"*Buongiorno!*" Derio cries out to them merrily with a big smile on his face. Their faces go beet red as they try not to stare.

We climb onto the bike in the parking lot and laugh all the way back to the house.

That day we prepare a big lunch for the kids upon their return, even though we know they'll probably be full from a night of overeating. While Derio goes to pick them up, I get everything ready and create a bruschetta bar of sorts, grilling bread and preparing an assortment of amazing toppings. The two of us decided earlier that we would have a talk with the twins about our status. After all, Derio introduced me yesterday as his girl-friend, and that sort of news apparently travels fast around here.

And does it ever. As it turns out, we don't have to bring it up at all. After Derio arrives with the twins, we sit down to eat outside under the pergola, which is blooming beautifully thanks to my long-dormant green thumb. Nero the cat, who has started coming back now that Annabella occasionally puts out milk for him, watches us from the patio ledge, his tail flicking. As the kids tell us about their fun times, Alfonso abruptly breaks the ice.

He looks at me and Derio before taking a bite of his bread, which he has piled obscenely high with toppings. Apparently they didn't overeat enough (Annabella said it was because most of the food Alfonso made wasn't very good).

"Are you two boyfriend and girlfriend?" he asks.

Derio and I exchange a look across the table. I raise my brow. He raises his.

"What makes you ask that?" asks Derio.

"*Allora*," Alfonso says, pausing to take a bite of his bread. Red oil from sundried tomatoes runs down his chin and half the toppings slide off onto the plate. He doesn't seem to notice. "Signora Bagglia said you were. So I believed her."

"Is it true?" Annabella asks, looking between the two of us. "Are you in *loooooove*?"

If it's possible for Derio and me to both blush at the same time, well, I think we just did. The boyfriend-girlfriend question is a lot easier to deal with than the love one. We're both aware we haven't said those words to each other yet.

I clear my throat. "We were planning to tell you. We just decided last night that you are old enough and responsible enough to know," I tell them, my voice extra serious. "So yes, we are boyfriend and girlfriend and we like each other very, very much."

"I knew it," Alfonso says, scooping up the tomatoes and slices of porchetta and stuffing them directly into his mouth. "I saw you kissing once."

"You did not," I admonish him. We've been so careful!

"You were kissing each other with your eyes," he says and then makes overly suggestive looks at the two of us.

I can't help laughing. "We were not. Now finish your food."

He shrugs and somehow manages to put more food in his mouth.

"Is it okay?" Derio asks, looking at the two of them. "That Amber and I are together? We really care about each other and we really care about you."

"It's okay," Alfonso admits cheerily.

"I like it," says Annabella. "It is like a fairy tale."

"Which fairy tale?" I ask.

"*Il Principe Ranocchio*," she says.

"*The Frog Prince?*" Derio translates, letting out a small laugh. "Am I the frog?"

Annabella nods, smiling cheekily at the two of us. "And she is the pretty princess."

Derio makes an overly disgruntled face. "I don't think that is very fair." He waits for a beat, then croaks, "Ribbit."

We all burst out laughing.

Later that night, Derio and I say goodnight to the twins before going to his room, where I am to sleep, permanently, from now on. As we are leaving Annabella's room, she calls out after us.

"Can Amber stay with us forever?"

Derio slips a comforting arm around me in the dark.

"I hope so," he says solemnly as he holds me close to him.

When we're in bed, after we've made love, I roll over onto my side and he pulls me against him, spooning me.

"I will find a way for us," he whispers gruffly in my ear. It sends a shiver down my back. "So you can stay."

"Promise?"

He kisses the back of my head, breathing in deeply. "Promise."

CHAPTER SEVENTEEN

I dream I am falling, as I always do. There is no scene that is set, no common reoccurrence, not this time. It's just me falling into the black, into the abyss. I scream but it falls with me, sucked into the darkness. The terror is not knowing when you're going to hit, when you're going to land—when it's going to hurt.

When I wake up, gasping for breath, I realize the dream is still going on. I look at the man beside me, sleeping soundly for once, and I know I'm awake and this is my life and I'm falling. Down, down, down.

I'm falling in love with Derio. My mind, body, and soul are tumbling over and over with my heart and he is the only thing in front of me. It's just him. It's always him. He invades my thoughts and my hopes and my beliefs. He's the hand I'm always reaching for and the skin I itch to touch. He's a boy of broken dreams and shattered years and I want so much to soothe his pain. I want to let him in. I want him to let me in. I want to heal this man and make him fall the way I am falling for him.

Sometimes I think I might be close. Sometimes he looks at me with such tenderness that I hope runs deep, straight into his heart. We need each other's bodies, but I want him to need my soul. To take what I'm giving him and give it right back. I want to feel loved like I never have before.

But I don't know how he feels. All I know is that I am falling in love with him. Every second, every minute, every day. It's terrifying but it's real. It's the worst of my fears with the best of my dreams. And beneath it all is the inevitable crash. Because at the end of the day, whether I love him or he loves me, only one fact remains:

I can't stay here.

I breathe in deeply and stare at Derio. We're in his bedroom, wrapped in soft, thick blankets. The door to the patio is open and the sea breeze wafts in, whirred around by the fans overhead. Crickets provide an endless choir that I don't even hear anymore.

I get out of bed, carefully untangling my legs from his so I don't wake him and then walk out to the balcony. I don't know what time of night it is but it must be deep in the middle of it. Everything is so calm. The sea is spread out before me like a sheet of velvet, dark ink blue that mirrors the sky. The moon is resting in the corner, nearly full and bathing the water in pale white.

Somewhere a dog barks and the crickets pause for a moment before starting up again. There is no other noise. The breeze in my hair is cool and carries the scent of sage and rosemary up the hillside.

I don't want to leave.

I feel Derio's presence before I hear him. I turn my head slightly to let him know I know he's there and he wraps his arms around my stomach, holding me from behind. He presses his lips into the back of my head and I relax into his touch.

"Couldn't sleep?" he murmurs.

"Bad dream," I say.

"Oh no! What about?" He holds me tighter.

I wrap my fingers around his strong forearms and close my eyes. "Falling. That's all."

"Well, you are awake now and I have you," he whispers. "You have nothing to worry about. And I meant what I said the other night. I will find a way to keep you here, just as long as you want to stay."

I nod my head but my throat feels thick, my feelings choked up. I want to believe in him. I don't want to think about anything else.

He turns me around and holds me so I'm pressed up against him. "I love to see those eyes," he says, his own crinkled and kind at the corners as he peers down at me. "Ah, there they are. You are so beautiful, Amber, and you do not even know it. In a way, that makes you even more beautiful. You glow, even now, even in the dark." He runs his palm over my head and cups the back of it protectively. "*Mia leonessa*."

He leans down and kisses me. His lips are warm and soothing and so wonderfully familiar now. I crave them like I crave his voice, his touch, his energy.

He pulls away slowly, leaving my lips begging for more. "Come back to bed with me. Let me make love to you," he murmurs. A long time ago I would have laughed if someone said that to me. But from Derio's lips, it's not funny. It's honest and it's real. I immediately turn to putty in his hands, my body responding to his voice like Pavlov's dog.

He leads me back into the blue dark depths of the room, back to bed, where we make love until the horizon glows pink.

The children are playing in their game room, Derio is riding on his motorbike, and I'm trying to come up with something fun for today's English lesson when my cell phone rings. It hasn't rung for a very long time and the sound of it immediately fills my body with dread. I know who it is even before I look.

Yup. My parents.

I sigh, loudly. Actually, I almost vomit. This isn't going to go over well. I've been ignoring their e-mails for weeks now, trying to push them, push reality, out of my life, but I guess they've reached their breaking point and actually need to speak with me.

I ready myself and then answer the phone.

"Hey," I say brightly. Maybe too brightly.

"Amber," my mother cries out on the other end. She sounds so far away—which, technically, she is.

"Hi, Mom, how are you?"

"Amber!" her voice is shrill now. "Where are you? Why haven't you written to us? We have been worried sick about you! Why haven't you called?"

"Why haven't you called before now?" I retort.

"Don't you start with me, young lady," she says, and I have flashbacks to a million teenage moments. "Even your friend Angela says she hasn't heard from you."

"Again," I say, losing my patience already, "she hasn't contacted me. And since when do you start harassing my friends for information?"

"I was not *harassing* her," she says, "though it's nice to know you're just as dramatic as ever."

"Whatever."

"Where are you?" she repeats.

"I'm in Capri," I tell her. "I said that in my last e-mail."

"You're still there?"

"Yes."

"I thought you would have moved on by now. I had a

cousin who went there once and she said it was just a rock in the middle of the ocean. She got food poisoning. Don't eat the fish there."

I roll my eyes. I don't even know where to begin. "I really love this place, actually. And I got a job that pays really well."

"A job?" she repeats incredulously. "Doing what?"

"I'm a nanny."

There's a pause and then she bursts into patronizing laughter. "Are you kidding? A nanny? You? You're always threatening to burn your uterus to deny us any grandchildren. Not that you've ever come close to that with anyone." She adds that last part under her breath.

I'm used to it and shrug it off. "Well, I happen to like these kids, very much."

"Well, who are they, what are their names?"

"Alfonso and Annabella."

"How typical."

"Well, they are Italian, you know."

"How old are they?"

"Seven."

"I just don't believe it. Wait till I tell your father when he gets home. He's going to have a heart attack."

"Why is this so funny? I'm doing it. I've been doing it for over a month now."

"Right. Which brings me to the question: When are you coming home?"

My throat closes up, making it hard to swallow. "I don't know."

"Well, you have to know, Amber. When is your flight?"

"I haven't booked it yet."

"Why not?" she screeches. "You're supposed to have a return flight."

"Well, I was waiting to save up money. I kind of ran out of it for a while, when you guys cut me off."

"That's when you were supposed to make your plans to come home. You shouldn't be wasting your time working there when you could be working here and actually building toward something. Your future, perhaps? Remember that?"

"I remember," I say through clenched teeth.

"So get your ticket right away. You can't stay in Europe longer than three months or you'll be deported. How long has it been now?"

Since she can't quite remember, I'm tempted to lie. "I have time," I say.

"Do you have enough money for your flight?"

"Yes, don't worry about it." And that's not a lie. Since I took on the nanny position, Derio pays me a thousand euros a month. We both find it kind of weird but he insists he keep paying me so there are no misunderstandings. Besides, the job is hard and deserves to be rewarded. I take the money because everything he says is true. Plus, I do eventually need to go home.

Or do I? I can't go an hour now without asking myself that. It's just too bad I can never come up with an answer.

"You know your father is going to ask me these things and when I can't give him a straight answer, he's going to call you."

"So let him call," I say and make a mental note to never pick up the phone again.

"How is your weight?" she asks.

I sigh. "Fine."

"You know Italy is a fattening country. All that bread and pasta and dessert." She sounds so suspicious that it pisses me off.

"I've gained ten glorious pounds since I've come here!" I

nearly yell through the phone. I've actually lost about five, but she doesn't need to know that.

She nearly gasps. "Amber, that's terrible."

"It isn't," I say. "The men here *loooove* it."

"Don't tell me you've fallen in love with an Italian boy. They're unfaithful lovers. Don't let anyone tell you otherwise."

I can't listen to this anymore. "I'm going to go now, Mom."

"Amber, you better be careful. Are you using protection?"

"Bye, Mom, I love you."

"Amber."

"*Arrivederci*!" I cry out and then hang up the phone. I wish it were a good old-fashioned rotary so I could really slam down the receiver.

I look over to the fridge and see Annabella standing there, eyes wide.

"Who were you talking to?" she asks.

"My mother," I grumble, sitting back down on the stool and going through my makeshift lesson planner.

"Is she not very nice?"

I shrug. "She can be. But she can also be very annoying." I look over at her, suddenly wary about talking about mothers.

She climbs onto the seat next to me. "Sometimes my mama and I would fight."

"It's very normal for girls and boys to fight with their parents," I tell her.

She nods, suddenly looking very small. "Yes."

"What did you fight about?"

She sits there and her bottom lip starts to quiver. I freeze, unsure of what to do. Then she cries out, "I don't remember." Big fat tears spill down her face and she looks at me. "I don't remember what we fought about. Sometimes I don't remember my mama." She sobs. "I'm afraid I'll forget her."

"Oh, sweetie," I say to her and pull her into me, hugging her tightly. Tears well up in my own eyes. "You'll never forget your mother. I promise you, you won't."

She wails something in Italian and I hold her closer. "It's okay, you can cry," I tell her over and over and it works. She cries. She cries for a long time, until the front of my T-shirt is soaked with tears.

Eventually, though, her tears dry up. I clean her face, kiss her forehead, and then give her a nice bowl of homemade pistachio gelato.

After that she seems almost lighter, like a weight has been lifted off her shoulders. She has a few bites then asks if she can put a few licks outside for Nero. I let her.

Meanwhile, my own heart feels heavier.

Derio gets back from his motorbike ride around noon but says he wants to do some work in the study. He has a very impassioned look in his eye and twitchy fingers and I know there is some kind of creative urge flowing through him that I shouldn't stand in the way of.

I decide to take Alfonso and Annabella into town. Annabella is more subdued but Alfonso is getting a bit hyperactive from being in the house, so I promise to take them to ride the funicular, which isn't much fun as an adult but apparently a lot of fun for a child.

I immediately regret my decision. Since it's mid-August now, the island is at capacity and everyone from the tourists to the locals are sweaty and irritable. We are shoved along the overcrowded streets of Capri town, pushed through the Piazzetta, and crammed into the funicular with a bunch of angry, smelly people.

When the car eventually unloads, the throngs of people make it hard to keep hold of the kids. Eventually, I have to let go of Alfonso and Annabella, though I keep them in my line of sight.

"Annabella, Alfonso, stay close," I tell them.

But there is a new crowd coming in and soon I find myself out by the marina and the kids are nowhere in sight.

Oh shit.

Shit.

Shit.

"Annabella!" I yell. "Alfonso!" I whirl around wildly, scanning the crowd to find them. I don't see them anywhere. I just see person after person, faceless, nameless people, and none of them are the twins.

Oh my God. Oh my God, oh my God.

I can't lose them like this. They have to be somewhere.

I quickly run through the crowd, trying to push people aside. I make my way to the marina's edge as more people pile off the ferries, dragging suitcases. I move along the edge and cross the road to the Bar Grotta Azzurra and take the stairs that lead up to a higher part of the road. I stop halfway and use the vantage point to look everywhere.

There are no children. Alfonso was wearing a blue shirt and Annabella was in a red-and-yellow dress. They would stand out in this sea of people but they aren't there at all.

I yell for them again, not caring if people are looking at me like I'm crazy. I am crazy. I'm losing my mind. How can they just disappear? Where could they go? Don't they know to stay in one place, to look for me?

Oh my God—the thought strikes my heart like lightning—*what if someone took them? Can you kidnap people on Capri? Maybe if the next ferry is leaving soon.*

I jog down the stairs and start sprinting to the crowd and onto the concrete jetty that leads to the ferries. I make no apologies for nearly bowling over couples and the elderly alike. I run to the ferry ramps and try to ask the attendants if they've seen two children. I hope I describe them well enough, switching between Italian and English.

They tell me they haven't. They're very understanding, trying to calm me down, but can't help me as they take the tickets. They tell me that they will help me look for them after the ferry pulls away. I'm grateful to them but I can't sit around and wait as person after person comes to board the ship.

I take off back down the jetty, looking everywhere. By now my heart feels like it's on its last legs and I can barely even breathe. The pins and needles of a panic attack are sneaking up on me. I have no choice but to call Derio, but he's going to kill me for losing them.

"Derio," I cry out into the phone. "Please, I'm at Marina Grande. I lost the twins, I can't find them."

"I'll leave now," he says. That's it. I stagger back over to the steps where I was earlier, which I figure is the best spot to see them or him, and try and catch my breath. The world pulses around me, gray fringing the corner of my vision. I'm panicking, trying to keep myself together, but I can barely keep my heart in my rib cage, my lungs in my chest.

I lost them. Did I lose them?

They're gone. Are they gone?

I'm an idiot. I'm not cut out for this. No one could lose two seven-year-olds on Capri but me. My mother was right to laugh. This is ridiculous. What have I been doing all this time, playing house? I can't take care of kids. I can't even take care of myself half the time.

I lost them. Oh God, what if something happens to them?

Derio is going to kill me. I've let him down. I've let the twins down. I've let myself down.

Why did I ever fool myself into thinking I could do this?

The questions, the words, spin around in my head over and over again until I realize I'm not even looking for them anymore. I'm lost in self-pity and I hate myself even more for it.

Suddenly, Derio appears at the bottom of the stairs, looking frazzled, and I can't help bursting into tears at the sight of him. He quickly runs up to me and pulls me to him.

"Shhh," he says, patting my head. "It's okay. It's going to be fine. Tell me what happened." He pulls away and holds me at arm's length, stooping over to peer at me.

I can't even wipe the snot from my nose. "There were so many people," I say, trying to breathe, "we got off the train and, and, I lost them. I let go of their hands, there were too many people, and I lost them."

"Okay," he says, keeping calm although his voice is shaking slightly. "That helps. They can't be far."

I shake my head. "Yes. No. I don't know. I checked the ferries and they hadn't seen them. I thought maybe someone kidnapped them."

"This isn't America," he says. "That rarely happens here. They are here somewhere and it's our job now to find them. Have you contacted the police?"

I shake my head, the tears spilling to the ground. "No, I just called you."

"You did the right thing," he says and straightens up, looking around. "We will go and find them together. We will search the marina and the beach and the shops and we will find them. If we don't we will contact the police and get the island searching for them. They won't get far."

I nod and let Derio lead me away from the stairs and down the road that curves back down to the marina. Instead of heading back to where I had been before, he steers us toward the beach where we've gone a few times. Like always, it's packed with people and makes looking for the twins almost as challenging as before. The two of us scour the beach, occasionally calling out their names.

"Not here," Derio says, taking my hand and holding it tight. "Let's look the other way now."

He's so calm and collected, trying to comfort me of all people, the one who lost his brother and sister, when he's the one who deserves all the comfort.

We walk past taxis and tourists and cafés and head toward the other part of the marina and the other port where the car and commercial ferries dock.

It's there that we see two familiar faces.

Alfonso is staring at the cars being loaded onto the ferry, obviously intrigued, but Annabella is scanning the area around us. When she sees us, her face lights up and she starts waving wildly, pulling on Alfonso's sleeve until he sees us, too.

They run toward us and we run toward them, Annabella running to hug me and Alfonso hugging Derio.

"Oh my God," I cry, holding on to her and feeling relief overtake my shame, "I am so happy to see you!"

"We were lost!" Alfonso cries out as Derio ruffles his hair with a big grin on his face.

"We thought we saw you," Annabella says, eyes wide and excited. "But it wasn't you. I guess I was . . . confused. She had your hair." She points at my curls. "But it wasn't you. Then we couldn't find you." She looks at Alfonso. "We were going to ask someone for help but Alfonso wanted to look at the ships."

"I want to be a captain," Alfonso announces, thankfully oblivious to the horror I just went through.

"I am glad you came," Annabella says, grabbing on to my hand. "We have no money for the train and I did not want to walk up that hill back home."

Oh. Well, I guess that should make me feel a little bit better, knowing they could have found their way home anyway.

When we get back to the funicular, Derio has to take his bike since he rode it here. I assure him I'll be fine with the kids going home—they certainly don't seem any worse for wear. But as I walk with them through Capri town, grasping them harder than ever, I know I'm not fine at all. Something has changed in me. Whatever confidence I had earned—falsely— over this job has now been shot dead.

Later on in bed, Derio tells me over and over again that it could happen to anyone. That I did a good job and that I shouldn't beat myself up over it. He tells me that here, people don't worry so much and that the twins are more capable than I might think. He reminds me that this is Italy, not America, and Capri is a very safe place.

But for all that, I don't feel it. And when he tries to initiate sex later, for the first time I pull away from him, uninterested. All I can hear in my head as I lie there in the dark is my mother's laughter over the phone, my dad's words echoing that I'm useless, helpless. I can't seem to shake the guilt, nor can I shake that feeling of hanging on the edge. Something could have gone horribly wrong today and it was only by luck that it didn't. I walked a tightrope with people's lives and I didn't even know it.

I dream again that I am falling.

CHAPTER EIGHTEEN

True to my mother's words, my father does call me. Again and again. I don't pick up, though. I can't afford to hear his voice now, not after what happened a few days ago, when I lost the twins.

You'd think I'd just get over it. So I lost them. It ended well. It's not a big deal. Time to move on.

But I can't move on. I can't get it out of my head. To be honest, I think it's making me a little bit mental. When I go out with the twins into the town, I freeze up. I either make sure Derio comes with me or I keep a crazy grip on their hands, barking at them like a freaked-out seal if they even stray an inch away from me. The twins are starting to think I'm a bit overbearing and overprotective but I feel like I can't afford not to be anymore.

Losing them, however briefly, has frightened the life out of me and it's becoming harder and harder to let it go. It's like I lost one fear and replaced it with another.

Not that all my fears have been replaced. There is the fear of losing Derio, which looms greater now than ever. Next week will be my last chance to leave the country before I become an illegal alien. Derio says he's still looking into it but he hasn't come up with anything yet. On my end, it doesn't look good either.

I did go out for drinks with Shay one night, after I randomly ran into her on the street. It was nice to be able to take a load off and have some girl time while Derio watched the kids but it didn't take long before she was crying her eyes out on my shoulder. It turns out that she and her boyfriend broke up the other night and she was trying to decide what to do. He was going back to the States but she could either stay in Italy and risk getting deported if she was found out, or go to a country outside Schengen law, like the Ukraine or Romania or the UK, for three months and then pop back in when the visa had reset itself. The last thing she wanted to do was go home, which put her in the same boat as me.

Unfortunately, the only solution that she had for me was to just stay as long as I wanted and then take my chances—just like she would be—when it came time to leave and hope the Italian officials wouldn't care or notice when I came into the EU. With the date coming up so soon, it looks like I'm not really going to have a choice in this matter.

A part of me, though—the part that listens to my parents—tells me to do the responsible thing and just leave before I'm forced to. In some ways, I'm kind of kidding myself if I think I can stay on Capri and play house with Derio forever. The fact remains that they aren't my children, and I'm not qualified to raise them or be anything more to them than a glorified babysitter. I'm not married or engaged to Derio and I don't belong in Italy. I'm an American and can't stay here forever. Eventually, something will have to give.

But so far, the responsible part of me isn't winning. Though it wants to do the right thing and go back home and make plans for a future that makes sense to me, I manage to push it away. And when I look at Derio, when he whispers sweet Italian nothings in my ear and makes love to me on our moon-splashed bed, all I can think about is how lucky I am to have him and how terrible it would be to leave.

I would break my own damn heart.

"*Mia leonessa è pensierosa*," Derio says to me as he brings my iced latte to the patio table. He places it down in front of me then brings my head close to him and kisses the top of it affectionately.

"I'm just thinking," I say, taking a sip of the latte. He makes the best kind, with lots of rich milk in a blender with ice and a spoonful of Nutella. I make a happy little sound and smack my lips. It's perfect on a hot day like today when you're hot as hell and the energy reserves are running low.

He sits down next to me and I ask, "Where are the kids?"

"Watching some show," he says. Then he smiles broadly. "I forgot to tell you, Signora DiFabbia called earlier when you were in the shower."

"Who is Signora DiFabbia?"

"She used to run one of the bookstores and was friends with my mother. She has a daughter, Gia, the same age as Annabella and Alfonso. She was at the cooking event for the children and said Gia would like to be friends with Annabella."

I sit up straighter. "Really? That's great!" I pause. "Not for Alfonso, though."

"Well, she invited the both of them to come over later in the week. I told Alfonso this but he said he would rather not hang out with girls anyway. He says he has some friend that maybe he will call. He is a well-liked kid, he just hangs around Annabella so much so he has never really reached out to others before. This might give him the push he needs." He sighs to himself. "I hope this does not mean they will want iPhones now." But he's smiling as he says this.

"They have iPads," I point out.

"True, but once kids start texting each other, then you have a problem. When I was younger I didn't have any of that.

If I wanted to play with a friend, I was even lucky to call them. Usually, I had to go bang on their door."

"So Italy was backwards in the eighties, huh?" I muse.

"Italy is still backwards," he points out. "But I love it." He pauses. "Don't you?"

I nod, taking another delicious sip. "I do." *But not more than I love you*, I think.

"Of course, you don't have too much to compare it to," he notes, sitting back in his chair and folding his hands behind his head.

"Not true," I point out. "I mean, I've seen more of the world at this point than you."

He grins and gives me a sidelong glance. "Is that so?"

"Unless you're suddenly going to tell me you've been to New Zealand, Australia, Southeast Asia, and the rest of Europe."

"I have been to the rest of Europe," he says smartly. "Even the little countries you missed. And I have been to Singapore, Thailand, India, and Sri Lanka."

Show-off, I think. "But have you been to the States?"

He rolls his eyes. "No."

"Didn't think so," I tell him haughtily and noisily slurp down the rest of the coffee.

"You would like Florence," he says.

I shrug. "I'm sure I'll go someday."

"How about tomorrow?"

I glance at him. "Are you going to send me and the kids off to Florence tomorrow? Because I'm not sure I'm up for that again."

His eyes soften. "I know you've been having a hard time because of what happened, Amber. I wouldn't do that to you when you've been feeling this way. Your feelings are very powerful, you know. I can feel them everywhere you are." He pauses and gets up, looming over me and blocking out the sunlight. "But I do think you need to get off this rock. I am going with you."

I stare at him dumbly, trying to think of the right thing to say to that. "You're coming to Florence with me?"

He nods. "I am at least going to try. And if we do not make it as far as Florence, it does not matter. But I am getting off the island, with your help."

"I hate to act like my father and play the psychology card here, but . . . are you sure you're not better off going to a doctor first? A shrink to deal with your fears? Maybe the kids could go, too . . ."

He looks off into the distance with a grim twist to his lips. "No. No, they would only put us all on medication and I believe in figuring things out for yourself first." He glances back at me. "Besides, they all suggest you face your fears. You have with yours. Now it's time for me." He holds out his hand for me. "Come with me, Amber."

I take it and he brings me to my feet. "Of course I'm going to come with you. I'm glad. I'm happy and I think this is absolutely what you need to do to move on. I'm just . . . surprised. That's all."

And it's the truth, though I'm also a bit nervous for Derio. I know how I was with my fear of heights and that was just the occasional panic attack. It didn't directly affect my life. With him, his fears have affected everything. But I promise to be there for him, through it all, just as he was there for me.

Florence ends up being too far away for two nights— Annabella was adamant she not miss her playdate with Gia

DiFabbia so we settle on Naples for the night. I know it's not really a destination city and has a lot of crime and riffraff but Derio tells the kids they can visit Pompeii the next day and they get all excited and flail their hands about seeing the mummified bodies covered in ash, which makes up for it.

Derio assures me we are staying at a gorgeous hotel in one of the nicer parts of town, with its own balcony overlooking some piazza or something. I honestly don't care where we stay—just like the twins, I am thrilled to be stepping off this island, especially with my man by my side.

We pack light, knowing luggage carts are hard to hire during peak tourist season on Via Tragara, and leave early in the morning before the heat gets too bad. Soon we're down at the Marina Grande and Derio is staring at the ferry with trepidation. I look around nervously as well, remembering how I lost the children.

But they don't care and they drag us along. Even though the hydrofoil is a much faster and more convenient way to get to Naples, we're taking the car ferry because of its size and sturdiness—anything to make this easier on Derio.

"Are you ready?" I ask him. I reach out and squeeze his hand. He squeezes back.

"We will find out," he says. He gives me a stiff smile. I know how badly he wants to believe himself but the fear is jockeying for prime position.

"Whatever you need to do," I tell him softly. And whether that means breaking down and crying or having a screaming fit or demanding the boat turn around, I will stick by him one hundred percent.

We walk down the ramp, our tickets already purchased, and step foot onto the ferry. Because of its size, it doesn't bow or wobble with the small waves that come into the tiny harbor. It feels like we are still on land. We go and find a row of seats in the middle of the ship, far away from the windows, just in case.

"Alfonso, Annabella," I say to the kids, leaning over Derio as he drums nervously on his knees. "Promise to keep your voices down during the trip and behave. Don't have your iPads too loud."

Derio closes his eyes. "It's fine."

I ignore him and make sure to look each twin in the eye. "This is a big deal for your brother. I know it doesn't seem like it but it is. You'll promise to be good and help him, won't you?"

They both nod and look at Derio. "We promise," they say in unison. Then they get out their iPads, put their brightly-colored headphones on, and start playing their games, content to pass the voyage that way.

I lean into Derio. "Do you want me to get you anything?"

Just then the ferry's engines rumble louder, ready to push off.

He keeps his eyes closed but grabs my hands. "Just don't leave me," he whispers.

"You know I won't."

The voyage feels far longer than an hour. Even though the sea is relatively calm and you can barely feel the waves as the boat cuts through them, Derio has his eyes closed for almost the entire journey. His grip on my hand is one of the G.I. Joe, kung fu variety. He tries to keep his breaths deep and slow, in through the nose and out through the mouth. I don't dare leave his side and I don't want to keep staring at him either, so I stare straight ahead and try to pass him some calming vibes.

The closer we get to Naples, the city rising up from the port like a dirty oasis, the happier I get. When we dock with a creaking, rusted *thud*, I let out a little cheer. The twins join in, clapping their hands. And Derio slowly opens one eye.

"Did we make it?" he asks.

"Yes!" we all cry out.

He exhales like he's been holding his breath the whole time and breaks out into an amazing grin. He laughs and leans back in his chair, wiping the sweat from his brow.

"You made it," I tell him, kissing the top of his hand.

He brings my hand to his lips and kisses it, eyes maintaining deep contact with mine. "But not without you."

When we disembark the ferry, Derio nearly kisses the ground. He looks astounded and stands at the base of the boat, staring at the city that lines the marina. It's noisy and dusty and hot and busy, cars honking, people yelling, exhaust clinging to the air, and garbage rustling past us on the stiff breeze. But it's the first civilization I've seen in a month and the first he's seen in over a year. We are on the mainland. The dirty wind here whispers *freedom* in our ears.

We hail a cab from the terminal parking lot but not before Derio pops into a coffee shop and quickly downs a cold beer. "Best beer I've ever had," he says, seeming utterly refreshed now. I don't think I've seen him stop smiling.

The taxi ride to the hotel is a trip and a half. The kids are delighted as the driver seems to have no regard for traffic lights, or other cars, or pedestrians, or roads, or even life itself. Somehow we make it to an elegant yellow hotel up on the surrounding hills and nearly collapse onto the bed.

The twins bounce around on their beds in the adjoining room until I yell at them to stop (they're tall for seven-year-olds and smacking their heads on the ceiling wouldn't be the best start to our mini-vacation) and I flip through a guidebook, trying to figure out what to do. Tomorrow is Pompeii, which I might be the most excited about out of all of us, but we have half a day and night here in Naples to explore. Of course, the truth is I don't mind just walking around the city and taking in the fact that I'm in the city. I don't care if it's full of beggars and pickpocketing children. I just want to feel that excitement thread through the air, the novelty of something new.

"Put that away," Derio tells me derisively. "I know Napoli like the back of my hand."

"So you'll be the tour guide?"

"I'll be the tour guide."

We start out by getting food because we're all starving. Since Naples is famous all over Italy—and the world—for their pizza, we find a pizzeria where I have *pizza napoletana marinara*, made with the juiciest tomatoes I've ever tasted, washed down with beer and Neapolitan espresso, which is strong enough to give a woman balls. Then we stroll downward through the streets, licking cones of gelato that drip down our arms until we come to the Piazza del Plebiscito. The square is so big and open, enclosed by the giant *duomo* of the royal palace and a curved colonnade, with rows of ochre, terracotta, pink, and lemon-yellow buildings beyond it. Derio tells the kids of a tradition and gets them to close their eyes and walk through the middle of two bronze statues of horses without bumping into them. Of course, the twins take this challenge—I was about to do it myself—but it's harder than it looks and Alfonso comes dangerously close to walking into not only one of the statues but a crowd of Japanese tourists who are snapping pics. Naturally, being the worrier I am now, I yell at him to stop and open his eyes.

"There is a slope to the piazza," Derio says, laughing. "It's not as easy as it looks."

"You're a meanie," I tell him.

He wraps his arms around me and pulls me into him, pressing a long, wet kiss on my lips. "Oh yes, I am so very cruel," he murmurs.

"You're the Beast," I remind him playfully while I attempt to remove myself from his grabby hands. The kids are marveling at the bronze horses now but I'm not sure I want to be molested in the middle of a busy piazza.

"I thought I was a frog," he remarks, not willing to let go so easily.

"You're all those things."

"And a great tickler."

His long fingers deftly find the tender spots on my sides, and I giggle. "Stop it," I tell him. *"Basta!"*

"It is so good to see you smile."

"You're tickling me, it's impossible not to," I tell him, finally swatting his hands away. "Don't you understand how tickling works?"

He sticks his hands in his shorts pockets and tilts his head as he looks at me. "No, I mean today. You have been smiling all day. I haven't seen you smile in some time."

His words bring me back to reality. I look around, feeling so very hot all of a sudden, the late-afternoon sun baking the square. "I've had a lot on my mind."

"You should think of things that make you smile, then."

"It's not that simple."

"It can be," he says, stepping toward me just as the kids come running over.

"Fa troppo caldo," Alfonso complains, throwing his arms around.

"It's too hot," Annabella translates, looking at me for approval.

I nod. "It *is* hot."

Derio takes a moment to peel his eyes off of me, though something is still on his mind, then he says to the twins, "*Allora*, why don't we go where it's cool, then: underground. *Sotterraneo. Cripta. Catacombe.*" He makes a scary face.

The way he says it makes even me feel a bit apprehensive but the twins cry out excitedly, obviously intrigued by the bones and creepy passages of the catacombs. I just want someplace cool. As long as there are no spiders ready to drop on me, I'm good.

We end up taking a cab since we're tired and it's all the way uphill to the Basilica of Santa Maria della Sanità. We manage to get in for the last tour of the catacombs of San Gaudioso, which is all in Italian, but I don't care—looking at the skulls and skeletons is pretty self-explanatory. It's pretty macabre but it's well kept, no spiders or creepy bugs anywhere, with ambient lighting down the passageways and a lot of old paintings and frescoes on the walls depicting saints and burials. I take discreet pics with my phone and remind myself to start writing in my travel blog again. I'd been so busy with Derio and the twins that the whole "traveler" part of my persona had completely slipped my mind.

When we pop back aboveground about an hour later, relieved to have fresh air, the sun is low on the horizon and the heat hugs instead of strangles us. We take the kids to a nearby park and find a bench to sit on while they play on the playground and chase each other around the grass.

"I like it here," I tell him, head on his shoulder as we look out over the city and the bay. Capri sits in the background, barely visible through all the haze. "But I wouldn't want to move here."

"Me neither," he says. "Where would you like to move?"

I shrug. "I don't know. In Italy, you mean?"

"Yes."

"I'd like to see a few places. Cinque Terre sounds nice. I've always wanted to go to Venice. Florence, of course. Tuscany. Umbria. Sorrento and Positano were really pretty."

"Not Capri?"

I glance up at him. His expression is solemn but curious. "Well, I live on Capri now."

"But will you live there forever?" he asks.

"Forever is a long time," I say, looking back at the view. Being with him feels so right. But part of me doesn't want to be a nanny forever. There is so much more to see and do. Of course, now I can't imagine doing anything, going to any of these places, without him by my side.

"And what if you can stay here?" he asks. "Legally. Would you?"

I swallow. A few weeks ago I would have said yes with no question. Now I'm not so sure. What changed? I look up at him and think that it can't be my feelings for him. "How could I stay?"

"We prove to the government that we are serious about each other. We can call upon witnesses like Signora Bagglia, or your friend Shay, or maybe even Felisa if I can ever get ahold of her. We have pictures. The government looks more kindly on love than they do employment."

Love?

He cups my face in his warm hand and looks deep into my eyes, so intently that I think he can see every hidden layer I have deep inside.

"Amber," he says in a low, husky voice. "I am madly in love with you."

My eyes widen. My heart fizzes like popped champagne.

"I knew I would fall hard for you, from the moment we first met. That's probably why you got under my skin so fast. I knew I couldn't let someone like you go. You were supposed to teach the twins, but you ended up teaching me."

"About what?" I whisper as his lips come closer to mine.

"About love," he says, gently tucking a strand of hair behind my ear. "About life. About dreams and fears. And family. You taught me about everything I had forgotten and things I'd never known. And the only way I can repay you is with my heart. You one hundred percent have my heart. It may not be worth much coming from a troubled man like me, but it's real and it's yours. *Ti amo, mia leonessa.*"

He kisses me and it's flush with tenderness. His look, his words, this kiss—it all reaches deep into my chest, into my soul, and shakes me loose. I feel like there's a sun rising inside me and it's so close to banishing the clouds for good.

If only I could let it.

I have to let it.

We break apart just long enough for me to whisper, "I love you, too."

His breath hitches and when I look at his eyes, so dark and beautiful, they are wavering with emotion. "Is this true?"

A wide, delirious grin breaks across my face. "Yes. *Si. Ti amo.* I love you, Derio, I love you."

And then, as he kisses me again, so passionately that my toes curl and my heart somersaults, it hits me like a fiery sledgehammer. I am in love with this man. This man loves me.

He loves me.

That night, while the twins are asleep in the other room, we make quiet love to each other. It is a night I will never forget as he undresses me by the open curtains, the moonlight streaming in and making us glow silver. He does this slowly, carefully, as if we have all the time in the world. His hands and lips and eyes make love to my body before the rest of him can begin.

There is a desperate, needy undercurrent to our love-making, the term feeling so official now that we are drowning in our words of love for each other: I love you, *ti amo, hai conquistato il mio cuore.* I love that last one. He whispers it to me moments before he comes—*you have conquered my heart.*

This feels like the biggest prize of all.

And my heart . . . well, he conquered mine a long time ago.

CHAPTER NINETEEN

Love makes you do foolish things. That's why there are so many movies, plays, and songs written about it. When you're in love, you don't think straight. But in some cases, you think more clearly than ever.

Love makes you bold.

The next morning, at the end of our trip to Pompeii in the shadow of Mount Vesuvius, we watch Annabella as she brings cups of water for the stray dogs that roam around the place, hiding out in the shade.

"I think you have a little animal lover on your hands. Maybe she'll be a vet," I tell Derio.

He smiles at this but it falters at the corners. I realize I've said this as if I won't be around in the future.

As we walk out of the grounds, grabbing fresh lemon sodas from food carts, Derio hugs me close to him and says, "You know what?"

"What?"

"I think I'm going to race again."

I can't help stopping in my tracks. "What?!"

He grins at me and nods. "Yes. I think it makes sense. I am here when I never thought I would be, I have your heart when I never thought I would. I think it's time for me to go back to racing."

He looks at the kids, who are staring at him with big eyes.

"What do you all think?" he asks. "Me back on a motorcycle." He makes the motion with his hands and grumbles like an engine.

"Cool!" Alfonso says.

Annabella is more reserved. "Are you going to get hurt?"

I hate to admit it but that's what I'm afraid of, too. I look at him for his answer.

"I may get some bumps and bruises," he explains, putting his hand on her shoulder. "But I will not get hurt. I promise you." He fixes a steady gaze on me. "And I promise you. I will take it slow and easy. I need time to build myself up again, if I ever get to where I once was. I won't be a fool this time."

But I am certain that being a fool at times was what got Derio to all those championships. I'm sure there are a million analogies about life and racing but I know that you can't get anywhere without taking risks, even ones that don't seem foolish at the time.

He leans in closer to me. "This will be good," he says softly. "Trust me. Taking time off has taught me a lot, just as you have. You make me feel so brave, so bold. Free. I don't have to do this for fame or for money or to keep a wife happy. I can do it for the fun of the ride, for the joy of it all." And I can see in his eyes that the joy is slowly being rekindled. Even if this will make me worry about him, I could never deny him his joy.

"I trust you," I tell him, kissing him on the cheek. "Do what makes you happy. Do what makes you feel alive."

He brings his lips to my ear. "You make me happy. You make me feel alive," he murmurs, his mouth grazing me.

The kids are looking at us with unamused expressions.

"All right," I say, taking a quick sip of my lemon soda. "Who wants to go back to Capri and go swimming in the pool!?"

"*Si, si!*" the twins cry out.

"*Si!*" Derio raises his hand. I punch him lightly in the arm and we go to catch the train back to Naples.

What I've learned about Derio is when he gets an idea to do something he jumps into it one hundred and ten percent. He lives like he loves, with passion and perseverance and complete commitment.

After we come back from Naples, he's like a changed man. Actually he had a minor panic attack on the ferry ride back since we took the hydrofoil and hit a patch of rougher water. But he pushed through it, and when we got back to Capri, he started going after his motorcycle dreams with gusto.

First he starts going out on the bike more, early in the mornings, just zipping around the island and racing the sunrise. He still spends time in his library on occasion, editing the manuscript, but for the most part he's either on his bike, talking about his bike, or fixing his bike.

Apparently he had more than a few of them but sold them after he quit, so he makes it his mission to start getting them back. Meanwhile, he pursues our plan for me to stay here by asking Shay and Signora Bagglia to write testimonies about our relationship. They do so happily, even though Shay hands hers over with tears in her eyes, still hurting after Danny left. I make a promise to come to the bar more in the near future.

But the near future always seems out of reach. With Derio back to racing, he takes frequent day trips to Naples . . . then Sorrento . . . then Salerno. There's only so much training you can do on Capri, but his frequent trips to the professional tracks in Salerno means he's gone for two or three nights at a time.

And me? Well, I am stuck firmly in the position of nanny, looking after the children in Capri. We both agreed that the tracks aren't a good place for kids to hang out, and Derio needs his space to get back into the game.

And I feel for him, I really do. It can't be easy to give up everything to take care of your brother and sister when it was never in the cards. As much as he tries to do his best by them, he's still their older brother. He's not their father and they're not his kids.

But I'm not their mother either, though it's beginning to feel like it. And not in a good way. Because as close as I have gotten to them, there's always this constant reminder that they aren't mine. They had wonderful, successful parents and I'm getting paid to take care of them. If you took away the financial aspect . . . well, it's a pickle. Do I really want to give up my whole life to take care of someone else's kids, no matter how I feel about them?

I honestly don't know. But I'm asking myself that question more and more these days, especially when Derio is gone and I'm in the big house all alone with them.

September ushers in a week of fog that wraps around the whole island and doesn't seem to let go. It's wonderful at first—the temperature is cooler, the sun isn't in your eyes, and there are fewer tourists on the streets. But it overstays its welcome and becomes claustrophobic.

Derio has been gone for three days at a famous racetrack in Tuscany but he's supposed to arrive back here sometime in the early evening. I've prepared one of the dishes we learned in our cooking class, roast chicken with olives, and it looks like it's turning out beautifully. Though I'm wearing a dress and light cardigan, underneath I'm wearing a racy bra-and-panties set I picked up yesterday at an end-of-season sale at Prada. I want to welcome him home in style. This week, of all the weeks, has been the hardest, and though I've been texting him, it sometimes takes him forever to respond. I love him so much but it feels like the bond we share is slowly fraying as we spend more time apart.

I can't let that happen. And sexy lingerie is always a good Band-Aid.

"When is Derio coming? I'm hungry," Alfonso grumbles as he sits down at the table, staring at the empty plate.

"He'll be here any minute," I tell him. "Where is your sister?"

"She's on her iPad, talking to Gia."

The kids have started school again which has helped me out a bit, having them occupied during the day. Annabella has become good friends with Gia, though I forbid her from using any Internet chat devices to talk to her friends. Call me old-fashioned but I just don't think she's old enough for that kind of communication yet.

Of course, Alfonso is bitter that she's made a friend and that's why he's tattling on her.

"You wait here," I tell him and then pop my head around the staircase. "Annabella!" I yell. "No Internet, remember? Put it away and come down here!"

Alfonso has a smug smile on his face and I shake my finger at him. "Don't think I didn't notice what you did."

He mouths, *What?* in mock surprise just as my cell phone rings.

It's Derio.

"Hey," I answer happily.

"Amber," he says and he doesn't sound as happy as I am. "I am in Naples. It is too foggy for the ferries to run. I am sorry but I won't be coming home tonight."

I can hear people talking to him in the background. "Really?"

"Yes, the ferries aren't running anymore. You can check. I came here early just in case but they aren't sailing until tomorrow, if the fog clears."

My heart sinks in my stomach like a stone. I can't believe how disappointed I feel. "Oh."

"I am so sorry," he says.

"I miss you. I made a special dinner and everything," I tell him, struggling to hide the hurt in my voice. I know it's not his fault that it's foggy but I can't rationalize my disappointment.

"I miss you, too," he says. "I love you and I wish I could be there. You know this."

"I know," I repeat despondently. The talking in the background gets louder. "Who is that?" I ask.

"Paolo and Andre. They drove me here," he explains. "Paolo lives outside Naples, I will stay with him tonight."

Sure, you get to stay with your friends tonight, but what about me? I think. Now I sound as bitter as Alfonso.

"Well, I'll take pictures of the dinner for you and you can pretend that you ate it," I tell him.

"Amber, please. This is not my fault."

"No, of course not," I say. "I've got to go, your brother and sister are starving. See you tomorrow." And then I hang up the phone.

Alfonso is frowning at me. "He isn't coming?"

I sigh and shake my head. "No."

Annabella comes into the kitchen. "Where is Derio?"

"Not coming," Alfonso says loudly. "He doesn't care about us anymore."

I fold my arms. "You guys, that just isn't true. He loves you."

"But you're upset," Alfonso says. "So why can we not be upset?"

"You're right," I tell them. "Be upset. But he still loves you."

"And he still loves you, yes?" he asks.

"Yes," I mumble. I pick up my phone and decide to text Shay.

> Hey, sorry I never showed up at the bar the other night.
> Derio is gone all the time and I have the kids. Do you
> want to come over after your shift? I can save some dinner
> for you.

I wait and take the chicken out of the oven. It does smell and look divine, the skin a gorgeous crispy brown, the olives plump and juicy. I take a picture of it with my phone to show Derio later and get a reply text from Shay.

> Not working tonight. They hired someone else to replace
> me. I can come over now? I'll bring the wine.

I tell her to hurry her ass over. The house she was renting with Danny is on one of the streets near Marina Grande so it shouldn't take her long. Even so, the three of us can't hold off eating any longer. We dig into the food and it's just as amazing as it looks.

This is what you're missing, I text to Derio, along with the picture I took.

But there is no response from him.

Luckily, Shay shows up with two bottles of wine—which means she means business—just as we're done eating and helps me do the dishes and put everything away. Annabella and Alfonso are fascinated by the pretty girl but eventually tire of us talking and go up to their rooms for the night.

It's too dark and foggy out to relax on the patio so we stay in the kitchen to drink and talk. Shay does most of the talking at first. She's brokenhearted over Danny and has no idea what to do with herself.

"But you have to go somewhere," I tell her. "You can't stay here."

She frowns at me, her pink lips pouting. "Why not?"

"Would you want to stay on Capri if it reminded you of the last place you were in love? I don't know, I think I'd feel so . . . trapped. If we break up, I'm definitely not sticking around this rock. I love it and all but . . . it's not home without him."

She appraises me through her long lashes. "Are you breaking up?"

"No," I quickly say, taking a gulp of my wine. "Not at all. I'm just saying."

She sighs. "Yeah. You're right, though. I won't be staying here for long. But if I go back home there's a tiny chance I won't be allowed in Europe for a while so I might as well stay here while I can."

"What are you going to do?"

She shrugs and looks at her nails, which are painted bright coral. Actually, she's wearing a fair amount of makeup, which is a change because when I first met her she wasn't wearing much at all. I guess she's trying to make herself feel pretty after losing Danny. I know I always lost revenge weight after a relationship went wrong.

"I was thinking I would go up to Scandinavia. Finland, Sweden, Norway." She gets this faraway look in her eyes. "I had an ex-boyfriend in high school I was madly in love with. He was from Norway. I've been interested in the country ever since."

I raise my brow. "Hunting down your ex-boyfriend in Norway sounds like a recipe for disaster."

She rolls her eyes. "I'm not saying I would hunt him down. I don't even know where he lives, if he lives there at all. But it's a beautiful country, and maybe I'll meet a sexy Viking. They can't all be assholes who cheat on you." She spits out that last part and then her face crumbles.

"Oh, Shay," I whisper. "Did Danny cheat on you?"

She shakes her head. "It doesn't matter." She blinks, looking up at the ceiling, and waves her fingers at her eyes. It seems to keep her tears at bay. "I'm not staying here."

I raise my glass. "Well, it will be a shame to see you go."

She gives me a grateful smile and clinks her glass against mine. "I know. I wish we'd gotten to know each other better."

I take a sip of wine, wanting to finish the whole glass in one go. It's just one of those kind of nights. "That's my fault. You kept inviting me but I just couldn't find the time."

"It's no one's fault," she says. "It's just life." She looks around her at the kitchen and the rest of the house. "I don't understand how you can do this, to be honest. I mean, the kids are sweet but you're practically their mother."

"I know."

"And that wasn't really in the job description. Would you have applied for the position at all if you knew you were going to be a nanny like this?"

"No."

"And you're not even a nanny, Amber. You're like . . . I don't know. A superhero. I know you get paid for this but how long are you planning to keep this up?"

I frown and my chest gets this cold feeling. "What do you mean?"

She purses her lips together before speaking. "I mean, you're with Derio. You love him, don't you? But he's never here and you're the one taking on all the work. I know you don't want to let the kids or him down, but didn't you have other dreams or plans for your life? Even if you can get this visa to stay here longer, can you continue in this role? You're so young but suddenly you're here and you're thrust into this situation." She pauses and sends me a sheepish glance. "I'm sorry. I know I don't even know you that well to be making all these assumptions. I just . . . I feel like one day you're going to crack, you know? I know what it's like to resent someone you love. It was Danny's idea to travel, not mine. And the first month out here, I hated it. I missed my home, my friends, my family. Even my old stupid job at the bookstore. I missed speaking English and having people understand me and I missed my favorite brand of yogurt. And I hated Danny for making me come here. Obviously, I got over it but that resentment was really strong. We almost broke up then. I should have taken that as a sign."

I'm listening to what she's saying and taking it all in. It's filling that cold space in my chest and making it freeze. "I don't know," I tell her. "I don't know what the future holds. All I know is right now, I'm really unhappy. And I want him to be happy. I just wish I could be, too. With the racing now, it just seems like either he's happy or we're both not."

"So what would you do if you could do anything?" she asks, smacking her palms on the table, her bracelets jangling loudly. "Pretend there was a nanny here taking care of them and you had another job. And you were still with Derio. What would you do?"

I try to think. "I'm not sure. I haven't really had a chance to think for myself lately." I glance out at the dark mist through the back doors. "I really enjoy plants. Maybe I could go into gardening or landscaping. Run a nursery. Grow olives and limes and almonds. Maybe floral arranging."

She shakes a long fingernail at me. "Do you see your face right now? You're glowing. You've got the same look from when you first met Derio."

When I first met Derio. I ignore that, swallowing it down like crusty bread. "I guess it's just something else I could do. Besides this."

"You don't have to do this job, Amber," she says emphatically. "I know you feel a lot of guilt because the kids rely on you and you're helping out Derio. But he could pay someone else. You could get a job doing something you love or at least something more enjoyable. That's the way it should be. Don't you think it's kind of weird that your boyfriend is employing you?" I shake my head, though I'm lying. "It's not right, it's making something like love—which, I know, is extremely messy and complicated—even harder than it has to be. I'm not saying Derio doesn't deserve things, too. He's still in his twenties; he doesn't have to give up his whole life for them. There is no shame in having that outside help to ensure they have the best life possible. Good grief, do you think the twins want to grow up knowing you had to sacrifice everything for them when you never asked for this, or wanted this, in the first place?"

With a shaking hand, I drain the rest of my glass. "I don't want you to be right," I mumble.

"I don't want to be right either. And I hope I'm not. But if I am, maybe it's best to talk about this situation with Derio before it all implodes. Because it will. I don't want to seem mean but . . . have you looked in the mirror?"

I look down at my dress.

"Not your dress," she says. "Your face. You look like a nervous wreck. Your eyes are all bloodshot and you look like you haven't slept for days. You have dark circles like whoa."

Now I feel like crying. "I haven't slept well lately," I say meekly.

"I know," she says and puts her arm around me, giving me a quick hug. "You deserve all the sleep in the world. You are working so hard and doing so much. I just don't want anyone to take advantage of you. Maybe I'm just all fired up because of me and Danny, so just take what I'm saying with a grain of salt. You know for the last month, he didn't work at all? He was just coasting along on my paycheck, like he used to do." She sighs heavily. "Men are rat bastards. But we love them anyway, don't we?"

She raises her glass to me and I halfheartedly toast her with my empty glass.

Derio isn't a rat bastard. And I do love him. A lot. A terrible amount.

But after Shay's words, my heart feels underwater.

Because what if love isn't enough?

When Derio comes back the next afternoon, I don't even hear him until he's right behind me. I'm still reeling over what happened moments earlier, my heart racing and my eyes on the edge of tears.

"Amber?" he says softly. "Didn't you hear me come in?"

I don't move or speak. I just stare blankly in front of me and try to breathe.

He sits down beside me on the living room couch and puts his hand on my knee.

"What is wrong? I'm here now," he whispers.

I slowly turn my head to look at him, blinking. Outside the sun is shining, the fog blown away by a strong breeze. The same breeze snakes in through the open door to the patio and ruffles the thick hair off his forehead.

"I had a fight," I say emptily. "With the twins."

He frowns and holds on to my hand. My other one is holding a wineglass, filled to the brim. "Oh? What happened?"

I take in a deep breath and put down the wine. "Alfonso got in a fight at school with another boy. Apparently the boy had called him gay or a girl or something like that because he hangs around his sister all the time. So Alfonso hit him." I look at Derio, suddenly angry that he wasn't there to help me when he should have been. "Do you know what that was like for me? The teacher called me in and I had to go. Hardly anyone spoke English. The other parents were yelling at me about Alfonso. It was horrible! And embarrassing! And I couldn't fucking do a thing about it!"

Derio's eyes widen at my screeching, dumbfounded by my outburst. But fuck him, he wasn't there, he didn't have to go through it. It was so fucking humiliating being called in there like that when I couldn't even understand what the headmaster was saying over the phone.

Derio tries to hug me but I break away from his grasp and stand up. I'm not done yet.

"So I have to bring him home early and then drag him with me back to school to pick up Annabella. Of course that caused even more problems with the parents, who thought I was bringing him back to gloat or something. So they started yelling at me in the streets."

Derio shoots to his feet now, his eyes flashing with anger. "Who are the parents? Who is the kid? They can't treat you like that."

"Well, they did!" I retort. "And I don't know, go talk to Alfonso, he's your brother, not mine."

He blinks at me and I continue. "And then Annabella starts acting up. I told her not to use the iPad to talk to Gia and she starts using it anyway, right in front of me. So I take it away from her. Then she tells me that she hates me and she won't listen to me because I'm not her mother." I pause, taking in a deep breath. "And I'll never be her mother."

Derio's heart looks like it's been shattered. "I am so sorry," he says heavily, trying to pull me close to him. I let him wrap his arms around me but I don't hug him back. I don't need his comfort right now. I need him to make this all right. I am so angry it feels like I've drunk a vat of acid and it's eating me alive. It's a dangerous kind of anger, the kind that takes years off your life.

He should have been here. He should be here helping me. These aren't my kids, Annabella is right, and I know that. I don't know what I'm doing. I shouldn't be doing this at all.

Tears spring to my eyes and everything inside me hurts. "I'm going to take a nap. You take care of them now."

"I will. I will speak to them and let them know how important you are, how wonderful—"

I raise my hand, cutting him off, and start walking away. "It doesn't matter. I need to lie down. You've been gone for too long."

"I know," he pleads. "I know, I know, but some things can't be helped."

I give him a tired look over my shoulder. "And some things can be helped." I walk up the stairs and he follows me.

"Derio," I say to him as I go into the room, ready to close the door on his face. "I really need to be alone right now. Please."

"Okay," he says softly, and I can tell the twins are poking their heads out of the room. I don't look at them. "I love you."

I only smile at him in return and close the door, locking it.

Then I collapse onto the bed and cry myself into a long, deep sleep.

CHAPTER TWENTY

I haven't seen Derio for a week.

It's now the end of September and Capri has become bearable again. The streets aren't crowded, the sun is warm, and the air sparkles with new clarity. There are still tourists at Dior and Louis Vuitton and all the restaurants are still open but there is a peace to the island now. If my own heart weren't breaking, I think I'd fall in love with Capri all over again.

But that isn't the case. My heart is breaking, slowly, degrading like the ancient ruins. There is a wedge between me and the twins, something I bet I could repair if I tried. But I haven't tried. I'm still licking my wounds over Annabella's words, still scarred by the experience with Alfonso. I know it's all part of parenting and that kids get into fights and say hateful things all the time. But I am not their parent. That much is clear.

Derio has talked to them. He has assured me that I have done nothing wrong. He even made them apologize, and I know the twins meant it. I know they don't mean me any harm. But I just don't care anymore. There's a wall going up around me that's deflecting everything that comes my way, good or bad. It's keeping me numb, which is preferable at the moment.

Unfortunately, Derio comes with the good or bad and I am growing numb to him, too. I'm tired of being overworked, tired of missing him. I know the racing brings him joy and I know he's doing really well as he gears up for his first race.

True to his word, he is taking things slowly and the race, which is in three days, will be low-key, at least compared to the competitions he used to be in. He doesn't even seem to mind competing at a lower level.

But while he's all smiles, I have none. I want to see him happy, I do. In fact, if it weren't for his happiness, I wouldn't be here at all. It's just that I wonder how much unhappiness I can take before it starts to matter. When should I put my needs first? It feels like I haven't for a while but I'm worried what it will mean if I do.

The truth is, I'm lonely. And there is nothing worse than being lonely in a big house, with responsibility at your feet, while the man you love is out there pursuing his passion. And you're left alone to forget about yours.

It doesn't help that I'm in a foreign land, a place that I can't call home. It also doesn't help that the only friend I had on the island has left, heading for Norway. It doesn't help that some nights, like tonight, I drink alone on the patio, staring at the empty sea, waiting for my phone to ring, for a text to come in. But he's been so busy; they're few and far between.

Shay was right. There is a breaking point for me. I feel like I'm tiptoeing along it, high-wire, above a fathomless drop. One false move, one overreaction, and I'm gone.

Sometimes you might not even see the push coming.

Tonight, I'm out on the patio, draining another glass of wine with a cat that isn't really my cat and waiting for my prince to show up. He should have been here an hour ago, when the ferry docked. He was to come home for one night, just to see me, before heading off to prepare for the race. I'm supposed to go with him while the twins stay with Gia's mother, Signora DiFabbia.

Even though I'm nervous about the race, I'm looking forward to it like nothing else. The night after, I can finally be alone with him, I can finally have him. He'll be mine and just mine. And then I will slowly, carefully, break to him how I'm feeling and how I can't go on like this. I don't want to leave him or the twins but there has to be another way, an easier way, for everybody.

Derio does love me. I know this. At least, I *knew* this. He will have to listen. He will have to understand. As long as he's on board, we can work through this.

I contemplate bringing it all up with him tonight but I'm feeling a bit emotional thanks to the wine and the vast emptiness of the blue dark around me. I just want him home, I want to collapse in his arms and I want his sweet words and steady resolve to bring me back around. I want to stop being numb and start letting him in again, to return to the way things were before we became emboldened by love.

I sigh, feeling worry bubble up inside me, and send him yet another text. Still no reply. I call him again. Still goes to voice mail. Even the professional tone of his voice in the greeting mocks me.

I get up, thinking about walking down to the Marina Grande, but the funicular isn't running anymore and it's a long walk when you take the road. I could take the bus, though, so I head inside to look at the bus schedule when my phone rings. It's a number I don't recognize.

"*Pronto*," I say, answering it like the Italians do.

The man's voice on the other end is speaking so fast in Italian that I can barely work out the words.

"I'm sorry," I apologize. "I don't know much Italian. *Non parlo Italiano.*"

"Sorry, sorry," the man says in a heavy accent. "Is this Amber?"

"Yes, this is Amber."

"I am Derio's friend, Paolo."

"Oh, hello, Paolo," I say uneasily, having never spoken to him before.

"Hi, hi," he says quickly. "Listen, I am with Derio and he is fine. We were drinking at the bar and he missed the last ferry. So very sorry, he is staying with me tonight in Napoli."

My heart curls angrily. "Why are you calling me? Why isn't he?"

"He is too drunk," he says with a little laugh. "We had too much fun after practice, you see. You know how it goes and you know how he is."

Actually, Derio's drinking has gone down by half since I started nannying but I don't bother bringing that up. That's not the point. The point is that right now he's supposed to be with me but was having too much fun getting drunk with his friend to even catch the damn boat.

"So what do I do now?" I ask him. "He's supposed to come here and then I'm supposed to go back with him for the race."

"Uh," Paolo says, obviously picking up on the simmering rage in my voice. "I don't know. I guess you will have to come meet him. It is just north of Rome, not too far." He pauses. "Listen, he will call you in the morning. Okay, Amber? Very sorry but I take good care of him. Goodnight. *Buonanotte*."

"*Buonanotte*," I nearly spit out and hang up the phone. Just in Rome, not too far? It's not like I've been to Rome since my backpacking days and it's not like it's just a short train ride away.

That vat of burning acid inside me? It's bubbling again.

I let out a growl that causes Nero to dart into the rosemary and then I dial Paolo's number.

"*Pronto*," he says.

"Paolo, it's Amber."

"Hi, Amber—"

"Listen," I say sharply. "When Derio wakes up, you tell him to take the first ferry in the morning back to me. Or else I'm not going to Rome and I may not even be here at all. Do you understand? *Capisci*?"

"*Capisco*," he says warily. "I will, but he—"

"Just do it or he'll have you to blame." Then I hang up, feeling better this time.

Have you ever gone to bed angry? I mean so angry that it's physically painful? It's probably the worst feeling in the world. Your face is red and your body is hot and your heart races like it's trying to puncture you with each beat. Your skin pulses with rage and all you want to do is sleep and forget about it. But you can't. Not right away. And when you do, the anger seeps into your bloodstream, ensuring you'll feel no peace even after you close your eyes.

That night, I fell asleep with a painful, angry heart and I woke up much the same way. There was no bright light of morning to clear the cobwebs, none of that positivity or optimism that comes with a new day. There wasn't even that fuzzy moment of ignorance when you believe everything is all right. No, I woke up slightly hung over and stark, raving mad.

And I let the anger consume me. I got up, made the kids a lazy breakfast of Nutella and toast, walked them to school, and then hurried back to the house so I could rage in privacy and not in the Capri sunshine, which seemed too happy and bright for my mood.

Meanwhile, I had gotten a million texts from Derio and a few missed calls. I answered one text with, *If you don't come here it's all over*, and that's it.

I know it's the not the kind of thing to say over text. I know Derio's pet peeve is big matters taking to small technology. I know he hates ultimatums and threats and he's the first person to get defensive. But if he can't see how serious this situation has become, then we have a problem. Actually, we already have a problem; we just have a bigger one now as well. The kind that can't be fixed. You can only patch a hole so many times before you just have to walk away.

I was ready to walk away now, but it wouldn't be without a fight.

Unfortunately, when Derio shows up—and for a while there I really thought he wouldn't—he isn't happy at all. And not in the groveling, I-did-you-wrong kind of way but in the pissed-off, already-on-the-defensive kind of way. The worst kind.

I'm sitting in the kitchen, nursing one of too many espressos, when he walks inside and throws his duffel bag down on the ground.

"What the hell is wrong with you?" he asks.

I'm already raring to go. I immediately get up, almost knocking over my coffee. "What's wrong with me?" I ask snidely. "What happened to the good old-fashioned *mi dispiace*?"

He glowers at me, all black arched eyebrows and dark searing eyes; I'd forgotten how good he looks when he's pissed off. "Paolo explained what happened."

"Yes, he did. Because you were too drunk."

"I didn't mean to get drunk."

"I'm sure that's why you ended up in a bar."

He crosses his arms across his chest and straightens up. This makes him look massive and imposing but I'm not fooled. All the best douchebags look like studs at one time or another. "We had a good day and we were celebrating. We got carried away. It wasn't a big deal."

"Oh, it wasn't a big deal," I repeat. "Not to you. What about to me? I haven't seen you for a fucking week and you get too drunk on the night you're supposed to come here? To spend time with me?" Suddenly, all the anger is pooling into tears. I don't like it. I like it better when I'm a raging beast, not a sappy girl on the verge of a meltdown. I try to blink them back and control the wavering in my voice. "You had time to go to a bar with your friend, who you've been with all this time, instead of catching an earlier ferry home. Why didn't you come home? You knew I was waiting for you. Didn't you want to see me? Or your brother and sister, for that matter?"

He swallows hard and looks away, his shoulders slouching, and he doesn't look so massive anymore. Instead, he looks as defeated as I feel. "I just want to have some fun," he says quietly.

"Well, that's all fucking great for you!" I say, too loud for my own good. "But what about me? I want to have fun, too. Instead I'm stuck here with the kids while you're out there living your dream and getting drunk with friends and having fun without me."

"But this is your job," he says to me, and I feel the color drain out of my face. "You are paid to be here to take care of them. You do your job and I do mine."

My eyes burn like fire while moisture floods my mouth. I swallow. "So that's what this is?" I say quietly. "It comes down to my job? You do what you do and I do what I'm supposed to do?"

"That's why you're here, is it not?" he asks, and I'm stunned he even thinks to say this out loud.

"No," I say, shaking my head. "I'm here because of you."

He sighs and runs his hand through his hair. "Well, if you are here because of me then you must take the bad with the good. You don't understand, Amber. I have been tied to this house, to them, to this island, for over a year. I have given up everything and I have finally gotten it back. Now you want me to give it up all over again?"

"That is not what I'm saying!" I tell him angrily. "I'm not asking you to give up anything. I'm asking you to cut me some slack. To help me out. To fucking come home when you say you're going to come home. I mean, it's been a week, Derio. *A week*. Didn't you want to see me? Didn't you miss me?"

He nods, looking away. "I did. I do. But I was going to see you in Rome. I don't see the big deal. I knew you would be fine here with the children."

"But I'm not fine!" I yell. "I am not fine. I haven't been fine for a long time now. Derio, I am fucking miserable being stuck in this goddamn empty house for weeks on end. I am only here because of you. Not the money, not even the twins, even though I love them dearly. I'm here because of you. I have given up everything to make sure you can do what you love, and meanwhile I've lost the thing that I love the most: you."

He stares at me. "You haven't lost me."

"Then you've lost me," I say. "Either way, it's gone."

He frowns in disbelief. "What are you saying?"

I breathe out slowly, in disbelief at what I'm about to say. "I'm saying that I can't do this anymore. This was never the role I wanted but I stuck by it to be with you. Now you're barely here and I have to do it all by myself. It's not worth it, Derio. I'm not cut out for this kind of job. The twins are too much responsibility and I just can't handle it. I was never meant to be the nanny. I'm not the right person."

"Look," he says quickly, stepping closer to me. There's a wildness in his eyes. "Just because you lost them one time—"

"That one time was enough!" I snap. "It made me realize that my parents were right. That I can't handle it, and I'm not cut out for anything like this. I'm useless, helpless. I'm not their mother and I'm reminded of that every day. I can't handle their activities or anything to do with school, I don't speak the language, and I'm not from here."

"You can learn," he suggests. "You know so much already."

"I don't *want* to be their nanny!" I tell him. "That's what it comes down to. I don't want to do it anymore. I want them in my life and I want to be with you, but this just isn't working."

He's silent, his eyes roving all over the kitchen as if searching for something, and I am desperate for him to understand, to put himself in my shoes.

"So the twins aren't good enough for you?" he finally says. "You don't care what happens to them? You're just going to abandon them, like our parents did?"

I feel like I've been slapped in the face. Holy hell, I did not see this coming.

"What are you talking about? No."

"Do you know what this is going to do to them?" he cries out, his features strained by pure agony. "This will kill them. You can't leave them! You can't possibly be that selfish!"

I jerk my head back, the words cutting deep. "I'm not selfish," I manage to choke out.

"You are," he says. "And you're leaving me. After everything, you're leaving me."

I stare at him and my soul feels bereft. I shake my head, tears spilling down my face. "I never said I was leaving you, Derio. I never said that's what I wanted to do." I take in a deep breath. It hurts. "But I'm leaving you now."

"What?" he asks breathlessly.

I brush past him out of the kitchen, trying to keep it together before I start bawling, but he grabs my arm and stops me.

"You aren't leaving," he says, his voice breaking. "What I said, I didn't mean it."

"But you did," I say. "And I do, too. This is for the best."

"For you!" he suddenly yells. "This is the best for you! What about me?"

"This is the best for everyone in the end," I tell him. "This never would have worked, not with me. Felisa knew what she was doing."

"Felisa is gone!" he yells, his face red, his eyes pained. "And I love you. I love you."

"Even if that's true," I tell him, trying to gather what little strength I have to make it up the stairs, "sometimes love is not enough."

"*Mia leonessa*," he says in a broken whisper as I go up the stairs. But that's all he says. He doesn't come after me. I pack my bags as quickly as I can, trying my hardest not to cry. I can't lose it here, not in this house. I have to get off this island, get away and clear my head. I know I have enough money saved now in my makeshift piggy bank—a hollowed-out book—to buy a ticket home at a travel agency. Derio still owes me a bit more but he can keep it. It's not worth it. It would only remind me of why I was here to begin with—as the hired help. A job that, somewhere along the way, turned into something more, something messy, something heart-wrenching.

I close my bag and zip it shut and take a moment to breathe before swinging it over my shoulders. I haven't carried it in months, and the weight of it feels so foreign. It was such a big part of me for so long, a part of my life, and now it feels like a hug from an old friend. But even my backpack can't comfort me. It just reminds me of the person I was before. I'm not sure I like her much either.

I look around our room—Derio's room—knowing I'm probably leaving half of my stuff behind, but I don't care. These things can be replaced; the memories can't.

I ready myself before I step out into the hall and am relieved to feel that sense of numbness come over me like a cloak. I rely on it to get me down the stairs and to the front door. I don't want to see Derio if I can help it.

But, of course, he steps out of his office, his eyes red and wet, and calls out to me.

"Don't go," he says quietly. "Please."

He is breaking and I am broken. I can hear it, I can feel it. But even though I know he means for me to stay, wants me to stay, I can't. Not anymore. Call it stubbornness or doing the right thing, but the voices deep inside of me are telling me to get out of here. That the situation is too messy to navigate. That we won't be able to work through it. That our love, our beautiful, passionate love, won't be enough to sustain us through the hard times. This moment is already proving that, after all.

I'm packed, with one foot out the door.

I have been pushed off the tightrope.

Now the fall begins.

"Goodbye," I whisper to him as I turn the door handle. "Tell the twins I'm sorry."

And then I steal out past the sad lemon trees, all which seem to weep yellow tears for me, and walk down the Via Tragara for the last time, heading for the ferry, for the mainland, for freedom. For home.

CHAPTER TWENTY-ONE

I'm curled up in the fetal position in a hotel in Naples, letting the pain pass through me in sharp, thorny ribbons. It hurts. It really fucking hurts. Heartache is so physically real that it needs to be recognized as a sickness, an ailment, a cancer of love. A broken heart is a sad, angry, powerful thing that shakes you by the collar and demands your respect, and it's pummeling me into the mattress, shattering me to pieces. It's as real as the actual heart in my chest.

In some ways, it's more real because it flows throughout your whole body, wrapping around your bones and your organs and your blood. It's in everything you do, every breath you take. I can't drink, I can't eat, I can't sleep. I just hurt as my mind turns over and over what I've done and what it means. I keep seeing the look on Derio's face, his heartbreak at my own hands, and I'm suffering all over again.

And again and again and again.

I think about everything I'm giving up by walking away and doing the so-called right thing. The twins, the love of my life. Everything changed for me on that island, and a part of me is afraid I'm throwing in the towel too soon.

But the other part feels wise and in control. It tells me it never would have worked, that this was a long time coming, that it was always going to end this way. A vacation romance, nothing more, nothing less. There was never a need for it to get complicated. But complicated, it is, and like a coward I ran when the going got tough.

You didn't run, I tell myself. *You chose to go because you had to go. Derio could have come after you but he didn't.*

Derio also has a brother and sister to deal with now, the day before the race. I wince, knowing I might have screwed up his first race in over a year. I tell myself there will be others, that he will win them, and all will be fine. But I don't believe it; I just feel guilty.

Guilt, sorrow, emptiness; they surround me in that tiny room as darkness falls over the city.

I think about the way he loved me.

Because he really did love me.

He really *does* love me.

I fall asleep clinging to that thought, like maybe one day it could save me.

I don't know how I manage to get everything done the next day but I do. I book my ticket home for tomorrow evening, then I call my parents and give them the so-called good news. My father is especially happy, telling me he's proud of me for knowing when to come home and even recognizing that it must have been hard for me to leave my job. Of course, he said it in a way that made it seem like I was fooling around at a summer camp, but whatever. My heart is too heavy to argue with him.

I send an e-mail to Shay telling her what's going on, then realize I have no one else to tell. There's Angela, but I haven't spoken to her properly in so long that it feels weird to do so—it's better if I just call her once I get home.

Home. The concept seems so weird now. The idea of living in the suburbs, in that cul-de-sac with my parents, where everyone's green lawns are the same color and the backyard fences all end at the same height and the roofs all have cheap red tile, feels stifling and somehow more claustrophobic than living on a rock in the middle of the Mediterranean Sea.

Am I doing the right thing? I ask myself as I pay for my ticket.

Am I doing the right thing? I ask myself after I hang up the phone with my parents.

Am I doing the right thing? I ask myself after seeing the one text Derio has sent to me since I left, which I ignore.

Senza di te, non sono niente. Si prega di tornare da me.

Without you, I am nothing. Please come back to me.

How am I supposed to respond to that? *Thank you for making me cry into my coffee?* Because that's exactly what happens.

But sometimes you never know if you're doing the right thing until after you've done it. And I know this is definitely one of those times.

In the afternoon, I decide to drag myself out for some pizza—I can still taste the glorious slice I had when I was here with Derio and the twins, and I start craving it, as if all the feelings of happiness, love, and security are wrapped up in that thin, oven-baked crust.

While there are a lot of pizzerias in the neighborhood, I'm looking for a place that sells authentic Neapolitan pizza. The government has imposed some quality-control standards regulating what is considered proper Neapolitan pizza, so I need to make damn sure I eat the right thing.

I finally find one with a vintage, mint-colored sign and go inside.

Vorrei uno pezza de pizza margherita, per favore, I mouth the words to myself as I walk under whirring fans, the smell of garlic and fresh dough hitting my nostrils. I'm not even sure if I'm saying it right, but I'm going to try. My mind feels completely fogged up, like all the Italian I've learned has gone out the window, and I can't think straight.

I get to the counter of the shop, barely noticing that the handful of patrons are all gathered by a TV in the corner as a sportscaster speaks rapid-fire Italian. The sound of his voice gives me a headache; I'm definitely not going to miss how loudly the Italians speak.

"*Vorrei uno pezza*," I say, forgetting the rest. The steely-eyed, Dalí-mustached man at the counter picks out a slice with mushrooms. Not what I wanted, but I'm not going to say anything. It's still probably delicious and the man looks like he wouldn't speak English to me, even if he knew how.

I slide two euros toward him and take the slice, turning around to the condiment station to put on some red pepper flakes, when I hear the sportscaster on the TV yell the name "Desiderio Larosa."

I nearly drop my pizza, and as I turn to look at the screen, it hits me that of course he is racing today. It must be televised. It's a feeling that makes me both happy and sick.

But when I turn around to look at the screen, the sickness turns to stomach-churning nausea. They're showing an accident on the racetrack.

A motorcycle is on fire.

One racer is trapped beneath the front wheel, the flames licking his legs. He's not moving.

Another motorcycle is flipped on its side, its racer thrown a few feet away onto the grass. He's also not moving.

People are rushing to the scene, and someone is dragging the body of the man on fire away while another person sprays him down with foam. Others are running to the other man on the track, leaning over him, gesturing wildly.

And still neither man moves.

The caption underneath says *Desiderio Larosa e Roberto Casadei. Un uomo morto, l'altro ferito gravemente.*

Morto.

Morto.

"Someone please!" I suddenly yell across the shop. "What is happening, tell me what is happening!"

The people in the shop look at each other in shock and I feel the walls start to close in on me. The TV station flashes to a picture of the hospital in Rome and someone being taken out of an ambulance, but I can't see who it is. This must not be live but it didn't happen long ago either.

Morto.

Dead.

Not Derio. No.

"Someone please!" I scream again, and a middle-aged woman comes over to me, babbling in Italian and trying to comfort me.

"No, no," I tell her, grabbing onto her shirt. "I don't speak Italian. Derio, Desiderio Larosa, is he dead? *Morto, morto?* I know him, he's my *amore. Mio amore!*" I thud my fist against my heart. "Is he dead? *Morto?*"

She has tears in her eyes and she nods. "*Si, si, mi dispiace.*"

I look at everyone else in the pizzeria. They all seem solemn, some looking at the screen and shaking their heads, others eyeing me with pity and sorrow.

This is not happening. They are all wrong. They have to

be. I stare back at the screen, blinking, feeling an icy sheet of shock wash over me. The woman beside me pats my shoulder and keeps telling me she's sorry.

This can't be happening.

I can't breathe.

I'm going to vomit.

Suddenly, I'm curled over, clutching my chest, my stomach, my heart.

No, no, no.

Another person comes to my side, a man, but I don't see him. I don't feel him as he leads me over to a chair and sits me down. Someone gives me water. The middle-aged woman is crying. The steely-eyed man brings me a fresh slice of pizza.

When I can finally raise my head, I stare at the screen, trying to read it, interpret it. They keep showing the crash in slow motion. The racer on the outside is passing on a corner and his bike skids out and goes flying into the racer on the inside. He's ejected into the air and lands in a way that you know he can't survive. He's completely limp. His bike crashes into the other bike and the other one bursts into flames, flipping into the air with the other racer until it smashes down on him.

Seconds later, as the fire starts up the racer's leg, medics run over. It's a replay of the scene that had caught my attention.

Derio always said his weakness was passing on the outside during a turn. That's how he was injured the last time. Derio always wore red when he was racing before. The man who went flying through the air was wearing red. Derio is taller and more muscular than most Italian racers. The man who landed on his head, motionless, has the same figure.

The man who went flying is the man who is dead. I can see that now as the sheet is placed over him. I can see the wrist of the man who is taken into the hospital, the man who survived the accident, albeit badly injured, and he's wearing a silver bracelet, like one of those medical alert ones. Derio doesn't wear one of those.

My heart sinks.

Derio doesn't wear one of those.

I burst into tears. It comes suddenly, like a bomb gone off inside of me, and I am ripped apart violently, ruined and destroyed. I am gutted, like a dying fish, my very being cut out, yanked out, discarded on the floor.

My grief is too powerful, too devastating for me to survive. I can't, I can't, I can't.

I can only cry. The pizzeria fills with my wails, the inhuman cries coming out of me that I don't even recognize.

Eventually, someone mentions getting a doctor and I think they mean for me. I can't stay here anymore. Before they can call someone or take me somewhere, I burst out of the pizzeria and into the chaos of the streets.

I can hear them yelling after me in concern but I can't stay there. I have to leave. I wildly hail a cab, arms flailing, and throw myself into the backseat. When the door closes I feel like I'm hidden from the world, if just for a moment.

The cab driver is listening to cheesy Italian pop music and has rosary beads hanging from his mirror. He's asking where I want to go but I don't know. I want to go back in time, when Derio was alive and I had his love, but I don't think he can take me there.

I tell him Rome. I want to go to Rome.

He tells me I'm crazy and can't take me there, but he can take me to the train station. I start crying again, banging my head against the window. He's frightened now, unsure what to do, and I yell at him that my boyfriend is dead and he is in Rome and would he please take me?

His voice softens but is still firm. I frantically dig through my purse and pull out a wad of euros. There are three hundred of them. I reach over the seats, tears blurring my vision, and shove them in his hand. "*Per favore*," I plead.

He looks at the money and nods. "Okay."

Rome is not a hop, skip, and a jump away. It's a two-and-a-half-hour cab ride up the highway, which I spend drowning in guilt. Derio made a mistake during the race and it was all because of me. He wasn't thinking clearly, he couldn't have been. What was I thinking? Breaking up with him right before his first race in a year? Couldn't it have waited? Would it have killed me not to be so selfish for once?

It killed *him*. My selfishness killed him.

It.

Killed.

Him.

And Derio died on that track, alone. He died in the horrible way I left him, thinking he wasn't worth it, thinking I didn't love him, wondering how he was going to take care of the twins without me there. He died with a broken heart.

He died with my broken heart.

I didn't think it was possible for my heart to break any further, but now it has been completely obliterated, turned to dust, the ashes swept away into the abyss.

The driver asks where I am going once we reach the crowded outskirts of Rome and I repeat the name of the hospital I saw on the news. He nods and then starts asking what happened, why I am going, but I don't know enough to respond to him. I can only cry to myself, trying to hide those strong, rolling sobs that rip the air from my lungs.

When he pulls up to the hospital, I see a crowd of reporters outside. No one pays attention to me and I slip inside while they talk excitedly to an exhausted-looking doctor.

I don't know where I'm going. Compared to the small Capri hospital I went to, the Rome one is a whirl of confusion, full of baffled cries and painful whimpers and the smell of iodine and sour skin. I start wandering through the halls, ignoring the nurses who glance my way, knowing if I even make eye contact with them they'll ask me why I'm here and haul me away.

I think I want to find the morgue. Maybe the emergency room. I want to find Derio. I want him to be alive so I can tell him I'm sorry. I want so much but can afford so little.

I end up in a long hallway past the noise and smells of the ER waiting room. The hall hums with fluorescent lights.

Then I see her, leaning against the wall, hugging herself. Felisa.

I start running toward her, amazed that she's here but craving the embrace of someone I know in a land where I don't really know anyone.

"Felisa!" I cry out, and when I see the tears streaming down her face, I know the truth.

It nearly knocks me off my feet.

Instead, I collide into her and she wraps her arms around me and cries. I cry. We don't have to say anything, I can feel her grief just as I feel mine, raw and bleeding.

Finally, she pulls apart and smooths down my hair affectionately. "I look for you," she says, her English thick and mangled. She clears her throat. "I am sorry, my English is not used much. I thought you would be here."

"I was in Naples," I tell her, afraid to tell her any more than that. That I left him, that I'm a deserter.

"I saw it on the news," she says, taking a heavy breath. "I was with my partner, Lorenzo, in Umbria. I made him drive me here right away." Tears well in her eyes again, and if I had any more left in me I would cry at the sight of an old, strong woman like herself moved to such grief. "He is like a son to me. I never should have left him. Or the twins. Or you."

We have far too much in common now. We're drowning in the mire of our guilty consciences.

"I left him, too," I admit and the words burn through my throat. "Just last night. I couldn't handle it anymore and I snapped. We broke up. We were together, you know. After you left. We fell in love and this is all my fault."

Without you, I am nothing. Please come back to me.

His last text cuts painfully across my mind, digging in like barbed wire.

I can never go back to him now.

"It is no one's fault but mine," Felisa says, staring up at the ceiling. She looks at me and sighs. "You know, I knew he was in love with you. From the beginning. You made his eyes light up, just like the sun coming through a cloud. I had never seen that before. I thought you were a blessing."

"I was a curse," I spit out bitterly, wiping my nose on my shoulder.

She digs into her purse and hands me a tissue. "You mean more to him than I think you know."

I can't even be bothered to correct her use of present tense.

"Where are the children?" she asks me.

I shrug helplessly. "I don't know. If they are not here he would have left them with someone on Capri. Maybe Signora Bagglia or Signora DiFabbia." The realization that they are truly orphans almost floors me. I look at her. "Should I go back to them? They have no one now, no one at all."

"If you don't, I will," she says, her head held high. "I just have to convince Lorenzo. It is funny, but like Derio, Lorenzo is afraid of the sea. Or like Derio *was*."

I don't understand how anything can be funny now, nor understand how Felisa's eyes can grow so warm when she says Lorenzo's name. How can her guilt, her sorrow, allow her even a moment of happiness? I feel like I'm six feet underground and buried alive, my screams lost in the dirt.

"No," I say quietly, and in my heart I find the truth. "I have to go back. I am the one who should take care of them. They need me. And now I need them." I can't even imagine how they are going to handle the news. "Do you think they will let me?"

"Who?"

"I don't know, the government. Do you think they will let me take care of them? Do I have to adopt them?"

She frowns at me and wipes a tear away from her eyes with long, wrinkled fingers. "If you want to be their nanny again, then be their nanny. I am sure Derio wouldn't mind. He would be happy."

"Yes, he would be happy if he were alive, but that doesn't have much pull now."

Felisa's eyes nearly bug out of her head. "If he were alive?!"

I wonder if she's gone senile in the stress of it all. "I don't think the government will care what Derio would have wanted if he's . . . he's . . . passed on. Unless I was in his will?"

"Passed on?" she repeats, her hand clutching at her collar.

Now I have to frown. Maybe she doesn't know the extent of it. "He's dead." Saying the words nearly breaks me open.

"No," she says wildly, shaking her head. "He is not. They would have told me."

I give her a hopeless look. "It was on the news."

"Yes," she says and gestures down the hall. "And they brought him here. He has burns, a bad shoulder, and broken leg but he is not dead." She arches her brow and gives me an incredulous look. "*Mamma mia.*"

Hope wants to bloom inside of me. But it can't, it can't . . . "But the man who died, he was wearing red and he passed on the outside and this man, this man on the other bike, he was wearing a bracelet," I tell her fervently.

"Yes, it was a shame," she says. "Poor soul. These kind of things don't happen so often but when they do, they are very bad."

"But the bracelet!"

She sniffles and gives me a look of impatience. "Derio has a rare blood type. He wears a medical bracelet when he races in case of accidents. Like this one."

"He's not dead?"

"*Santo cielo*!" she curses. "He is not dead!"

I can't contain the hope now. My smile is larger than life. "But you are crying!"

"Because he is hurt!" she snaps. "And I should have been there for him. I don't like to see my poor boy hurt, he has been through so much."

"But—" I start.

"He is not dead," she assures me. She nods at the nearest door. "They have treated him for his burns on his leg. It is broken, too, which is a problem with the healing. They put his shoulder back in. Soon they will come out and tell us how he is. But he is stable and he is alive and I am sure when we are allowed to see him, he will be happy to see us. I hope so, anyway."

I suddenly feel faint and the hallway is starting to spin. I grab for the wall and slowly lower myself so I'm sitting on the floor, my legs splayed out in front of me.

He's not dead.

My heart is leaping inside my chest like an animal that's been set free. I start crying again but these are happy tears. These are the best tears. I feel terrible that he's so hurt, that he's going through this all over again, and the injuries sound bad, especially the burn. But even if half of his body melted away, I wouldn't care.

He's alive. *Alive*.

My Derio.

Felisa stares down at me and smiles like I'm the biggest fool. "So what are your plans now?"

"I'm going to stay here," I tell her without thinking.

She nods. "You said you were in Naples. Where were you going?"

"Home," I say softly. I give her a worried look. "I was going home."

"You can still go."

"No!" I nearly yell it, wiping the tears away with the heel of my palm. "No, I can't go home now. I can't leave him like this. And the twins need me. I wasn't kidding when I said I would go back and look after them."

"I know you weren't. I can see it in your eyes. You are very kind. Very determined. Stubborn. Like Derio. That's why you work so well together." She exhales and straightens her shoulders, staring at the door. "You will wait with me first, until we can see him. I know both Signora Bagglia and Signora DiFabbia. I will call them and find the twins and tell them what has happened. It is better that I do it, so the language does not get crossed."

I'm more than okay with that.

"Then," she continues, "you will go back to Capri. I will stay here, me and Lorenzo, and make sure Derio is all right."

I frown and slowly get to my feet and dust off my butt. "Should I bring the twins here?"

She shakes her head. "Unless Derio gets worse, don't take them out of school. They need some, how you say, time to be normal. I am sure he will be transferred to the hospital in Naples, and seeing him will be easier then."

"He has friends from Naples," I tell her.

She doesn't look impressed. "Yes, I met them earlier. Stupid men. All the men who race are stupid. But what can you do?" She gives me a kind look. "I know you say things were not good between you but he is going to need you now more than ever. Can you be there for him?"

I swallow, feeling a strength burn through me. "I'm not going anywhere."

Even if it means heading backward, not forward, I am not going anywhere.

CHAPTER TWENTY-TWO

We wait for hours in the hospital. I meet Lorenzo, a funny little man with big false teeth and kind squinty eyes, who speaks no English at all, but he and Felisa seem to be madly in love. Which is cute and all, but seeing them embrace makes me itch for Derio even more. Ever since I learned that he isn't dead, which still feels fragile, like a truth that could be blown away, I've gone from pure joy and relief to a nearly uncontrollable urge to see him, like I can't see or breathe or think properly until I do.

But the hours are long and the doctors tell us little. It's always "soon." But at least Derio seems to be pulling through. I knew he would. That man has a fire inside him.

After a while I think about the hotel in Naples with all my stuff in it and realize I'll probably have to stay in Rome overnight, though I don't have anything with me other than a purse. I also realize that if I'm going back to Capri to look after the twins while Derio recuperates, then I'm going to have to cancel my flight. At this stage in the game, there's no way I can get the ticket refunded—all that money will have to go to waste.

I go outside into the alley, where two orderlies are on their smoking break, dial home, and wait.

My mother immediately answers with a "What's wrong?"

"Nothing," I tell her quickly. "But I only have two minutes on my plan and I need to make this quick before they charge me an arm and a leg." I can hear my dad in the background asking her who it is. When she tells him Amber, I know he's going to pick up the phone in the other room. They like to tag team me.

"Why are you calling?" she asks me. "Is your flight canceled? I thought it was tomorrow."

"Amber," my father says, picking up the line, "I'm going to be a bit late picking you up from the airport. I didn't account for the hockey game. That means extra traffic, you know."

"That's fine," I say, taking in a deep breath. "Because I'm not coming home."

The line goes silent. Just for a moment. Just long enough for my words to sink in.

"I knew it," my mother says in a hush.

"Amber, please. Explain what you mean," says my dad, his voice taking on that dry quality, the doctor-of-psychology one he uses when he needs to make himself look more important than he is.

"There was an accident, and Derio was involved. Motorcycle racing, it's really big here and he's hurt. Pretty badly. I'm actually at a hospital in Rome right now."

"You're in Rome?" my mother squeaks.

"Yes, I had to see him. I saw it on the news. It was horrible. I thought he was dead. But his old nanny is here, Felisa, the woman who hired me for the job. He's just really hurt. The other guy actually died. God, it's just terrible."

"You made a commitment to come home," my father says. "I know what you're saying is sad and you feel bad, perhaps you're even displacing your guilt, but if he's all right and he has someone, then you need to come home."

"I made a commitment to those children," I tell them, feeling frustrated. He always pretends he knows what's best for me, even though he doesn't even know what's best for himself.

"You made a commitment to your parents," he says. "And you need to honor that commitment."

"No," I tell him. "I promised those kids I would take care of them, I'm the one who ran away when the situation got too hard."

"You ran away because you realized you were wasting your life!" he yells, and I'm stunned into silence. He sounds ferocious, even over the phone. "This whole trip has been a waste of your time, and you know it. Whatever you're looking for, Amber, it's not out there. I should know. I traveled, too, and never found it. You might think you're smarter and braver than your parents, but you're not. I've seen the world and I've learned you can't be a butterfly drifting from flower to flower. What you need, what you want, is at home. You'll find it by using your goddamn degree and getting a proper, well-paying job and building a life for yourself here. Do you really think you can be a nanny? It's a sad, sorry position with no respect and lousy pay. You are better than that. You have an education and you have brains. It's time you use them. Be responsible for once in your life and come home!"

More silence. Months ago I would have cried at his outburst but I barely flinch at his words. I watch the orderlies stub out their cigarettes and laugh heartily at some private joke. This is surreal. I'm in Rome, waiting on Derio to come out of a situation where he almost died, and my father is yelling at me like I'm not here at all. Like I'm standing in the kitchen and complaining about what to do with my life, like I'm some teenager he can still talk down to and boss around. I still don't know what I want to do with my life, but I know I'll do it in time. But for now, there are bigger things than that.

"Harold," my mother says in a softly chiding tone.

I clear my throat, feeling all the power they ever held over me drain away. "I *am* being responsible," I say quietly but with more determination than I've ever felt before. "I have two children who depend on me and need me more than ever. And I have a man who I love, who loves me, who needs me just as much. I have a brain and I am using it, along with my heart. I'm sorry you're disappointed in me but I'm not sorry I'm staying. You always wanted me to do the right thing and grow up. Well, this is me growing up." The phone beeps at the two-minute mark. "Goodbye, Mom and Dad. I'll write to you in a few days."

Then I hang up the phone, put it on mute, and slip it back in my purse. I run after one of the orderlies and stop him.

"*Scusi,*" I say with a big smile. "*Hai una sigaretta?*"

The orderly looks at the other one, then shrugs. He brings a cigarette out of his pocket and gives it to me.

"*Grazie mille,*" I tell him. "*Sei un santo.*"

He grins at me, pleased at the compliment, and I grin right back, glad it wasn't lost in translation. I'm learning. I watch as they go inside and then stick the cigarette in my purse. When I see Derio, he's going to want this.

At around eleven p.m., Felisa insists I go to a hotel and get some sleep. I tell her I'm not going anywhere at this point and that she needs the rest. Lorenzo seems to agree—they aren't spring chickens—and I promise to call her if anything changes.

About an hour after they leave, the doctor comes into the waiting room, looking for them.

I stand up and wave at him. He's wiry and has bags under

his eyes and a bad hairline and speaks in an overly monotonous voice, which I personally find strange for an Italian. His hand gestures are also minimal.

"Do you speak English?" I ask him since he's only talked to Felisa in Italian.

He nods. "Yes, of course."

"*Buono*," I say. "I'm Derio . . . Desiderio Larosa's girlfriend, Amber MacLean."

He nods. "I was looking for the woman, Felisa."

"She went to a hotel. I told her I would stay behind. How is he?"

He seems to think about that for a moment, and I gear up for some horrible news. Then he looks around and puts his hand on my shoulder. "He is in good condition now. Usually we just let in immediate family at this stage. But I think you are the closest thing to that. Would you like to come see him? He doesn't look very pretty."

I nod eagerly and the doctor leads me down the hall.

We stop outside the room and he opens the door.

The blood inside me runs cold.

Derio is lying in the hospital bed in a green hospital gown with an IV running into one arm, seemingly asleep. There's a sling around his shoulder and his leg is elevated. The leg looks bad—really bad. It's raised but hasn't been placed into a cast yet. I can see many large pins sticking out of it, attached to an outer shell, like a cage. The skin itself is covered in layers of bandages.

The doctor nods at me. "We have set the bone this way while he's here but we have to treat the burn before the leg can be put into a cast. It's second-degree instead of third, thanks to the clothes he was wearing during the accident. Not many racers wear the right equipment, for fear it slows them down, but he did. We won't need to do a skin graft after all. But because it hasn't destroyed all of his nerves, he will be in a lot of pain. But his leg and shoulder will heal and become mobile again, with time. He's a lucky man." He looks at Derio, who is slowly waking up. "I hope you don't mind that she's here. I figured you wouldn't since you were calling for her earlier."

He was calling for me?

The doctor pats me on the shoulder and then leaves the room, leaving the door slightly open.

Suddenly, I feel scared. But when Derio sees me, his eyes light up like diamonds. The doctor was wrong. He still looks pretty. Actually, he looks gorgeous. He'll always look like that in my eyes.

"Amber," he says, his voice hoarse and barely audible.

"Don't talk," I tell him, coming over to his right side, which isn't in the sling. I stop beside him, one hand on his arm, the other at my mouth because I'm not sure if I'm going to cry or laugh or if I have the strength to even breathe. Tears fill my eyes, my vision of him becoming blurry, before they spill down my cheeks. He's so hurt. One side of his face is scratched raw along his cheekbone. Purple and red bruises flare out from his nose and eyes. His hair is greasy and seems to still have dirt in it. His lip is busted up. It's almost too much for me to take in all at once, but I have to remind myself that it could have been worse.

You thought he was dead, I tell myself. *But he's full of life.*

"I'm so glad you're here," he croaks, coughing.

"Shhh," I tell him, afraid to touch him anywhere except his arm, but his arm will do. I run my fingers down until I come to his hand. With effort, he wraps his fingers around mine. Despite everything, they are strong, warm, comforting.

"I must tell you," he says, "that when you stepped inside

this room, I thought I might have died. I thought I was in heaven."

"You're very much alive. How do you feel?"

"I am okay. I don't feel much pain, just . . . it is uncomfortable. My pride is bruised but I will not suffer for it. The other man is dead."

"I know," I whisper, holding his hand tightly and feeling those tears prickling hot at the corners of my eyes. "I thought you were dead. I was confused about the accident. I came all the way here from Naples when I heard, expecting to see you in the morgue."

"Would you have come if you knew I was alive?" he asks, regarding me warily.

"Of course I would have." I bite my lip, taking a deep, deep breath. "Derio, I am so sorry for what I did to you. You have no idea how badly I wish I could take it all back. I was frustrated and lonely and lost and so damn tired, and I snapped. I just snapped. I couldn't hold it in. I should have told you earlier, should have admitted that I was struggling and needed your help. But I didn't want to bother you and I didn't want to seem weak, like I couldn't do it all. I'm so sorry. I never wanted to leave you, or the twins, I just didn't know what else to do." I feel lighter having said that, but I don't know if it is enough. I stare at him, afraid.

"*Mia leonessa*," he whispers gently, bringing my hand up to his lips where he places a delicate kiss. "You don't have to say anything. I said things I did not mean. I lost my temper. I am guilty, very guilty, for putting you aside. I took you for granted but it still pulled on me, every day, that my racing was taking me away from you. I just assumed that you were okay and I should have seen you were not. I should have asked about you more. I should have been there. I was so caught up with proving to myself that I had my life back, I forgot about the very thing that makes this life so sweet. You." He squeezes my hand, his eyes tired but sad. "Amber, *tu sei il grande amore della mia vita. Senza di te, la vita non ha più senso.*"

"That sounds beautiful," I tell him. "But I have no idea what you said."

He gives me a soft smile. "You are the love of my life. Without you, life has no meaning." He breathes in deeply, seeming to get choked up. "And it is true. You are my life, my love, my everything. I thank God for bringing you to me, into our lives, and for showing us the way. I was a fool to forget that, even for a second. Amber, I love you far more than I can even say."

It's the honesty and sincerity in his words that undoes me. The tears spill down my cheeks. I am unable to contain them and I don't care. I want him to see them, see how he affects me. My heart beats loudly, alive and happy and free.

"Don't cry," he says, coughing, his eyes wet. "Or you will make me cry. I should have to tell the doctor I am in pain if he asks."

"These are good tears," I tell him. "Felisa and Lorenzo, her man friend, are here, too. I sent them to their hotel for the night. She's going to make sure you're okay. I'm going to make sure the twins are okay."

"You don't have to do that," he says adamantly. "The twins are with Signora DiFabbia. They are okay."

"I know, Felisa spoke to them. They know what happened but they're being well taken care of. Even so, that's not her job. It's my job. I'm going to Capri tomorrow."

"Tomorrow?" he repeats. "You aren't going home?"

I gently brush his hair off his face. "How could I go home when I never really wanted to in the first place? You are my home, Derio. And I will go back to Capri and take care of your brother and sister until you are well enough to return to me."

"And then what?"

"And then we'll figure it out. But we will do it together."

He blinks at me, rubbing his dry lips together. "I don't want you to leave me." He holds my hand tighter.

"I don't want to leave you either. But this, finally this, is the right thing to do." I lean over and kiss him on his forehead, and through all the sterile smells of the hospital, I smell him. Lemons, musk, and his natural woodsy scent. It's like Capri. It's like home.

"I want you to know," he says, his eyes drooping a little, "that I did not do anything reckless. I was very careful while racing. It just . . . happened."

"I know," I say. "They said the other racer took the corner too fast and crashed into you. Your extra gear is what saved you, and probably the fact that you weren't racing erratically. I know you weren't being reckless."

He blinks slowly. "But now I don't know what is best for me, for my future, for our future. Do I give it up again and risk it all?"

"I can't answer that, Derio. This is your life. Things happen even when you plan well ahead, even when you take all the precautions. Life is dangerous, even without being on a motorbike. Follow your heart and I will support you, no matter what. Your dreams are no less important than anyone else's."

He closes his eyes. "Thank you."

"I'm going to let you rest," I tell him. "And I'll be back tomorrow before I leave."

"Don't go," he says as I pull away.

I give him a look. "You know I'm not going anywhere." I'm about to leave when I remember something.

"Oh," I say quickly, reaching into my purse and pulling out the cigarette I bummed. "I forgot, I got this for you." I hand it to him. He takes it from me, examines it, and then snaps it in half between his fingers.

"No, thank you," he says with a quiet smile. "I think I am going to quit. I hear they are bad for your health."

"That doesn't sound very Italian," I tease him, though of course I'm relieved.

"No," he admits. "But it does sound like a man who wants to live as long as he can, with the woman he loves by his side."

We stare at each other for a moment, a current passing from my eyes to his and back again. It tells us everything else we can't figure out how to say. Some feelings transcend any language.

CHAPTER TWENTY-THREE

I've decided that October is my favorite month in Capri. It's still sunny and warm but the tourists are mostly gone and the island hums like a true community. The locals are friendlier and the visitors are, too. You can look out at the sea and see that deep, never-ending blue instead of hundreds of boats jetting to and fro. Sometimes it rains, but that's okay; I love the rain here. You can see it sweep in off the sea in sheets as it fills the air with the smells of hot stone and grass and lemon. The island seems to take a deep breath as the parched plants inhale the fresh rain, turning from brown to green.

I've been taking care of the twins on my own for three weeks now while Derio heals in the Naples hospital. There was a bit of a complication with his leg and then his shoulder, thanks to a previous dislocation (also due to racing, surprise, surprise), which was making him immobile for longer than they thought.

While he goes through his struggles on the mainland, I go through my struggles here. They're not the same, of course. They aren't even close. But just because I'm doing the right thing, doesn't mean it's easy. In fact, the right thing rarely is.

Annabella and Alfonso are forgiving and kind, though uncertain about me, about life, about everything. They worry for their brother and ask about him every day. They also seem to worry about me and think I'm going to leave them again. I keep promising them I won't but I can see they don't fully believe me. I don't blame them. They came home from school one day and saw everything packed up and gone, just like the day Felisa had left. It took a few days after my return for Annabella to stop crying. She blamed herself so much that she started to sound a lot like me. I realized that we both needed to start letting go of the guilt and move on.

Taking care of them is still a lot of work. My appreciation for moms grows more and more each day. But somehow I get it done. I try not to complain. I count my blessings. I feel important and useful and right, and that gets me through the tough days.

It doesn't help that my parents aren't being any more understanding about this whole thing, but at least their opinions don't bother me so much. Though my dad remains stubborn in his ways and isn't afraid to show it, my mother has started reaching out to me on her own. She's called me a few times, speaking in a quiet voice that suggests she's doing this in private, and has asked me about Italy—what it's like, how the people are, the best places to go. I think she wants to come visit; she sounds so wistful when she asks me what I'm doing. If she brings it up one day, I will encourage her to come over and spread her wings a bit. I know she's afraid to do it because of my father, but I just hope she learns to overcome that fear, as I have.

I'm trying to learn more Italian and stop being so shy and afraid when it comes to making friends here. I've been watching Alfonso and Annabella branch out and socialize, and I figure it's about time I do the same. Though Signora Bagglia is a lot older, I've become friends with her and often drop by her restaurant for a bite to eat during lunch or just to say hello. The free food is nice, too. I've also made friends with Cara, a young single mom who moved to Capri a year ago. Her son, Emilio, is a year younger than Alfonso, but so far they get along great. Cara's English is pretty good, too, and she's been a major force in helping my Italian along. She also enjoys a few glasses of wine and a good gossip about the people on the island, which is fun to listen to, especially when she gets worked up and her hands start flying around like lethal weapons.

Because of people like Cara and Signora Bagglia, I don't feel so alone anymore. I have a bit of extra help with the twins if I need it and I've stopped being afraid to ask. I also know I won't depend on Derio too much, emotionally, when he returns home, and that's crucial for me if I'm going to live here. I love him more and more each day, even though he's not here, but I can't let him be my everything. It's not fair to him when he already has so many to support.

He's supposed to come back tomorrow—Paolo is taking him on the ferry—so I'm racing around the house while the kids are at school, trying to get everything into tip-top shape. I've vacuumed, I've dusted, I've scrubbed, I've wiped, and I've cleaned. The whole villa sparkles, like a house of happy lemons. It at least smells fresh and citrusy; I've even picked a few from the lemon grove and placed them in bowls around the house.

Tonight, I plan on trying my hand at soufflé. I want everything to be perfect for his arrival, including me, which is why I'm shaving my legs, rubbing body scrub all over, and deep conditioning my hair so the curls are soft and shiny instead of the texture of steel wool. We haven't been with each other for a long time, and while I'm sure he's not in the best shape for me to fuck his brains out, that doesn't mean I'm not going to makes his eyes roll back and his toes curl. He doesn't even have to lift a finger.

I'm in the middle of flipping through a cookbook and looking for the perfect recipe, while wondering if I should paint my nails, when I hear the front door open. We don't lock our doors here during the day, but still, no neighbors or friends that I know of would just barge in the house without knocking first.

"Hello?" I call out, getting off the stool. My first instinct is to grab the nearest knife. I have a lot of choices in this kitchen.

"Amber?" I hear a woman's voice.

Felisa!

I round the corner and see her at the door, dragging a suitcase. Behind her comes Derio on crutches and behind him is Lorenzo, also with a suitcase and duffel bag.

"Oh my God," I say, completely shocked to see Derio, as well as them. "Let me help you." I run over to Felisa to take the suitcase but she bats my hand away.

"Tend to your *amore*," she says, nudging me toward Derio. "Lorenzo and I can take care of ourselves."

I'm smiling at Derio and he's grinning at me—looking sexy as hell with a full-on beard—but I'm still looking between Felisa and Lorenzo in surprise as Lorenzo shuffles past me and joins Felisa in the living room. "You're here early," I say to Derio. "Can I touch you or does it hurt?"

"Please touch me," Derio practically wails, his eyes glinting. "I am going crazy without you and the only ones who have touched me lately are doctors and the man from the hotel down the street who had too much fun getting me into his luggage cart." He nods in the direction of Via Tragara.

I laugh before I grab his face in my hands and kiss him hard. The minute my lips meet his it's like the entire world, full of its worries and expectations and lies and truths and victories and losses, fades away. He tastes and feels like my dreams and I can't help sighing and lean into him as my body shudders with relief.

Even on crutches, his body is strong and steady. I can hear his heart beating loudly in his chest and its rhythm brings me more peace. My love is home.

"You came home early," I whisper.

"I couldn't wait another minute," he says, kissing the top of my head. "I needed to see you. Plus, the nurses were so tired of me talking about you all the time, showing them your picture. They told me if I don't go home to see *mia leonessa*, they would personally put me on the boat and send me there. So I decided it was best for everyone's health if I left."

"Smart nurses," I remark, wrapping my arm around his waist. "How did you happen to come with Felisa and Lorenzo? I thought Lorenzo was afraid of water."

He nods. "He was. Still is, I think. But he did it for Felisa, much like I did it for you."

"You did that for yourself. To get back your life."

"And you are my life, Amber. Please don't ever forget that."

I pull away and look up at him. He's gazing down at me with so much love and sincerity, it breaks my heart in the most beautiful way possible.

"Things are going to change now," he says, clearing his throat. "For the better. Felisa and Lorenzo are here, not only to help me but to help you and the twins."

"What?" I ask, confused.

"Lorenzo was in a bad situation in Umbria. He lost the house he was renting and didn't have enough money to support the two of them. Felisa came back, asking if she could be a nanny again. She said that Lorenzo can cook very well and would help out as the chef. I told them of course they can work here. She is my family, always has been. They will live in your old room now that you are with me."

"They seriously want to work here?" I ask, feeling another weight rise off my shoulders.

He nods. "Yes. Is that okay with you?"

I rub my lips together. "Of course."

He reaches out and brushes my hair off my face. "Good. I know it will be a full house, but think of what the time will give you. Now you can follow your dreams and passion . . . and hopefully they won't lead you away from me."

"I don't really know my dreams," I tell him. "But I know you're in them."

"*Buono*," he says, smiling softly at me. "Then you are half-way there."

"And have you thought about your dreams?" I ask him carefully. "Have you decided to race again?"

He shrugs, looking pained. "I do not know. I want to, per-haps even in a lower division, more as a hobby than a career. But I still worry about another accident."

"But at least now you don't have to worry about the twins being alone. I'm here. And so are Felisa and Lorenzo."

"What do you want for me?" he asks quietly.

I give him a soft smile. "I want you to be happy."

"I already am." He kisses me again and then we join Felisa and Lorenzo in the living room.

"He told me your good news," I say to them.

"You don't mind?" Felisa asks, but there is a twinkle in her eye that tells me they would stay even if I did mind, bossy old thing that she is.

"Not at all," I say. I won't have to leave the kids or Derio or Capri, but I'm no longer held back from discovering myself.

I look at Derio and smile, big and bright. "I promise I'll get a job right away."

He lets out a small laugh. "It's okay, Amber. Take your time finding out what you want to do. You deserve it and I will support you through it. If you want to show off that green thumb of yours, maybe we can get you on board with one of the local nurseries. If you want to cook, well, maybe you'll have to fight Lorenzo for that."

Lorenzo looks over when he hears his name mentioned, but of course he doesn't understand what was said. Derio quickly translates for him and Lorenzo makes fighting fists. I make the fists back, laughing.

"I don't know," Felisa says as she gazes around her. "I'm not even sure if I can measure up to you now. This place is spotless." She picks up a white couch cushion and turns it over. There is a huge red wine stain there from the other night. I thought I was being clever. How did she know? She must have some super sixth sense for dirt and disorder.

I feel myself flush. "Well, we can't all be perfect."

"Ah, but you are perfect for me," Derio says, circling his free arm around me. He eyes Felisa and Lorenzo and tells them, "If you don't mind, I'm letting Amber take me to our room."

Felisa waves at us dismissively, turning her back to us.

Derio pats me on the butt. "Come on, let's go. I really need to lie down." I help him up the stairs to our bedroom and he says to me, "By the way, I have more good news for you."

"What? What could be better than you coming back home?"

"I spoke to someone who works in immigration. They are still going over our case and reviewing the files, but my contact, Federico, seems to think you have a very good chance at having your visa extended indefinitely."

"Really?" I cry out. I don't want to get my hopes up over this—it feels like I'm on the verge of winning the lottery—so I keep my squeals inside.

"We won't know for a few weeks," he says, "and of course this is just his feeling. But now I have a good feeling about it as well."

We go inside the room and he shuts the door behind us. I immediately throw myself at him, kissing him hard and deep, on his lips, his beard, his neck, his collarbone. My hands roam up and down his body, softer and thinner now thanks to weeks of being confined to bed and missing his daily workouts, but still strong. Still mine.

"Am I hurting you?" I murmur against his skin as my lips skirt the V-neck of his T-shirt and he lets out a gasp.

"No," he moans. "You feel like an angel. Don't stop."

I pull back and eye his cast on his leg below his long shorts. "Can you stand for this or do you need to lie down?" I start to undo his pants, my hands firmly gripping his erection. I've fucking missed him, missed this.

"I'm a strong man," he jokes, sounding breathless. "Of course I can stand."

I unzip his shorts and let them fall to the floor before I take his gorgeous cock out. My Italian Stallion. I'm going to make him forget he was ever in the hospital.

I eagerly place him in my wet mouth and start to give him the best head possible. His hands find my hair and make tight fists while he groans loudly.

Suddenly, his hand jerks and he says, "You know, I think I need to lie down. You're better than I remember."

I wipe my mouth and grin at him before leading him over

to the bed. I carefully push him down onto the thick duvet, his body beautifully bronzed against all the white, and finish him off. He comes hard and fast, spouting off a string of Italian curses, and I take all of him.

While he's breathing hard, murmuring sweet nothings, I curl up next to him. I rest my head on his chest as he catches his breath and stare out the open balcony doors to the island outside. A butterfly floats past on the fall breeze and I am reminded of what my father said, that I can't be a butterfly fluttering from flower to flower.

But I think I can be. It's just that I've found my flower. And now I call it home.

It is a weekend in November and Derio and I are in Positano on a mini getaway. I have just finished up a bowl of delicious mussels when the waiter brings out Prosecco for us. The sun is close to setting, and though the air brings a bite to it when the light fades, the days are still pleasant and warm.

The Prosecco is for the good news we received this week. Derio has finished editing *Racing the Sun* a few weeks ago and sent the book to his mother's old agent. They discussed what to do with the book since it still remains unfinished. Though Derio cleaned it up, he was unable or unwilling to write an ending, not without knowing what his mother intended. Her agent suggested that they actually cut the book by a few chapters to a place that had a bit more closure. It's still an open ending, but at least at that earlier spot the "Happily Ever After" is more pronounced and the readers can infer what happens next in their own imaginations. It's possible that Sophia Larosa didn't even know the ending herself, just that she wanted her characters to be happy.

Derio agreed, and with his permission, the agent sent the book to his mother's old publisher. Though it wasn't much of a surprise, they wanted the book and will publish it next year—one more shot for Derio's mother to have her work out there, where it belongs. The advance and royalties are going straight into a trust fund for Alfonso and Annabella.

Derio has also started racing again, though he's only training in a lower division, thanks to his injuries. He hopes to compete on occasion, but it will no longer be his career. He feels like his dream has been altered, but in a good way. He's able to follow his passion on a smaller scale, while still trying to figure out the next direction in his life.

The other good news is that I am officially allowed to stay in Italy for as long as I like, provided Derio and I stay together. And that won't be a problem. I can't see myself with anyone else but him. And though I have a lot of questions and curiosities about life, I find the answers now with him by my side.

I work part-time at a nursery that grows organic lemon trees for juice, supplying many of the healthier eateries on Capri and the mainland. It's fun work and really interesting, and though I don't know if I'll be working there forever, I know it's the first step in the right direction. Working with plants is a lot like being a nanny—there's a lot of patience and nurturing involved. But Felisa is in charge of that now, and Lorenzo is in charge of the cooking, and our house is starting to resemble an Italian sitcom, but I wouldn't have it any other way. It really feels like family in the *Villa dei Limoni Tristi*, even though we all manage to drive each other crazy from time to time.

"Let's catch the sunset," Derio says after he has paid. "We may have to race it."

He takes my hand and we shuffle out of the restaurant and down the boardwalk that cuts along the beach. I realize that we're at the same place where I first went to meet Felisa, all those months ago. My God, has everything changed since then, and in the most wonderful, surreal way. *La dolce vita* is entirely true.

We walk along the small dock and Derio hands his iPhone to a couple who are standing close by, asking them if they can please take our photo. I hand my phone to them, too, wanting one of my own, especially since I'm never satisfied with photos on the first try.

We pose at the end of the dock, knowing that the sun is almost gone, and I tickle Derio, trying to get him to smile naturally for the cameras. He always freezes up and doesn't show off how beautiful he really is.

I tickle his ribs but he's fast and tickles me back. I yelp and jump out of the way, but my foot hits the edge of the dock and I lose my balance.

Before I know what's going on, I'm pitching over and landing in the cold sea. Thankfully it's only about shoulder-high here, but still, I totally go under.

I burst through the surface, my feet finding the bottom, and look up at the dock, spitting out water and wiping the salt from my eyes. Derio is laughing his head off at me while the people on the dock look on in concern. Actually, the woman is concerned but the man is still taking pictures!

"It's not funny!" I yell at Derio, completely embarrassed. Who the hell would fall in the sea with their clothes on? Well, Amber MacLean would.

But Derio just shakes his head, and before I know what he's doing, he jumps off the dock, landing with a splash that completely swamps me. My hair is plastered against my head like a wet mop. He swims over and pulls me into him with a wicked look in his eyes. "You think I would let you have all the fun?" He gives me a wet, salty kiss and then looks over at the people on the dock. "*Un minuto, per favore*," he says, giving them a wave. Then he grins at me and presses his forehead against mine. "Where you go, I go," he says. "To the land, to the sea. Always and forever."

We turn to look at the horizon, just as the sun slips below it.

ACKNOWLEDGMENTS

Thanks to my assistant, Stephanie, for being such a good companion, even though she said she hated Italy every five minutes—she'll say this is true, but I think she secretly loved it—and the fact that she traveled with two huge suitcases . . . but we'll always have Lady Gaga and the disco cab. Thanks to my editor, Jhanteigh Kupihea, and my publicist at Atria, Ariele Fredman, for totally getting on board with this idea. To my super agent and the cutest girl around, Taylor Haggerty. To Shawna Vitale for being the first to experience Derio. To my parents for putting up with me for ten days at their house in Palm Springs, where I hammered out this book from morning to night. They eventually had to hide the Keurig K-cups from me because they grossly underestimated how much coffee writers need to function. To K.A. Tucker for always being a text away (Canadian authors must stick together!). To Danielle Sanchez for talking me down from great heights. To the Whores and the Kartel for being so badass. To Kelly St-Laurent for always being there. And to my husband, Scott, and my dog, Bruce, for being the best couple of guys a girl can have.

Ciao!

Printed in the United States
By Bookmasters